Praise for John Abel Mysteries

Stumbling Down the Road of Revenge

The author is equally adept at showing how ineptitude and apathy within the justice system affect innocent people.

Another suspenseful and surprising legal thriller in a consistently entertaining series.

Kirkus Reviews

Stumbling Down the Road of Revenge offers moral complexity and high-spirited thrills, delivering a satisfying justice in the end—though it looks different from what readers may expect.

Publishers Weekly

Road to Redemption or Wherever

In Cain's legal thriller, shocking allegations of abuse lead a defense attorney into a tangled web of secrets...A complex story with mature themes that stays true to its characters.

Kirkus Reviews

Cup of Malice

Cain delivers a tense crime thriller with a large cast of characters that will keep readers guessing....

Exciting and unpredictable, this is a thriller fans of the genre will enjoy.

An intensely intriguing Legal Thriller that fires on all cylinders, A Cup Of Malice is one of those rare novels that promises much from its opening pages and delivers beyond our expectations. Both pithy and suspenseful Cain writes with the authoritative voice of his experience and it's to his credit that his plot stands in contrast to many of today's thrillers which often seem simple-minded and lacking in genuine depth.

The Dead Judge and the Golden Buddha

In Cain's final installment of a crime-fiction trilogy, a judge's sudden, violent death rattles the local political establishment.Jason Olyphant, a skateboarder in Washington state who's notorious for his reckless stunts, becomes a murder suspect after a collision that apparently claims the life of Judge Alvin Hansen, a pillar of Hardin County's legal community...

He also demonstrates a flair for snappy dialogue, whether he's referencing a smile that "only a teacher's pet could appreciate" or dishing up chilling insights into the mentality of murder: "There is more to killing than just the killing." Another bold stroke is a revelation roughly halfway into the story, effectively transforming the tale from a whodunit to an old-school "howcatchem." Some fans may dismiss this maneuver as a Columbo-style move, but Cain's rapid-fire approach should be sufficient to overcome any objections. A fast-paced, engagingly written mystery.

Stumbling Down the Road of Revenge

John Abel Mysteries
by John Cain

The Dead Judge Rolled Over

The Dead Judge and the Raid Gone Bad

The Dead Judge and Golden Buddha

The Prosecutor and the Obsidian Knife

The Prosecutor, the Truck, & the Mermaid

The Prosecutor and the Gem Stones

All That the Rain Promised and More

The Curious Death of Silas Smith

A Cup of Malice

The Road to Redemption or Wherever

The Dead Judge Trilogy (Books 1, 2 & 3)

Stumbling Down the Road of Revenge

Stumbling Down the Road of Revenge

John Cain

John/Cain, Tacoma, WA

We can be redeemed only to the extent to which we see ourselves.

Martin Buber

A man that studieth revenge keeps his own wounds green

Francis Bacon

In memory of my mother
Dorothy Louise Cain
(1915-1951)

Disclaimer

This is a work of fiction. Any resemblance to the living or the dead or to places is a coincidence. Any reference to historical events, persons, or places is fictional. Harbor City and Hardin County are fictional political entities.

Acknowledgments

My friend, Barb Immermann, has helped me in many ways. Her patience is extraordinary. My sister, Suzannah Cain, has given me much help and assistance. I am very grateful that she is in my life. Dorothy Chant has given me invaluable proofreading assistance and an education in the need for commas when using non-restrictive phrases. My friends, Ann Carlsen, Bill Tammaro, Phil Dantes, Jim Heath , Jim Turner, and Bill Kelly, have each given me encouragement, and advice. I owe a debt to Mark Whitehill for his work and insights. My wife, Bobbi, has given me far more help and assistance than I can begin to mention. I am a lucky fellow to have her in my life. All typos and other errors and flaws are my sole responsibility.

Partial list of Characters

Alan Merwin, Assistant Chief of Police
Alfonso LaFontaine, lawyer
Alice Medford, Emma'sgrandmother
Amanda Bowman, John Abel's client
Billie Abel, John Abel's spouse
Calvin Green, criminal defense lawyer
Cheryl Boardman, Kyle' mother
Edmond Goldman, Court Commissioner
Ed Robinson, homeless veteran
Elizabeth Knight, Police Captain
Ellen Bowman, Amanda's grandmother
Emma Kelly, junior high school student
Erin Douglas, teenager
Frank McCoy, Police Sergeant
Ian Edgington, family law lawyer
Ian Franklin, psychologist
Isaac "Ike" Kelly, Emma Kelly's father
Gary Shipman, deceased man
Greg Madison, Court Commissioner
James Brinkmeyer, Prosecutor
Jimmy McDonald, teenager
Joe O'Conner, Randy O'Conner's father
John Abel, lawyer
Julia Carpenter, Court Commissioner
Laconia Jones, Police Lieutenant
Leon Pence, Hardin Sheriff's Deputy
Kathy Washington, Amanda's mother
Kyle Boardman, high school junior
Martin Wojciehowicz, Episcopalian Priest

Matthew Blackridge, psychologist
Mary Dugan, student
Raymond Knott, Police Technician
Randy O'Conner, alleged victim
Rick, Manager of the Bluebeard Café
Ron McBride, man of many talents
Sarah Shipman, former day care owner

Stumbling Down the Road of Revenge

1

Father Martin adjusted the bicycle clips on his blue jeans and admired the steel frame road bike that he had owned for many years. He considered himself frugal, but not cheap. He rode the bike for many years for day-to-day pleasure and participated in large bicycle events. He rode in the Seattle-to-Portland bicycle event several times, plus many times in the RAGBRI trip across Iowa. Neither he nor his wife bought expensive items, but what they bought, they bought to last. For instance, his steel candy-red Raleigh that he bought while in college. However, he had long since switched the original ten-speed gears for thirty-threes.

He was in his 60s, over six-foot tall with broad shoulders and a thin waist. At Yale he crewed on the B team. His hairline had long since receded past the back of his head, leaving him with a smooth dome and half wreath where his thick dark brown hair was at one time. He had thick eyebrows and a gray mustache. He always enjoyed the surprise of a new acquaintance when they realized that a regular looking guy like him was, in fact, an Episcopal priest with five children. He lived in a small city several miles from his church in Harbor City.

He adjusted his bike helmet and double-checked that his pant clips were secure, then headed toward Harbor City. His trip from home began on a county road with a wide shoulder that led to a quick descent toward a mile-long bridge with a protected walk and bike lane. He paused to look at the water and mountains to the south, and then gathered speed toward the bridge that led to a steep ascent and a busy four-lane street. After traveling on the arterial street, he crossed the street and rode through a two-block Veterans' Memorial Park filled with flowers, park benches, and the names of the Harbor City war dead neatly inscribed on bronze plaques. The park ended at a parking lot. From there, he crossed a street after pressing a 'walk' warning sign. He reached his church within a few blocks.

The route he took was longer than the route on the busy street, but much safer. At his age, he thought it best not to take chances with his life. When considering his life, he realized his journey had always consisted of taking safe and secure routes. But his efforts had not secured him from misfortune, such as the birth of a child with a chronic illness. Through his life's journey, his faith was tested from time to time such as when he had not become a Bishop. His life was not without some disappointments, but after every test of faith, his faith had grown stronger. Faith did not come with obvious or quick rewards. This was a message he always tried to convey to his parishioners and those he met outside the church. He was a strong believer that the church should be active in community affairs.

He was not the first to arrive at the church. On a bench near a Celtic cross sat a young woman with exotic features. Her skin was olive or light tan, and she had high cheekbones and large brown eyes. She was drinking from a Starbucks reusable mug. She was wearing a long-sleeved T-shirt under a light cotton dress.

"Good morning, Father Martin, or should I say Father Wojciehowicz?" she asked, standing up from the bench and smoothing down her dress.

2

"You can call me Martin or Father Martin or even Father Wojciehowicz. I am impressed. Most people stumble over my name."

"I used to watch reruns of Barney Miller, so the name Wojciehowicz doesn't trouble me. It is best if you don't look at the spelling of some names if you want to pronounce them correctly. Don't you think?" She smiled. She had very white teeth.

"Very true." Martin was good with names and faces. When he handed out the Eucharist, he always said the first name of the recipient, but he did not know the name of this person. "You have me at a disadvantage. Have we met?"

"No, but I have heard of you and want to make a confession."

"Are you Episcopalian?"

"No. Does it matter?"

"An Episcopalian priest can absolve persons of any denomination who make a sincere and faithful confession. So can a Catholic priest, as far as I know."

"No, you have to be Catholic to have your sins absolved. I checked up the street, and the priest was quite certain that I had to become Catholic to be absolved." She shook her head. "I did not attend much church growing up, and it seemed like a lot of work just to confess sins that God would already know about."

"I suppose so," said Martin. "Wait here while I open up the church doors. We can talk inside."

"May I bring my coffee?"

"Please. I will start some for myself. Just wait here, and I will be back in a few minutes."

He went to the side door and punched in a code. Inside, he traded his bicycling shirt for a shirt with a Roman collar. He let her in through the main

3

doors opening into the vestibule where a table sat with brochures on it. Posted on the wall were announcements of various activities.

"Did you have to dress up for my confession?"

"No, but this is what I wear when I am on duty."

"Aren't you always on duty? Like a policeman?"

"Obviously on duty, so to speak." He suspected he was being gently mocked, but was not certain. Perhaps she was flirting. "How did you learn about me or this church?"

Glancing at a board with a list of activities, she said, "You have AA meetings here twice a week. One in the morning, one in the evening."

"Is that how you learned of us?"

"Sure," she smiled.

"You seem young to have a drinking problem."

"You are never too young to have a spiritual problem."

"Well said. More than one member of my congregation is a member of AA. I read in *The Big Book* that once you recover from spiritual malady, you straighten out mentally and physically."

"Well, I am here to confess. That will help me overcome my spiritual malady."

"I hope so. What is your name?"

"Is that important?"

"It is a form of trust. If you trust me to absolve your sins, then you should trust me with your name."

"It is Amanda, and I may not really be an alcoholic."

"That is fine," said Martin. "Let's go to the chapel." He pointed down a narrow hallway.

The chapel was a small room with a large cross at the front, office chairs along the walls with a few haphazardly arranged in the center.

"I thought all chapels had pews."

"It is not a requirement."

"Shouldn't we sit in a confessional box?"

"Not required anymore. Not even by the Catholics. The Sacrament is known by many names, including penance, reconciliation and confession. Most official church publications usually refer to the Sacrament as Penance or Reconciliation, or Penance *and* Reconciliation because you cannot have one without the other. As you pointed out, God knows what you and I have done. Telling me what you have done is a method by which you become reconciled to God. It is not to inform God of your misdeeds, but to acknowledge to God that you are aware of your misdeeds and want forgiveness."

"I see," she said.

"I forgot something. I will be right back." He darted away and returned quickly with a white stole over his shoulders. "A special garment is not needed, but I like to wear a white stole, signifying a person's return to God."

"Confession will do that?"

"It is a matter of faith," said Martin and he sat down beside her. "Perhaps we should pray before we begin." Amanda nodded and bowed her head. "Come Holy Spirit into my soul so that I may honestly help the woman with me, and enlighten her mind that she may know the sins she ought to confess, and grant me your grace to understand them fully, humbly, and with a contrite heart. Help me to assist her to firmly resolve not to commit them again. Do you swear by your resolve to not commit your sin again?"

"I swear."

"So, what is it you seek reconciliation for with the Lord?"

"I killed my father."

"I beg your pardon, you what?"

"I killed my father. I won't do that again."

"Do the police know?"

"Yes, they heard me kill him. I was wearing a microphone. It was determined that I killed him in self-defense."

"Did you?" Martin gulped in a breath of air and added, "Did you kill him in self-defense?"

"I am not certain that is relevant. He abused me for years, and I killed him. He cannot abuse me anymore."

"Why are you are here?"

" The reason I am here is because I don't care that I killed him. There is just emptiness inside me. I want to care that I killed him. But I don't. I thought with him dead I could be free of him. I could be free of the years of him touching me, coming into my bedroom at night, telling me that he loved me, and I should not be afraid. It was so wrong. I believed that he loved me. How could he do what he did if he loved me? How can a parent give a child such shame?"

"I can't answer that."

"He is dead, but I am not free of him. I want God to make me feel the sorrow that I should feel."

"Have you talked to your mother about this? Did she know what was happening?"

"She was useless. She tried to help, but his power over me was too strong. She was weak. There was a custody battle, and the lawyer she hired was inept. He could not stop my father even when he had evidence of the abuse."

"Who was the lawyer?"

"John Abel. You know him. He comes here."

"Yes, I know Abel."

"This emptiness is dragging me down. I am tired all the time. I used to have energy. Now I sit alone and just stare at things. I go to the park; I see families having fun; and all I can do is watch and feel sad." She pulled up the sleeves of her T-shirt, revealing thin scars where she cut herself with razor blades. Some were fresh and some were very old and faded. "I cut myself to feel alive. I want to feel alive without shame and rage, but that is all I know."

"Of the seven deadly sins, sloth is the most insidious."

"I am not lazy."

"No, but another translation of sloth is self-pity. It is a subtle sin that masquerades as justified anger. You must conquer that great sin."

"How do I pray about it?"

"It will be hard, but I suggest you come here and talk to me more. I think once you find a way to help others, you will find that your self-hatred and self-loathing will leave you."

Amanda shook her head. "I don't think it will be that simple. Have I been absolved?"

Martin sighed. "I'm just a priest. If your intent is pure and you are serious about seeking forgiveness, then yes, but it is what is inside you that is important. There is no outward sign. When Moses came down from the mountain after being in God's presence, his face shone so brightly that he had to wear a veil. Absolution is not like that, but it is you and your acts that follow which determine the extent of your absolution. Just telling a priest your sins in confidence does not remove them. Your faith and your acts that follow are what's necessary for absolution. Without them, my words and prayers are meaningless."

"Then why confess to you?"

"Confession to a priest is a gateway."

"I murdered my father. I don't think anyone will hire me as a nurse or trust me to do good work."

"You must try; that is all God asks of us. You came for help. I can give you my sympathy, my blessing, and absolution as I am empowered to do by the teachings of my faith. Let us sit quietly and pray."

They prayed and before she left, he gave her a pamphlet about what an Episcopalian believes, along with a book of Common Prayer.

"Thank you."

"Please come back; I'm here every Sunday."

2

Abel was suddenly awake at 5:15am. This was fifteen minutes before it was time to rise and feed the dogs and cats. So, he did his best to lay quietly and not disturb his spouse, Billie. His best was not very good.

"You're breathing," she said, tapping him on the arm.

Removing his CPAP mask, Abel replied, "It's a habit."

"Stop it," she said.

"Breathing?"

"No, thinking. I can always tell when you are thinking. You breathe differently when you are thinking. It's disturbing. What were you thinking about?"

"I was thinking that I might get myself one of those pins that say, 'Ask me about my pronouns.'"

"You get one of those, I'd rip it off," she snorted. "Why would you want one?"

"The judges and commissioners all have signs in their courtrooms. 'Diversity is the law. Tell us your preferred pronouns and your request will be honored in this courtroom.'"

"And so?"

"I just wanted to mess with them. Chaucer, Shakespeare, and even Jane Austen used the singular 'they.' Some grammarians in the nineteen hundreds got together and decided English should be more like Latin. Why, I don't know. Maybe because they were feeling neglected. Anyway, they pushed for making 'they' only for plural usage and look where it has gotten us."

"It amazes me the things you know and don't know. We have four extra bags of granola in the pantry because you can't remember what we have and don't have when you go shopping. I don't think you look before shopping."

"I fall under the Costco spell."

"Counselor, if that is your defense, you have no defense."

"We already established that long ago. It is dry goods, and it won't go bad. I think it is important to know things and be concerned about things."

"Where has it gotten you? You are awake early thinking about things you don't really care about," laughed Billie.

"I just dislike a simple interaction getting all political. If I am talking to someone, I doubt that I am going to address him in the third person. It is the people who refer to themself as 'we' who really need watching."

Billie sighed. "Over half the prosecutors hate you because you helped put a prosecutor in prison. Now you want to mess with the judges. People have a right to be addressed as they see fit. It is not worse than when women demanded to have letters addressed as Ms. instead of Mrs."

"I suppose that's true," Abel muttered his agreement.

"You are not much of a curmudgeon."

"It's early," he said and went on, "I got a form the other day. It asked me what my preferred sex was at birth. I can tell you this, I remember having no preferences when I emerged from the birth canal."

Abel might have said more on the topic except for the interruption of Barney, a copper-colored golden retriever, bounding onto their bed, demanding to be petted. He was quickly joined by Henry and Atticus, littermates from the Dutch shepherd they had rescued out of California. The mother was, apparently, not only a bitch, but also a slut. Henry was stocky with the sable markings of a German shepherd. Atticus was lean and snow white.

Billie let the dogs outside, made coffee and gave Barney some medication. While she was doing this, Abel put out food for their cats and filled up the dog bowls. Within ten minutes, they were back in bed with coffee, morning papers, and their iPads. It was a routine that served them well.

Abel quickly breezed through the front section of the *Morning Herald* and placed it next to Billie who was looking at her iPad. Each year, the newspaper became thinner. More and more of the news was not original to the area, but taken from national news sources. If it was not for their love of the routine of a morning paper in their hands, they would have discontinued their print subscriptions long ago.

"I forgot to tell you that Juan Arnez sent you an email." Juan was the editor of the *Hardin County-Harbor City Bar News*. "Juan said they would run your editorial in the next *Bar News*, but they will add that the editorial represents your personal opinion and not that of the *Bar News*."

"And people wonder why lawyers never have statues made for their bravery."

Billie just shook her head. She knew what he wrote because she spent over an hour correcting his typos, misspellings, and grammatical mistakes. "I did warn you."

"You would like me to retire?"

"Judges are worse than the Pope when their infallibility is questioned."

11

Abel picked up his iPad and pulled up the article.

Chaos in the Courtroom

Laws come and go, but one judicial principle is constant. The further you go up the judicial food chain, the better the furniture and the fewer cases decided. The common assumption is that the loftier the court, the more people are affected by its ruling. The Dobbs ruling will affect not only the born but also the unborn, just as Roe v. Wade did before it. The recent Carpenter v. Colorado opinion may be cited in many protection order hearings for years to come.

The trial level courts are where most people experience justice, the results of which can be more consequential for the individuals than any other court ruling anywhere, ever. The butterfly effect suggests the movement of a butterfly's wings in Mexico may create a tornado in Texas. A brief appearance in court can have lifelong consequences for more than just the litigants.

Years ago, I brought a motion to limit a father's visitation time. Evidence from neutral witnesses, and the opinion of a psychologist indicated that the father's temporary visitation with the child should be revisited. Previously, my client, the mother, had raised concerns about possible abuse. Not only was my motion denied, but the commissioner warned that he and other commissioners were tired of hearing from me, and if I brought any more motions, I could face sanctions, plus my client's limited or supervised visitation. Faced with an unsympathetic guardian ad litem and the risks at trial, my client agreed to a split custody arrangement. Throughout her childhood, the child complained of recurring yeast infections. At a recent physical examination, a doctor opined that she had scarring, indicative of child abuse. What was decided in a very brief hearing years ago may have consequences that will last her a lifetime.

In The Art of Cross-Examination, Francis Wellman opines that there is never a contested case that does not mainly depend upon the skill with which an advocate conducts his cross-examination. Less than 5% of criminal cases in Superior Court go to trial. The majority of civil and domestic cases are decided by settlement or summary judgment rather than by trial or arbitration. It is not uncommon for a temporary order or a guardian ad litem's report to determine final orders. To a large extent, declarations take the place of direct testimony. Many lawyers seem to think that if they attach hearsay to a declaration, it is magically not hearsay, and perhaps for expediency, judges do not object. Administrative hearings admit what is considered reliable hearsay. In drafting declarations verisimilitude is the goal. One firm drafts statements that are pasted into a letter so it appears that an individual, and not a lawyer, wrote it to create the illusion of spontaneous, heartfelt support from a loved one. If Solomon had a crowded docket with a noon deadline, or relied upon a guardian ad litem's opinion, his ruling about the two women contesting the motherhood of a child might have been different – certainly less dramatic or instructive.

Former Harbor City Municipal Court Judge Gary Emory helped many by accurately assessing what a particular individual needed. A friend of mine appeared before him so often that Judge Emory addressed him by his first name. The judge offered to dismiss his legal financial obligations if he would attend five sessions of AA. My friend did that, and after a few slips, he now has over eighteen years of sobriety. He has helped many to change their lives, and the ones he has helped have helped others. The butterfly effect applies to small acts, whether intentional or not, resulting in significant consequences.

The butterfly effect is an allegory of the chaos theory. Its implications are far-reaching. In August of 1967, I lit a cigarette on the steps of a church I had never attended. A stranger bummed a smoke (he had never been to that church either), and that action began a friendship that lasted more than fifty years, until his death. Without his friendship, I would not be in the Northwest or have met my wife. Zen attentiveness is not needed. Small things, whether we know it or not, set in motion other events. Some are turning points in a person's life.

The commissioner's response to my motion has troubled me for years. "Indicative of abuse" is not proof of abuse. I always wished the allegations were investigated and not dismissed as a troublesome inconvenience. But I never questioned the commissioner's integrity or desire to make correct rulings. I do regret the lack of further investigation. As Herbert Spencer wrote, "Contempt prior to investigation is the surest road to ignorance."

Ours is a profession where winning is truth and truth is winning. Mistakes and errors in judgment are bound to happen. The persons who think they can never be deceived are the easiest to deceive. A chronic liar can be very persuasive. Even though a belief is deeply believed, that does not make it true. What seems to be outrageous can be true or partially true. We are a far more diverse society than when Wellman wrote his classic, *The Art of Cross-Examination*. It was published in 1903. Women's universal suffrage was seventeen years away. Government forms asking, "What was your gender preference at birth?" were more than a century away and not contemplated by anyone.

Even with cross-examination, mistakes and deception do occur, but without cross-examination, the opportunity to weigh the credibility of a litigant, a fact finder must rely upon their common sense and their expectations of human behavior. For example, when a mother seeks a restraining order, it is made against a backdrop of the common assumption that mothers usually have their children's best interests at heart and normally do not seek restraining orders unless necessary. On the other hand, roommates sometimes seek restraining orders

14

against one another to avoid the cost and expense of unlawful detainer actions. But exceptions do exist, and relying upon common sense to make a ruling based on observations of other people is unreliable. Declarations sometimes obscure what can easily be discovered by direct observation.

One Hardin County judge decided a case with the flip of a coin. The Judicial Commission reprimanded him for bringing disrespect upon the judicial process. I think he was reprimanded more for letting the cat out of the bag than for disrespect of the judicial system. Some cases are just too close to be sure, but a decision must be made. Fortunately, most cases are not that close.

As our world becomes more diverse, the possibilities for a proper judgment are more diverse, and this can be especially so when the litigants come from different backgrounds. The "reasonable man" of Wellman's era was essentially a white Protestant who, if that was all you had on a jury of today, might be a reason for an appellate challenge. As we continue to move away from a court system that relies upon direct contact between a litigant and fact finder, the more important it is for the fact finder to be sensitive to the culture, gender, and gender identification issues of the litigants. Juries consist of six or twelve jurors; judges don't have the benefit of their collective wisdom and insight. Lone fact finders often must rely upon their own knowledge, background and assumptions that they are heir to. Diversity, Equality and Inclusion (DEI) seminars may be helpful, but perhaps not as much as practical experience. Sometimes overcoming a college education is the greatest obstacle to a fair and just decision.

Clarence Darrow said, "Justice has nothing to do with what goes on in a courtroom; Justice is what comes out of a courtroom." I do not agree. I think what justice goes on in the courtroom determines what justice comes out. The majority of cases never rise to the level of appellate review, but their effect can be unmeasurable. Whatever the furnishing of the courtroom, it may be the most important courtroom your client ever enters. We never really know how momentous and far-reaching a decision may be. If when you rise up to speak, you do not believe what you are saying, you should sit down and be silent.

-John Abel

"I don't think it is so bad. It is common knowledge that judges don't always get things right. That is why we have the appellate courts."

"It may be common knowledge to some, but that doesn't mean judges and commissioners like to have their noses rubbed in their mistakes. Commissioner Goldman will know you are writing about him."

"I hope he does. Last time I saw him in action, he denied Gary Shipman a restraining order, and later that day Shipman was killed. Goldman needs to have his nose rubbed in his failings from time to time."

Barney jumped onto their bed with a red rubber ball in his mouth, "You are incorrigible," laughed Billie.

"I am not," said Abel.

"Not you. Barney," said Billie, pulling the ball from the dog's mouth and tossing it to the floor, causing the retriever to spring after it. "Well, actually you are too."

"Incorrigible?"

"Absolutely. Barney when he wants to play, and you when you have a client to defend."

3

Amanda was working at a Starbucks taking orders and preparing drinks when Detective Sergeant Frank McCoy and Captain Elizabeth Knight approached her about wearing a wire and inducing her father, Stephen Bowman, into admitting that he abused her when she was a child. In response to Amanda's statements, he admitted abusing her. But before they could congratulate themselves on their cleverness, they heard Amanda crying for help. When they reached the kitchen, she was huddled on the floor covered in her father's blood. Both carotid arteries were severed, and he bled out quickly. Knight and McCoy agreed that Amanda acted in self-defense. It was a far more reasonable explanation than that their plan had resulted in the death of a civilian. Declaring her action as self-defense was face-saving for them. Any other explanation would have likely ended their careers.

Within three days, Amanda returned to her work as a partner. Starbucks calls their baristas "partners" because for every year of employment, an employee receives a small stock bonus. Amanda thought that was nice, but would've preferred better hours, better wages, and better tips. What she would do with the rest of her life was uncertain. Yet, when her father's mother, Ellen Bowman, came into Starbucks, it quickly became evident that her future did not lie with Starbucks.

Elbowing past a young mother with a toddler in one hand and a Nordstrom shopping bag in the other, Ellen shouted. "So, this is where you work now?"

"Hello, grandmother."

17

"Do they know you killed your father?" Ellen yelled toward the customers. "Do they know that?"

"It was self-defense," Amanda whispered. "Please don't make a scene."

"You are a killer, and you don't want a scene?" shouted Ellen in an even louder voice.

"Ma'am, you will have to leave. Mall Security is on the way," said the manager.

"Did you know she killed her father?"

"We know, we know," said a coworker.

"Did you know that before she killed him with a knife, she poisoned him with antifreeze?" Turning to the line she had pushed past, she shouted, "That's right, she poisoned my son! Think about that when you are sipping your frappés. She poisoned him, and then after he survived with damaged kidneys, she slit his throat." Ellen emphasized her point by drawing a finger across the front of her throat.

"You will have to leave," said a security officer, grabbing her elbow. She shook it off.

"I will go. I will go. She also poisoned her employer, Ian Franklin. You can look it up."

"I was acquitted!" yelled Amanda.

"Enjoy your drinks!" shouted Ellen, stomping off with two security officers behind her. The following day, Amanda was given two weeks' pay and a warning not to apply at other Starbucks.

Amanda was young, attractive, and knew the basic skill of making espresso drinks. Within a week she was hired by the Bluebeard Café. The shop was located in a former mechanic's garage built in the thirties. The floor was concrete, and the walls were made of bricks. On hot days, the wide bay door was opened for the breeze. Not only was it a coffee shop; it also had a roasting area. Large bags of beans were stacked away from the seating area. Throughout the room were metal tables and wooden chairs. Some tables were for two customers to sit, and there were other larger tables. It was not far from the college, so many of the patrons spent their days drinking coffee, leaving for classes, and then returning to study or socialize. It was also near a middle school, so some of those students came in as well. The Italian drinks were popular, and the pastries were made by a well-known bakery. It was a hit with various people who, while they did not mingle, neither did they begrudge the others' presence.

Amanda thought getting fired from Starbucks was one of the best things that could have happened to her. She liked the loud music and chatter of the students. The manager, Rick, had taken a liking to her and was teaching her latte art. Within a month she had learned how to create a double heart with tulips on both sides.

For Rick, latte art was much more than pouring micro foam into a shot of espresso and making a pattern or design on the surface. He often compared latte art to the Tibetan Buddhist tradition of sand mandala, involving the creation and destruction of mandalas made from colored sand. On his forearm he had a multicolored tattoo of an espresso cup with a Yin and Yang sign in the center. All of the staff had tattoos of one kind or another.

Amanda thought from time to time of getting a tattoo. She had never really had a group of friends to hang out with, identify with, or be accepted by. If a tattoo would help her to gain more acceptance, it seemed like a small price to pay, even if she didn't really want one. She had not had time for extracurricular events. Growing up, she spent half her time with her mother, Kathy Washington, and half her time with her father, Stephen Bowman.

When she was at her mother's, her father called every day, reminding her that he missed her, and they should never be separated from each other. He often said her mother wanted her half-time only, so she would not have to pay child support to him.

Living half-time in two different households meant that she could not participate full-time in many activities. On the road so much, she did not have much time to socialize outside of class with girls or boys her age. Right before her senior year with her father's support, she refused to return to her mother's home. Her mother, knowing that courts seldom forced teenagers to do anything, had not fought to enforce the custody arrangement. She then entered a new school where friendships had already been solidified for many years, and she did not take part in extracurricular activities. She simply traded the isolation of traveling between homes for living in a single home where isolation from classmates was the rule. After school, her grandmother, Ellen, always picked her up and took her to her house or to her father's. He intensified her isolation from others by discouraging her from leaving the house without him or his mother.

When Amanda was fired from Starbucks, she was afraid. She never had much time on her own. When she moved away from her mother, for the first time in her life, she had to pay rent. But leaving Starbucks was not nearly as dramatic as she thought it would be. The Bluebeard, within days, felt like the place where she was meant to be.

Rick was a patient instructor. He taught her the basics of latte art. She soon learned the practical skills of latte art, like pouring the milk too slowly causes the milk to separate in the pitcher, resulting in lacerated milk. Raising the pitcher too quickly causes the milk to dive into the crema, rather than resting on top of the crema, Within a week, she had various techniques down, and could chat with customers and smile while make their drink. Rick was City Latte Art Champion three years in a row, and he was now the grand master who judged competitions. Within two months, Rick gave her a three-piece set of latte tools. He considered her skill at cutting edges in the foam ruthless and encouraged her to make her own designs. He could no longer compete, but he wanted her to compete in the upcoming latte design competition. He felt it was always nice to have a trophy on display near the cash register.

She enjoyed the work, the praise, and the joy her patterns gave the customers, and still she wondered if her joy would last. For Rick, the art was paramount and helped sell the beans he and his co-owner roasted and blended on the premises. Was this the joy in helping others that Father Martin had spoken of? She doubted it, and yet the work pleased her. Still, the emptiness of indifference that once protected her now seemed to drag her down into greater and greater levels of depression when she was not busy.

One day, an older man, somewhere in his late thirties or early forties, was near the espresso machines where she was working, staring at her as if he knew her. He was also wearing a gray suit and tie, unusual attire for the café.

"Yours is the decaf cappuccino," she said.

"Yes," he said.

"There are a couple orders ahead of yours. I will call it out when it's ready."

"You don't recognize me, do you?"

21

"You've been here before. You always order a large decaf cappuccino."

"That's right. You had a lot on your mind when I first saw you. I was a witness in your trial. I am glad you got off."

She took a closer look at him. Too much chatting with customers was not recommended by Rick. "That's right. Your wife died not long before the trial. I remember you now."

"This is my little girl, Emma. She just started kindergarten in elementary school. My name is Ike Kelly."

Amanda glanced at the little girl with a spoon of gelato in her mouth who waved back vigorously.

"She is cute." Amanda placed two Americanos on the counter and called out that the drinks were ready. A college-age boy, with a scarf around his neck (even though it was warm outside), fetched the cups and took them to a table where a girl with a silver nose ring and rose tattoo on her wrist waited. The Bluebeard clientele was never stereotypical.

Once the Americanos were made, Amanda thoroughly wiped the steamer nozzle clean and was making a vanilla latte. "Yours will be next," she said with a smile. The vanilla latte man came and went, and Amanda began to prepare the cappuccino.

"I am glad it worked out," Ike Kelly repeated. "It must have been hard knowing that you were innocent of what you were accused of."

"Innocence is relative when lawyers are involved," she replied and went back to work.

She used her tools to make a teddy bear design. "Decaf is more difficult to make a design with. If you had ordered a regular, the edges would be more defined," she said, smiling.

"I like to keep my hands steady, so I avoid caffeine in the afternoon," he said as he moved away.

As Ike moved away, Ellen Bowman suddenly stood in front of Amanda. Taking off a baseball cap, Bowman shook long gray hair over her shoulders. "You can fool all the people you want, but I know you are a killer. It took me a while to track you down, but now I know where you are."

As if on wings, Rick was at Amanda's side. "You need to leave."

"What? Will you call the police?"

"You should be so lucky."

"She killed my son. What do you think your customers will think of a murderer making their drinks?"

"This place is named after a man who killed six wives. I think they will be just fine if she makes them drinks. Your sonny boy abused her, and she was never charged with his death. So, buzz off!" He slammed her drip coffee down on the counter. "I made it to go. Buzz off!"

"She killed my son. She slit his throat."

"Buzz off! He needed killing."

Leaving her coffee cup on the counter Ellen left, knocking over a rack of free magazines and newspapers as she brushed past a teenager with a bright red mohawk.

The boy returned the magazines and newspapers to their rack and walked over to Amanda.

"Line starts over here," said Rick, pointing to the order spot several feet away. The boy ignored him.

"You're Amanda, aren't you?"

Amanda nodded, but looked puzzled. She knew who she was, but as to who he was, she had no idea.

"It's me, Kyle Boardman. You were the receptionist at Dr. Franklin's office. You gave my mom rice cakes and slipped me shortbread cookies when she wasn't looking."

"Kyle, of course," Amanda said. "I didn't recognize you."

"I have hair now, and I've grown a foot or so."

"And it's red," laughed Amanda.

"My dad used to give me buzz cuts every week. When we heard you tried to kill Franklin, we all cheered."

"I was accused of trying to kill Dr. Franklin," she said emphasizing the word *accused*, and added, "but I was acquitted."

"We were all glad you got off. Well, not everyone. We all hated him. All except Randy. Randy O'Conner, that is. He liked him."

"Is Randy the boy who used to come over to my desk all the time and try to peek down my blouse?"

"That's him. That's why we call him Rowdy Randy. He hasn't changed much."

"Drinks are backing up," said Rick. "Sport, if you're going to buy something, get in line."

"I'll be back. I'll bring others. I just wanted to be sure you were here." Kyle said, backing away and smiling.

4

Abel seldom deviated from his morning routine, so when he quickly scanned the paper and got out of bed, well ahead of his scheduled time of 7am, Billie was curious. Even Barney, who was in the middle, was curious.

"Going somewhere?" Billie asked.

"The sun rises at different times. Why shouldn't I? Good to change routines from time to time."

"Changing routines is not your strong suit."

At the foot of the bed were Atticus and Henry. He walked around the bed and petted them. "They are nice, but I miss Murphy."

Murphy was their dog for nine years. He was a big sweet golden retriever with thick fur. They'd gotten him the same day as Charlie, a red golden retriever, who had died at five years of age with bone cancer.

They got Barney to keep Murphy company a few years ago. They had taken Murphy in to get him fitted for a brace, and they walked out of the vet's office with a diagnosis of terminal bone cancer. He died quickly. Before they learned of his illness, they discovered Barney had a life shortening condition. His body could not process protein normally. He was on prescription dog food and daily medications. Neither Abel nor Billie ever considered not doing all that could be done for any dog. Because Barney had a shortened life expectancy, they got two dogs so that when he passed, the survivor dog would not be alone. To them this made sense.

"But why are you up early?" Billie asked.

"I still miss Murphy's thick fur. It has taken me a while to get used to the heat coming from Henry and Atticus."

"It took me a while to adjust because we decided that goldens are just too overbred. It is nice that we rescued a couple of mixed breeds. Now, answer my question. Why are you up early?"

"Commissioner Goldman asked me to come in and speak to him before court starts."

"I knew something was up. It was that article, wasn't it? I warned you there would be repercussions."

"I don't think half the lawyers in Hardin County even read the *Bar News*. I think he wants my advice on the Rules of Evidence."

"Really?"she intoned. "I missed the weather report. When did hell freeze over?"

"He might have inside information."

Abel arrived at the courthouse just as its doors to the public were opening. He displayed his bar card and skirted around the metal detectors which was just as well. He left his .38 revolver locked in his car, but forgot to take out his sturdy pocketknife, which by legal standards was considered a weapon. However, by his standards, it was an item not to be without. He owned several, but the one he carried most often was a wooden-handled Puma that Kathy Washington gave him upon her return from Germany with her mother and Amanda. Getting Amanda out of the country for a simple two-week trip was not easy. Before Stephen Bowman, Amanda's father, would sign off on an order allowing them to travel, he demanded that a cash bond be deposited with the court clerk. Amanda also had to have a cell phone where he could reach her daily, and he called her every day. Upon their return from Germany, Bowman insisted on picking her up soon after they landed. Like a jealous lover, he never relinquished control over her, even when she was out of his sight.

Commissioner Edmond Goldman was in the main first floor hallway leading to his chambers. Tapping his wristwatch, he said, "Glad you made it." Without waiting for a response from Abel, he opened the door and let Abel follow him. The narrow hallway was dimly lit and lined with shelves and boxes. They passed the back door to the courtroom where Goldman was presiding and went farther on to the commissioner's chambers of another courtroom. Every six months, the commissioners rotated to different courtrooms. He knew the commissioner who was presiding in the main courtroom, Room 100. He thought of the labyrinth Theseus had traveled to kill the Minotaur. Abel failed to keep pace with Goldman, so Goldman stopped for him to catch up. "Did you know that the Minotaur is the first Infernal Guardian Dante encounters within the walls of the City of Dis?"

"No, should I?"

"Everyone who administers justice should know Dante. Most people begin their journey through the family law court with a temporary hearing before a court commissioner."

"I studied economics and accounting before I went to law school. Knowing how to divide assets is important in my courtroom. A practical education is important. A knowledge of dead Italians, not so much. What's your point?"

"If you and Carpenter wanted to meet with me, why not tell me she would be here?"

"Would you have come?"

27

"Of course. Lead on."

Commissioner Julia Carpenter was behind a computer screen and took her time looking up at them. Unlike the Minotaur, she was small, boney and bulimic thin. Like the Minotaur, she was often angry and looked down on people, especially people who were too poor to afford a lawyer, as well as lawyers who did not appear sufficiently subservient to her expectations. Before she became a judicial officer, she and Abel crossed paths from time to time. She always impressed him as meticulous, but easily rattled when things did not go her way. Now she made a point of letting people know that in her courtroom things went her way.

"You must know why you are here."

"Ed invited me," replied Abel.

"You know what I mean."

Abel shook his head. "No, I don't."

Carpenter tilted her head toward Abel and held up a copy of the local *Bar News*. "Your article, Abel, your article. There are rules, Abel, and they are to be followed. You wrote this, didn't you?"

"Previously, my client, the mother, raised concerns about possible abuse. Not only was my motion denied, but the commissioner warned that he and other commissioners were tired of hearing from me. He said if I brought any more motions, I could face sanctions, and my client would get limited supervised visitation."

"I suppose. Sounds like something I would write. I think you may have added a word or two," said Abel. "Once I write something, I try not to remember it or look at it again."

Carpenter slammed the magazine on her desk as if attempting to slay a fly. Abel did not appear impressed.

28

"Yes, I wrote the whole article. What of it? Half the lawyers in this county don't even read the magazine. What I wrote is protected by the First Amendment and truth is a defense."

As if she did not hear him, Carpenter said in a loud voice, "This is what the *Rules of Professional Conduct* say about lying lawyers criticizing judicial officers, and I quote, 'A lawyer shall not make a statement that the lawyer knows to be false or with reckless disregard as to its truth or falsity concerning the qualifications, integrity, or record of a judge, adjudicatory officer or public legal officer,....' Did you know that?"

"What does that have to do with my article?"

"In the comment section, it is specifically noted, 'To maintain the fair and independent administration of justice, lawyers are encouraged to continue traditional efforts to defend judges and courts unjustly criticized.' What do you have to say to that? We are thinking about filing a bar complaint against you. You could be sanctioned or even disbarred."

"Again, let's say truth is a defense, and I have a First Amendment right to write what I did. I didn't even mention Ed by name."

"Commissioner Goldman," she snapped, rising out of her chair.

"Ed asked me to come here," responded Abel and went on, "What I wrote was true, not false. Bring a bar complaint, and I will prove that my criticism was more than fair. I could have said far more."

"What more could you have said?"

"Before the hearing, when Ed threatened me, I asked for a protection order stopping Stephen Bowman's visitation. The child was interviewed by

29

a counselor and disclosed troubling facts about how the father was bathing her."

"I have no recollection of that," said Carpenter.

"My motion and the declaration of the counselor is in the court file. You can look it up," said Abel. "I brought the motion, asking that his visitation be suspended so that more information could be gathered. You denied it. You said that visitation should proceed, and the father's mother should be present when the father was with the child. After that weekend, the child recanted all the statements she made."

"If the child recanted the allegations, then there you have it. There was nothing to be done. I was right not to grant your motion."

"Standard protocol is to isolate the child from the suspect so that a forensic exam could be done. That is what Child Protection Services do. That is what police investigators do. No one lets the suspect have custody of the child until an investigation is done."

"But it was the mother who had the child interviewed. Hardly a neutral source. She did not obtain a court order allowing the child to be interviewed."

"There was no order in place prohibiting the child from being interviewed by a counselor."

"Perhaps not, but getting the child interviewed without the father's permission or knowledge rankled me. It was underhanded. Not something I would do. Not something a decent family lawyer would do. It seemed sneaky. Like something you picked up from your criminal practice. This is a family court."

"You denied my request because you thought I violated some ethical standard in the sky. I was trying to protect a child. You disregarded classic protocol and sent the child off for the weekend with the father after I gave you evidence that he was not to be trusted."

"His mother was with them."

"And you trusted her, why?" Abel shouted.

"Because she was a mother," said Carpenter as if the answer was self-evident.

"If abuse is suspected, the suspected abuser is separated from the child. Neither of you followed that standard protocol." Abel unfolded a sheet of paper and waved it in front of them both. "I filed this with the court about a year after you sent the child back to the father." He pointed a finger at Carpenter and read the following:

Dear Mr. Abel:

You will recall that approximately 18 months ago I conducted psychological evaluations of both parties in this matter following allegations that Stephen Ray Bowman, 35, had sexually abused their minor child, Amanda Elizabeth Bowman, now 7. I did not recommend any changes in Mr. Bowman's access to Amanda at that time, as the findings of his evaluation were inconclusive. Actuarial assessment revealed him to be at a low risk to perpetrate acts of sexual abuse, and he appeared devoid of Axis I symptomatology. However, it was notable that Mr. Bowman was found deceptive on a sexual history polygraph, and he manifested certain problematic Axis II traits (e.g., marked feelings of personal inadequacy) that are associated with an incest offender. I concluded, as did the guardian ad litem, that the allegations of sexual abuse of Amanda by Mr. Bowman were "completely contaminated," primarily as a result of undue influence of the mother, Kathy Ursula Washington.

Recently, your office provided me with copies of the Jackson Police Department's Report No. 11-07849, which details observations of Mr. Bowman's contacts with Amanda on the Interurban Trail. According to two disinterested parties (i.e., unknown to Ms. Washington), Mr. Bowman was observed holding Amanda in a way that appeared markedly inappropriate (i.e., she was straddling his groin area, while he was perceived to be attempting to kiss her on the lips). The observers noted independently that Mr. Bowman and Amanda initially appeared to be a romantic couple rather than a father and a minor prepubescent child. One of the observers of Mr. Bowman's conduct was Jackson Police Officer Patrick B. Tubman; the other was a local middle school teacher.

As a result of these concerns, on July 29th, Amanda was interviewed by Forensic Child Interview Specialist Carolyn Northman of the Jackson County Prosecutor's Office. According to the summary of the interview prepared by Officer M. Vasey, Amanda disclosed that she was having some "hard times." Then she began crying and pointed to her private area, saying that her dad had hurt her "right here." What strikes the undersigned as incredulous is that despite these disclosures, the officer reported that "(a) There were no disclosures, and she left with her father, Stephen Bowman."

Another significant disclosure made in the interview was that Amanda reported she does not like it when her father puts a gun to her head and pulls the trigger. Interestingly, in an email received today from Ms. Washington, she indicated that Amanda disclosed that this happened again recently. Reportedly, Mr. Bowman "...threatened Amanda with a new gun and even clicked it. He told her that if she cries he will shoot." Learning this, the undersigned advised her to contact CPS immediately.

In summary, the new information gleaned from the July police reports and the resultant forensic interview, along with Ms. Washington's email received today, suggests the need *for further action in this matter by CPS and the court. The reports about Mr. Bowman's conduct suggest at the very least he would appear to need Risk Management Therapy, a targeted treatment in which he would learn appropriate parental boundaries.*

Your prompt attention to these concerns is greatly appreciated.

Very truly yours,
Mathew B. Blackridge
Licensed Psychologist
Certified Sex Offender Treatment Provider

"I filed this with the court and asked for a temporary restraining order, and you denied it, Ed. You denied it. Why? You know the protocol of isolating the potential victim from a perpetrator. That was all I asked for. Why didn't either of you grant me a simple request? You both know what you should have done. Why am I here? You want to file a bar complaint? File it, but you know what my response will be? Do what you want, but you can't give yourselves a better past. What you did had consequences, and you cannot change that. Why am I here?"

"We want to know what you told Amanda Bowman," said Goldman.

"She has been in the courthouse reviewing the court files," said Carpenter.

"She has sat in both our courtrooms watching us," added Goldman.

"The courtrooms are public as are the court files," said Abel. "Why are you so concerned?"

"She poisoned two people, her father and Ian Franklin, with antifreeze. When they didn't die, she shot Franklin in the knee and slit her father's throat," said Carpenter.

33

"She was acquitted of poisoning Franklin and shooting him in the knee. She was given a misdemeanor for her father's poisoning. As for slitting her father's throat, that was deemed self-defense; no charges were ever brought. For judicial officers, you seem to have little faith in the judicial process."

Carpenter fixed Abel with a cold stare. "But why is she there? She slit her father's throat. Why is she watching us?" Carpenter demanded.

"Does she threaten you or do anything other than observe? Does she follow you home?" asked Abel.

"No, just watch. That is all she does," said Goldman.

"Are you sure she doesn't follow you home?"

"Do you think she might?" gasped Carpenter.

"Now he's mocking us," said Goldman.

"Did you show her your article?" asked Carpenter.

"No," said Abel. "She hardly needed to read the article to know that you are not infallible."

By the time he left the commissioner's passageway and stepped into the main hall, Abel knew that he had stepped away from the practice of family law in Hardin County. Unlike Amanda, who had sought revenge for actual wrongs done to her, Carpenter and Goldman were petty people and would use their power to harm, if not him, then his clients, whenever he was before them. They were not the only family law commissioners in Hardin County, but the chance of appearing before them was great. He did not want his clients to suffer because of some vendetta against him.

5

Ike Kelly and Emma were soon such regulars at the Bluebeard Café that Emma had a drink named after her – steamed milk with a dash of vanilla, sprinkled with cinnamon, and Ike's business suits no longer merited second glances from the artist college students with rings in their noses. The two usually arrived in the mid-afternoon when Emma was done with her classes and Amanda's barista shift was soon to be over. Amanda had no sooner sat Ike's decaf cappuccino down, Emma's drink, and a glass of water for herself, than a woman she did not recognize approached their table. The woman was lean with a decidedly stiff posture, but when Emma shouted, "Grannie!" the woman was suddenly less stiff and smiled. At the corners of her eyes were small crow's feet.

"Alice," said Ike, standing up. "What a surprise!"

"I thought you might be here, and I was in the neighborhood. I thought I would drop by and say hello to my favorite granddaughter."

"How nice," said Ike and added, "this is Amanda, she works here. Amanda, this is Alice Medford, Tiffany's mother."

Amanda was wearing blue jeans and a red T-Shirt with the logo of a local rock band.

"Yes, I saw her behind the espresso machine. It must be nice to work in a place with a relaxed dress code."

"Yes, it is nice. I worked at Starbucks for a while. Would you care to join us?"

"Oh please, oh please," said Emma. "Amanda named a drink after me. See? It's on the board," she

35

said, pointing to the cash register. Taped to the machine was a sign written in bold black Sharpie suggesting, "Try an Emma – steamed milk with vanilla."

"I saw that," smiled Alice. With her face still frozen in a smile, she added, "I thought maybe Emma and I could sit together and let the two of you chat."

"You're more than welcome to sit with us," said Amanda.

"I see Emma so seldom. I thought a little time alone would be nice."

"Of course," said Ike. "Enjoy yourself with Grannie. We will be right here."

"Have a nice chat with your young friend," said Alice, giving Amanda a once-over with her eyes.

When they were across the room, Amanda said, "That was a surprise."

"Sort of," said Ike. "Ever since Alice and her husband filed a third-party custody lawsuit against me, I have felt like I was being watched. I thought it was my imagination, but her turning up here confirms that I was not mistaken."

"Why is she seeking custody of Emma?"

"She has never liked me. She and her husband were lifelong teachers. When she heard I was working in a bank she was pleased." He paused. "It wasn't like I was a hit man to the mob, but she made it clear that people who deal with money were less than people who devoted their lives to helping others, like doctors, nurses, police officers, firemen, and teachers."

"What about lawyers?"

"She definitely does not see lawyers as people who help other people. To her they are just in it for the money. Anyway, Tiffany did not portray me in the best light. I like to come home and have a beer. She told her mother I was an excessive drinker who cared more about having a drink than anything else. When Tiffany and the other parents were certain that Gary Shipman and Sarah Shipman had used their day care center to abuse the children, I was skeptical. I just did not act as Tiffany thought a loving father should act."

"Which was how?"

"She thought Emma was abused. The evidence seemed iffy at best. Ian Franklin, a child counselor, spent a lot of time convincing the children that they were abused, including Emma. He was paid big money by the State to investigate child abuse, and if he found none, his money pipeline would dry up. When the children were interviewed away from Franklin, and the parents nodded their heads telling them what to say, the children said they were not abused, or could not remember. They thought they were abused because their parents told them they were. Emma fell into that category."

Amanda added, "I was a receptionist for Franklin. I know what he did. He kept insisting that a child say they were abused. No matter how many times the child said they were not abused, he would press them to say that they were victims of abuse. Eventually he wore them down. But I am telling you what you already know."

He nodded that he did.

"I remember you. Tiffany was the one who brought Emma to the sessions, but I was there a few times. Why did you poison him with antifreeze? Was it because of what he did to the children, convincing them that they were victims when they were not?"

"For months we have chatted while Emma drank her steamed milk and you had your cappuccino, but we have never talked about these things. You have never asked me about Franklin."

"I was afraid that if I asked too much, you would not want to talk to me."

"So strange, Ike." Amanda paused. "We are drawn to each other by the darkness we have experienced, but all we talk about is the lighter things in our lives." She leaned close to him and whispered into his ear as lovers sometimes do. "We talk about things that we don't remember. We talk about your work in the bank. We talk about Emma's play at school and the words she is learning. Still, all of the time what we really have in common is the darker side of things we have not spoken about. On the day that Franklin was shot in the knee in the parking lot, he had just fired me. Commissioner Goldman humiliated me about what I experienced before. Goldman and Franklin made a point of telling me that I was just a girl in their eyes, and no one would believe me. They allowed me to be abused, rather than admit they made a mistake. Goldman and Franklin took the elevator to the parking garage. I took the stairs. I wanted to be alone and not see them again. When I went downstairs, I interrupted the man who just shot Franklin. He was looking for something on the ground. I know now that he was looking for a shell casing." Her hand landed on his knee and pressed inward as if her fingers were talons. "That man was you, Ike."

He gulped for air and wanted to look away, but her big brown eyes were fixed on him and he couldn't. He knew that this moment would come sooner or later. He knew that the more often she saw him and talked to him, the more she would be certain it was him in the stairwell. She only had a glimpse, yet he knew that sooner or later she would say what she just said. He could not deny what he did, not to her. "Yes," he said. "That was me."

"Grannie says she wants to take me to Disneyland. Can I go? Please? Don't say no, daddy." Tugging on his arm, Emma repeated, "Disneyland, daddy, can I go?"

"I wanted to talk to you first, but it just now blurted out of me," said Alice.

"That can happen," said Ike. "Can you come for dinner?"

"I have plans," said Alice.

"I meant Amanda."

"I am busy too," said Amanda.

"You seem distracted," said Alice to Ike. "A parent should always be in control."

"Thanks for the tip. We have to go. We have to go now," Ike said, grabbing Emma's hand and standing up.

6

Emma and a girl her age were playing hopscotch on a grid made with red chalk on the sidewalk leading to her front door, when Amanda pulled up in front. "Amanda," shouted Emma with glee, "Daddy said you were coming."

"Here I am," smiled Amanda.

"This is my friend, Kat. She lives in the house over there," she said, pointing to a house at the other end of the cul-de-sac. "Kat, this is Amanda. She makes drinks at the Bluebeard. I told you about her. She made a drink for me. It is called an 'Emma,'" she said proudly.

"You told me. Emma says you are nice," said Kat. In her hand she had a beanbag. "Do you know how to play?"

"I've played before," said Amanda.

Kat tossed the bag onto the fifth square. Without waiting for a dare, Amanda hopped on one foot to the fifth square, bent down on one leg, picked up the bag and hopped to the tenth square. Then she returned with all of her hops in the proper squares.

Laughing, Ike greeted Amanda from the front door and invited her inside. "Daddy, can Amanda be on our team?" asked Emma.

"Team?" quizzed Amanda.

"On Saturday mornings we have a neighborhood competition," replied Ike.

"Can she?" pursued Emma.

"We will see," said Ike. He glanced at his watch. "Fifteen more minutes, then you should come inside."

"Ok," said Emma.

On top of the stove, in a large cast iron pan, red sauce was simmering. Ike stirred the sauce a couple of times and turned the gas burner down.

"Would you like something to drink? I don't have any alcohol, but I have plenty of other things to drink. Some juice boxes that come with little straws?" he added with a smile.

"Water is fine."

From a Perrier bottle, he poured a glass for her, then poured one for himself. "Thank you for coming," he said. "After what you said in the café, I thought you might not want to come to my house."

An orange cat appeared at his feet and sat down. "This is Matlock. He is not shy."

She reached down to pet the cat, and he purred in response to her touch. "Have you had him long?"

"About two years. I got him after Tiffany died."

"Did you have another cat before Matlock?"

"Ishmael, but he died," Ike said. He quickly added, "So you recognized me from the stairwell. When?"

Amanda straightened up and moved closer to him, looking him in the eye, "About your shooting Franklin? You have nothing to fear from me. I didn't like him either."

"Why didn't you say anything?"

"I came down the stairwell and you were bent over, looking for something. I was in jail for nine months awaiting trial. I suppose some of the 'don't snitch' mentality rubbed off on me. You saw me and ran off. If I told them there was a man with a gun, no one would've believed me then. Why would they believe me now? If I were convicted of shooting Franklin, would you have come forward?"

"I'm not sure. I told myself that I would, but I am not sure."

"You shot him in the knee from twenty-five yards away. Where did you learn to shoot?"

"Air Force. I was on a shooting team."

"Can you teach me to shoot?" Ike nodded that he could. "It's nice that Emma is here. I knew when I saw her that I could trust you."

Ike nodded his agreement.

"Grannie is here," beamed Emma, skipping into the kitchen area. Behind her came Alice. She was not beaming when she saw Amanda so close to Ike.

"Ike, Emma told me you had a visitor."

"Why are you here?"

"To pick up Emma for a McDonald's Happy Meal and a stroll in the park. Didn't your lawyer tell you? My lawyer emailed him that I couldn't come tomorrow, so I came today to pick her up. Your lawyer didn't tell you? Sounds like your lawyer has other things to do."

"He is a good lawyer."

"Check your emails. You might have missed one. I know you are busy," said Alice. To Amanda she said, "You are the barista girl. Branching out into babysitting, are you?"

"Alice," exclaimed Ike.

"She is much younger than you. I have a right to know who is in my granddaughter's house."

"That is not a legal right," said Ike.

"It's a moral right. My daughter is dead, and I have the right to know what is going on in the house where my granddaughter lives. Amanda, have you been to college? Do you see yourself making lattes for life? Do you always go to the homes of customers?"

"Don't answer that," demanded Ike.

Pressing close to Ike, Amanda wrapped her arm around his arm. "No, I never have before. I first saw Ike when I was on trial for murder. He was a witness for the prosecution. I was attracted to his honesty. I was acquitted of all charges. Well, all but one, a misdemeanor. Hardly counts as a crime compared to the others I was charged with."

Alice's jaw dropped while waiting for a further explanation, but none came.

"While I was in jail for months, I didn't let myself think of the future. If the State had its way, I would have no future. Do I see myself making lattes all my life? I have no idea, but one thing I know is jail did not break me, and neither will snippy remarks from old women who have never been to jail."

"Well, I never," began Alice.

"I'm ready," said Emma, bounding into the room and taking her grandma's hand.

"Have her home by eight," said Ike, hoping for eight-thirty.

7

Commissioner Julia Carpenter was a diminutive woman. Her light brown hair was wavy in Shirley Temple curls. When her judicial assistant saw that she was at the door to her chambers waiting to be announced, he said, "All rise." It was an entrance she never tired of repeating.

As she ascended the steps to the judicial chair, she cradled in one arm working copies of pleadings she had reviewed, and she cradled a black seat cushion in the other arm. Without the cushion, the back of the chair would be above her head. She thought that demeaned the authority she wanted to project over the room.

She sat down and studied the large courtroom to be sure that all were standing. Satisfied that everyone was standing, she said, "You may be seated."

Her voice was high-pitched, but her tone firm and her stare cold. The courtroom was Room 100, the largest courtroom in Hardin County, several times larger than the other rooms used by the court commissioners and judges. Suggestions that it should be divided into smaller, more functional courtrooms were never seriously considered. From time to time, its expanse was needed for swearing in new lawyers or judges. Along one wall, in columns of four, were photographs of all the judges, past to present, who had served on the Hardin County Superior Court. Under each photograph was the name of the judge and length of service. This was a courtroom that no judge wanted subdivided.

Monday through Friday, the afternoon docket was always the same. Supplemental Proceedings were heard first. Supplemental Proceedings are when a debtor is summoned into court to provide, under oath, a list of their creditors with an accounting of their assets. In Hardin County, the debtors are sworn under oath and then sent off with the creditors to give testimony in a conference room. If there are issues, they return to the courtroom.

Otherwise, they are never seen again that day. After the last of the creditors to appear are sworn, probate and minor settlement matters are heard. Then, at the end of the docket came eviction hearings. Having evictions heard last was sensible. At the far back of the courtroom, coming in and out into a hallway, were lawyers for landlords and their renter clients, attempting to work out agreements that would forestall or ease their ejectment onto the street, with all that they owned.

Amanda sat in the center of the back bench, watching the proceedings. On the days when she was not at the Bluebeard Café, she was often in the courthouse watching the commissioners' hearings, the arraignments, and trials, both civil and criminal. The discrepancies in what opposing parties claimed fascinated her.

She would listen and watch and decide what the judge should do and wait to hear what the judge decided. Within only a few months, her predictions on what a judge would decide had improved. Occasionally, she thought she might pursue a career as a jury consultant, which she did not think required a college degree so much as an understanding of the depravity of human nature. Her father had taught her much as he attempted to convince her that his perverse love for her was love. While in jail waiting for trial, she had an opportunity to learn about the lengths that people go to deceive themselves and others. In the courtrooms, she learned even more about the lengths to which people will go to cover up their corruption, even from themselves, and the stupid ways they exposed themselves.

She came to the conclusion that she would be a good consultant when she read about a jury consultant who died in prison after taking his personal computer, loaded with child pornography, into a shop to be repaired. So wise, but so arrogant and forgetful. And to think that he was advising people about people. She could do that, and she thought that she could do better. Amanda's years of abuse by her father and hiding the truth from herself and others had given her insight into what people were really thinking, no matter what they said.

As the last debtor was sworn in and cautioned to be truthful, Commissioner Carpenter called out the first case name. A woman pushing a rolling infant seat with a fidgety child came forward.

Carpenter looked down at her and asked her to raise her right hand to be sworn under oath. The woman quickly did as she was told.

"Children are not supposed to be in this courtroom," the commissioner said.

"My babysitter canceled at the last moment."

"You should have found someone else."

"She canceled at the last minute, and I did not want to be late or not appear."

"Nevertheless, you should have planned ahead. You are the maternal grandmother?"

"Yes, my daughter uses drugs and abandoned her son by leaving him with me months ago."

"So you wrote in the pleadings. Where is the father?"

"He has never been a father. He's never paid support." In the infant seat, the child cried out and the woman hoisted him onto her hip.

"This is why we don't allow children in the courtroom. You couldn't find a day care center?"

"No, they cost money."

"So, you didn't look for one, did you?"

"No, Your Madam." Seeing the judicial assistant roll his eyes toward the sign that said, 'Address the court as YOUR HONOR,' she corrected herself and said, "Your Honor, there wasn't really time."

"Where is the father?"

"I don't know. He disappeared before Jimmy, Jimmy is my grandson, was born."

"You still have to serve him before you can go forward."

"I don't know where he is. How do I tell him?"

"I do not give advice. I rule on the law and your motion for guardianship before me is incorrect. I am not granting your request. You have to go."

"You are dismissing the case?"

"I am not granting your request. If you don't do things correctly, it may be dismissed at a later date."

In tears, the woman rushed toward the back of the courtroom while Carpenter glared at her.

At the back of the room, Amanda stopped her, and they spoke for only a few moments. While Amanda spoke, the woman nodded. She was smiling as she left the large room.

"Come here," demanded Carpenter.

Amanda pointed at her chest.

47

"Yes, you, come here," demanded Carpenter.

Amanda walked forward, not slowly, but clearly not as quickly as Carpenter would have liked. She tapped her pen loudly on the bench as Amanda approached. Amanda was wearing a silver cross and chain outside of her black sweater.

"What is your name?" demanded Carpenter.

"You know who I am," said Amanda.

"State your name for the record."

"Amanda Bowman."

"You are not a lawyer. It is illegal for you to give legal advice. Did you give that woman legal advice?"

"I told her about the free legal clinic on Thursday nights in the law library, where it is legal for lawyers to give legal advice."

With her eyes, Carpenter scanned the lawyers in the room looking for a smile or snicker. Finding none, she said. "Ms. Bowman, I am ordering you to stay in the courtroom until the end of the docket. We can talk more then."

"Alright." Amanda saw the judicial assistant roll his eyes toward the sign directing subservience. She repeated, "Alright."

Carpenter waved her hand for Amanda to remove herself.

The remainder of the afternoon docket went quickly. The lawyers on the minor settlement docket were experienced, and the sums settled on seemed reasonable. In one case, an inexperienced lawyer had neglected to have the child and the child's parents present for the order approving the settlement. Carpenter quickly told them to reschedule the hearing with the parents present.

48

After all the settlements were complete, Carpenter approved the opening of two probate matters for which the surviving spouse was the only heir. Before the unlawful detainer docket was called, Carpenter instructed the judicial assistant to request that security stand at the door and make sure Amanda did not slip away.

An unlawful detainer action is a quick proceeding to evict a person, usually for nonpayment of rent. During the Pandemic, various laws and city ordinances were passed that delayed the eviction of a person for nonpayment of rent. When the cases were finally heard, there were many reasons for nonpayment of rent, such as illness, slow pay on benefits, and so on. In the end, if the money was owed, the request for eviction was granted. Once a tenant admitted they owed money, things moved quickly because whatever excuse that was offered by the tenant was never good enough. Such is the law, and Carpenter was quick to point that out. Each time she signed an eviction order, with the compassion of an indifferent executioner delivering death with a single stroke, Carpenter would say, "You did not pay your rent; what did you expect? Landlords have a right to payment."

After the last lawyer walked out of the room, Carpenter commanded, "Come forward."

Closely followed by the sheriff's deputy, Amanda quickly reached the front of the barrier that separated her from the commissioner.

"Why are you here?"

"You told me not to leave."

"Don't be smart with me. You know what I mean. You have been in my courtroom before. Why are you coming here?"

"I come to observe and learn. I have observed in other courtrooms too."

"Why?"

"I am considering a career in the law. I want to know what I am getting into."

"Have you reviewed the divorce court file of your parents in the clerk's office?"

Amanda remained silent.

"That is a question," snapped Carpenter. Her irritation at Amanda's silence echoed in the large, empty courtroom.

"Sorry, I thought it was a statement. Yes, I have reviewed the court file."

"Then you must know that Abel did not appeal any of the rulings made by me or Commissioner Goldman."

Amanda nodded.

"Speak up. We are recording this discussion."

As if on cue, the judicial assistant pointed to a green light on a microphone.

"Yes, I am aware of that," said Amanda.

"He could have sought a trial, but he and your mother reached an agreement with your father as to shared custody."

"Yes, that is in the court file," agreed Amanda.

"He wrote an article blaming us for whatever may have happened to you as the result of a shared custody arrangement."

"I was not aware of that," said Amanda. "I will look for it. Was it published?"

"The point is that Commissioner Goldman and I relied upon the statements on file and the recommendation of the parenting investigator in making our rulings. If Abel didn't like what we did, then he should have asked a judge to review our rulings. That is the proper way for a lawyer to act.

Abel did not act properly, and he got the rulings he deserved. Do you understand that?"

"I understand you are saying that you are blameless."

"Exactly." Hearing no further response, Carpenter added, "The courtrooms are public courtrooms, but if I suspect you are attempting to intimidate me or any judicial officer, I will make certain that you are prosecuted. Do you understand?"

"Yes, ma'am."

"You may go," said Carpenter as she walked to her chambers carrying a metal water flask in one hand and her seat cushion in the other.

For the next hour, Carpenter reviewed working papers for the following morning's docket. It was a full docket, which meant each side would have little more than eight minutes to argue their case, setting the course of their case, just as a slight deviation in terrain near a spring sets the course of a river. The parent who is awarded temporary custody usually ends up with final custody. She took her work seriously and was often disgusted by the attempts of rookie attorneys to gloss over the deficiencies of their clients by needlessly attacking the integrity of the opposing counsel. The work was never-ending, but at 4:30pm she quit, satisfied that during the next morning's arguments she could ask clarifying questions if need be.

The passageway from her chambers to the main hallway passed by a door to Goldman's chambers. She looked in and without entering told Goldman about disciplining Amanda. "I don't think she will cause us any trouble," she said in conclusion.

"Perhaps," said Goldman. "She did slit her father's throat. So, who knows? Beyond our courtrooms it's a big world."

"Even if you granted Shipman the restraining order he wanted, he might have been killed anyway."

"I am just saying we need to be careful. That's all."

"I am not going to live in fear," Carpenter said and closed the door. Before she left the City-County Building, she asked for an escort to her car in the parking garage. The same guard, who had earlier been in the courtroom, escorted her from the building across the short walkway to the parking garage. "This is probably being overly cautious, but I just don't want a confrontation," she said.

"I understand," said the guard. "If you don't already carry pepper spray or even a gun, you might think about getting one of them."

"Do you think those are necessary?"

"I couldn't say," said the deputy.

They took the elevator to the third floor. Before stepping off, the deputy got out and looked both ways. Carpenter's car, a BMW, was a few parking spaces from the elevator. Scratched in deep gouges on the hood was the word BITCH.

8

The next day, Commissioner Carpenter rushed through the afternoon docket and left the County-City Building without reviewing the court files for the following morning. Her appointment at the MAACO shop was for four o'clock, and she did not want to be late. The sooner she could have her car repaired, the better it would be. More than once, she noticed judges in their shared area of the parking garage snickering as they walked past the word BITCH on the hood of her BMW.

She was in a hurry and did not notice a large black van following her as she pulled onto a street behind the courthouse. The van had tinted side windows. From its dents, multi-colored paint and scrapings, it appeared to be no stranger to minor and moderate collisions. The van kept at least one car back as she traveled to the MAACO body shop.

The shop was several blocks away, located near a shopping mall and the main post office. When she pulled into the MAACO lot, the van went by, turned left past the post office, then circled back behind the post office, near a homeless encampment. Then it parked with a view of the MAACO entrance.

The MAACO shop was set back from the main street with an office and several large work bays. In front of the shop there was a gated lot for vehicles in temporary storage. A large sign on the gate stated that MAACO accepted no responsibility for damage to vehicles stored on the lot. Carpenter parked in an angled stall in front of the office.

"I'm Commissioner Julia Carpenter. I have an appointment," she said to a person at the front desk.

"I'm Maggie. I will be with you in just a moment." However, she continued   talking on the phone. "Let's schedule you for an appointment, and we can give you an estimate for the work. Until the expert sees your car we can't give you an estimate, and you will need to decide what quality of work you want done." She looked up at Carpenter and raised a finger, the universal signal for "wait just a moment." Into the phone she said, "At MAACO, we offer three affordable auto paint packages tailored to your specific needs and budget concerns: Basic, Preferred, and Premium."

Carpenter remembered that was exactly what she said to her when she called. It was word for word what she read on their website. She wondered whether it was disingenuous to say the same thing over and over to each customer or merely a lack of creativity.

The receptionist paused, glanced at the card on her desk, and read from it. "What makes each of the three services unique all comes down to two factors: longevity of the paint, including warranty/durability, and the appearance of the paint, including gloss, color match and metallic appearance. This is a complicated business, but MAACO has operated for years with satisfied customers for generations. If you bring your car in, a technician can answer your questions in person. Yes. Very good. Thursday at 9am will work for us. See you then, and thank you for considering us." The woman smiled and looked up at Carpenter.

"I have a 4pm appointment," said Carpenter, glancing up at a large wall clock that showed the time was ten past four.

"The clock is fast," smiled the receptionist. "I'll buzz Joe. What with the heavy rains and potholes and the Department of Transportation laying new gravel and tar on county roads, we are backed up like you wouldn't believe."

"I am sure I couldn't," said Carpenter.

The receptionist smiled, pressed the intercom button on her phone and said, "Your four o'clock, Commissioner Julia Carpenter, is here, Joe. Please hurry."

Fifteen minutes later, Joe O'Conner appeared, wiping his hands on a pink cleaning rag. He was in his late thirties or early forties with muscular shoulders and a slight belly that extended beyond his belt. He stretched out a hand that Carpenter ignored.

"My car's in stall number three."

"Let's look at it, shall we?" Joe said and pointed to the door.

Walking to the vehicle, he said, "It's a BMW," when he was several feet from reaching the car.

"Yes, I told the woman when I booked the appointment. Is it a problem?"

"The woman at the front desk is my wife, Maggie. She is filling in today. I'm sure she didn't make the appointment. It looks good from here."

"Look at the hood."

When he saw the damage to the hood, he whistled softly. Carpenter hated whistling. "Someone sure had it in for you."

"Yes, she does."

"You know who it was? I hope she has money to pay for the repair."

"I doubt she does."

"Why the hate?"

Carpenter shook her head. "She blames me for her life. I am a court commissioner and ruled long ago that her father could have visitation rights.

Eventually he and his ex-wife agreed on shared custody. She now claims, years after my involvement, that the father abused her. She was in my courtroom yesterday for no reason other than to harass me. We spoke today, and I thought the matter was resolved, but when I went out to my car, this was there," she said, pointing at the hood.

"That sounds a lot like a case I was involved in. My son, Randy, was at a day care center and abused by the owners. A receptionist at his counselor's office was accused of killing one of the owners, Gary Shipman. Perhaps you have heard of the case?"

"Who hasn't in Hardin County?"

"She stole my gun from my car and used it to kill Shipman on Halloween night. At the trial I testified that she must have taken the gun from my car when I was at a meeting with her boss, Ian Franklin, the counselor."

"I know him well. He is a very respected counselor. She was accused of shooting him."

"I can't believe she got off. When I testified, she just sat, cold and indifferent, as if nothing I said about her caused her any concern. Pretty girl, mind you, but she has antifreeze in her blood," said Joe, shaking his head.

"That's funny," chuckled Carpenter. "She was accused of trying to poison her father and Ian with antifreeze."

"I know," said Joe. "Maggie thinks it's bad to make that a joke, but that is how I feel. She tried to kill Franklin, and she actually killed her father, yet she walked free. If she is after you, you should be careful."

"Thanks, but about my car?"

Joe bent down so his eyes were even with the hood of the car and then stood up. "Those are deep gouges. Some are down into the primer. The lighter scratches could be buffed out, but the deeper ones have to be filled in and painted over by a body shop certified to work on BMWs. My shop doesn't have that certification. You will have to take it to a BMW dealer. Another alternative is finding a hood that matches your car color, model and make, then swapping them out. BMW makes over 165 colors of green alone. The chance of finding a match for your car is unlikely."

"I should have been told this over the phone," Carpenter said.

"I'm sorry you weren't. Maggie makes the appointments; she doesn't give advice over the phone."

"Can you just repaint the car with a premium paint job?"

"I could do that, but you would not be satisfied. BMW exclusively powder coats the clear coat onto their cars, using an advanced clear coat called Enviracryl by PPG. BMW uses a premium refinish brand. MAACO does not have that. You have an expensive car and if I repainted it, it would lose at least $10,000 to $15,000 in value. You would be dissatisfied, and when you wanted to have it repainted by a certified BMW auto body shop, they may tell you they can't because you used an inferior product."

"I see MAACO advertisements all the time."

"We do good work, but we don't do luxury cars like this." Joe shook his head sadly. "I have the names and addresses of the body shops that work on BMWs. There are only a few. I think the best is in Victoria, Canada."

"Canada?"

"To really repair the damage, I think the paint will have to be stripped down and repainted from scratch. Premium paint lasts many years, but it does fade. You will never get a perfect match with the paint you have. The best thing to do is have the entire car repainted."

"How expensive is that?"

"I don't know. You have a quality car. You can drive it forever with the marring."

"That is not an option," she said.

"Then think of a week's vacation in Victoria. I understand it is a lovely city. I will get you the phone numbers."

When Carpenter left the MAACO lot, she turned left and headed toward Interstate 5 to go south. At the on-ramp, the black van from earlier pulled up behind her. As she slowed down a bit to enter the traffic flow, the blare of the black van's horn startled her. She looked in the rearview mirror. The driver was a woman with long black hair, but her face was obscured by her middle finger. Carpenter sped up and the black van dropped back and let a couple of cars come between them. When she exited to head west, the van was tailgating her. Again, she sped up and in the rearview mirror she saw the black van switch lanes. Was she being followed, or was it just her imagination?

The traffic headed west was thick with commuters heading home from work. If she was being followed, she did not want the driver to know where she lived. Carpenter drove past her normal exit from the interstate and passed under a large pedestrian two-lane overpass called Freedom Bridge. It connected the National Guard camp with the Fort Clark Army base. Yellow ribbons were sometimes tied to the railing and patriotic gatherings were common.

Especially when troops were being deployed or returning from overseas. Today, however, there was a large banner that read, "Free Gaza." Carpenter clucked her tongue as she passed under as if a banner would make a difference thousands of miles away. And, even if Israel was gone from Gaza, would life be better under the thumb of Iran, where women were ordered to cover under a veil? Not exactly progress from the distant colonial days of British rule, when Palestinian men and women were doctors and intellectuals.

She took the exit and headed south. She did not see the van and breathed a sigh of relief. The traffic was two lanes, bumper-to-bumper, going south.

Stuck behind a gravel truck in the right lane, she looked for an opening. There was a pause in the left lane of traffic, so she darted into the left-hand lane, only to find that the black van had opened the lane for her. She began to weave in and out of the traffic. At a key intersection, she went south past a sign that signaled the arterial turning west. She found herself on a blacktop road, leaving housing developments behind for farmland.

At a T-intersection, she had a choice of heading west or east on a recently graveled road. She chose to go west. As she sped up, the ricochet of the loose gravel intensified.

Her cell phone was in her purse. With her eyes on the road, she fumbled for it. If she saw the van again, she wanted to call 911 and if she didn't, she wanted to ask Siri for directions. She stopped several yards short of an intersection with a smaller gravel road. At the end of a narrow lane was a white farmhouse. She glanced up and in her rearview mirror the van was far behind her, but gaining.

She gunned her engine, sending gravel into the culverts on either side and spun onto a smaller gravel road. This narrow road was thick with gravel. Her tires spun, and she fishtailed across the road, heading toward a ditch. She pulled the steering wheel to the right and continued to accelerate to keep the car from heading straight into the ditch. If she nosed into the ditch, she was certain that she would be trapped. She raced her car at an angle along the embankment of the ditch.

The black van in the road began to race side-by-side with her. She could see the driver above giving her the middle finger as it passed by. The hand blocked her view, but she saw enough to be sure it was Amanda mocking her.

The driver's hand lowered and pointed down the road. Carpenter looked and saw that she was headed toward a stone culvert. The van pulled ahead of her, and she cranked the steering wheel to the right, sending the BMW back onto the road. The car started to raise up. She pressed her hand onto the passenger seat, attempting to push the car back down, and then the car flipped onto its top. The airbag deployed, pinning her into the seat as the car slid along the gravel road. She heard glass breaking, and then there was darkness. All around her was the sound of metal and rocks scraping against each other.

Finally, the car stopped. There was silence, as if nothing of interest had happened. She was in darkness. She was blinded temporarily, then she opened her eyes. She remembered the action movies she had seen with cars exploding. She found herself upside down in her car, pressed against the back of her seat by her airbag and the seat belt. She jerked on the seat belt latch and pounded on the airbag, deflating it ever so slowly as she screamed and screamed for help. But no one came. Finally, she freed herself from the restraints and fell, striking her nose against the steering wheel that was below her. The fear of burning alive was all she could think of. She kicked at the passenger door. She expected the door to burst open; it was what doors always did in the movies.

The door didn't budge. She crawled around and from an upside-down position, she unlocked the door and scrambled out onto her hands and knees on the gravel of the narrow road. She looked up and down the road. She was alone, more alone than she had ever felt before in her life.

The heel of her foot was bruised. Carpenter limped toward the farmhouse she had passed by earlier, looking over her shoulder for the black van. She knocked on the door several times before an older woman appeared, wiping her hands on her apron.

"I crashed my car. I was being chased."

"At the intersection?"

"Yes."

"I told the road crew they put too much gravel on that road. Yours is the third car this month. I will get you a paper towel."

"I don't need a paper towel. I need the police," snapped Carpenter.

"You have cornstarch or talcum powder all over your face from the airbag. I recognize the signs."

"I was being chased!" Carpenter screamed.

"It is a bad intersection, dear. Come in, we'll call the police and your husband. Do you have a husband?"

"I was being chased."

"It is a bad intersection. Would you like some pie while we wait?" asked the woman.

"I was chased. Didn't you see the black van?"

The woman shook her head and again offered Carpenter the healing powers of pie.

9

By the time Deputy Leon Pence arrived at the farmhouse, Carpenter was on her third cup of whiskey-laced coffee and her second piece of pie.

"You took your time getting here," said Carpenter.

"Only two deputies are regularly assigned to this area of Hardin County. I was in Harbor City dropping off a prisoner. I was told there were no real injuries. Just some scrapes and bruises."

"That is what I said," said the owner of the farmhouse.

"What does she know?" exclaimed Carpenter.

"Mabel's a retired nurse. She knows a lot," said Deputy Pence. "Tell me what happened."

"I was run off the road and almost killed."

"Do you know who did it?"

"It was Amanda Bowman. She gave me the finger as she was driving past me."

"She gave you the finger as she ran you off the road?"

"I was in the ditch trying to get out when she drove past me, giving me the finger."

"How fast were you going when she did that?"

"Ten or fifteen miles an hour, I suppose. Shouldn't you be putting out a call that she be arrested?"

The deputy scratched his head for a moment. "I need to gather a few more facts. Let's go to the scene of the accident…"

"It was no accident. It was an assault."

"Ms. Carpenter…"

"It's Commissioner Carpenter. I am a court commissioner.

"Fine then. Commissioner Carpenter, let's go to where your car is, and you can walk me through what happened. Can you do that?"

"I can if it will hurry you up and get Bowman arrested. I am a court commissioner. I know what I am talking about. She assaulted me."

Pence drove her to her car. The windows of his car were closed. "Have you been drinking?"

"Mabel gave me some coffee with whiskey."

"You weren't drinking before the accident?"

"Of course not."

"Would you mind doing a field sobriety test for me?"

"Yes, I would mind very much, thank you."

The deputy nodded as if he were satisfied. He instructed Carpenter to stand by the side of his car. He walked around the upside-down BMW, taking pictures with a large camera. He took close-ups of each side of the car. He walked to the intersection that was about two football fields away. Then he walked back, taking pictures of each side of the road and tire tracks that led into the culvert. He walked along the side of the road snapping pictures of the culvert and the road where the car had emerged, then flipped onto its top. He surveyed the terrain, and he took pictures of the skid marks left by the car as it slid along the road to a stop.

Returning to Carpenter, he asked, "How fast were you going when you turned the corner?"

"Very slowly. It is a T-Intersection. I was just accelerating when the car sideswiped me."

"You were on the right side of the road?"

"Yes, of course, this isn't England."

"And you were sideswiped, forcing you into the culvert?"

"Yes, that's correct. It was an assault."

"You went into the culvert on the left side of the road."

"So?"

"That would mean you had to have been hit on the right side of the road to have been forced onto the left culvert."

"That is what happened."

"I didn't see any transfer of black paint to your car on either side."

"Are you an expert?"

"I have training."

"Training," she sniffed. "You better call for an accident reconstruction expert."

"We usually don't call for them unless there is bodily injury or death."

"I could have been killed."

"How fast were you going?"

"Ten or fifteen miles an hour."

"Your car should have stopped yards back near the intersection."

"I was pursued, and I tried to escape. I couldn't very well stop and let her attack me in the culvert. So, I attempted to drive out of the ditch, and the car flipped over when I got to the road."

"When did she give you the finger?"

"When I was driving along the ditch."

"At an angle?"

"Of course, I was at an angle. She drove past me and gave me the finger, and then she pointed to the stone culvert. I saw that I was headed toward it, so I stepped on the accelerator and cranked the steering wheel onto the road."

"That is when your car flipped?"

"Exactly. Now, will you put out a BOLO for Amanda Bowman?"

The deputy shook his head. "The accident just didn't happen the way you say it did. I would like you to take a field sobriety test."

"What if I refuse?"

"You might lose your driver's license."

"I was given whiskey after the accident. Mabel can tell you."

"I will take that into consideration."

Carpenter fell backwards against the side of the patrol car. "This cannot be happening. I feel dizzy."

"I will call for an aid car."

"You need to have forensics out here. Someone who has more than just 'some' training."

"To be sure, I am going to do that," said the deputy.

10

The ex parte courtroom was a small room, with only a few rows for seating and no counsel tables in front of the bench.

It was about the size of a restaurant specializing in take-out or home delivery. There was not much seating room. This was the courtroom where emergency motions were heard and agreed orders signed. When Commissioner Greg Madison entered, the lawyers rose quickly to their feet out of respect for him and the robe he wore. He was in his early sixties, and he was the commissioner for more than two decades. He was stout with round features and soft-spoken. In elementary school, he was a double Dutch jump rope champion. At noon he went to the YMCA to play basketball. Throughout his life, he had done athletic things, but never looked like an athlete.

He understood the law better than most, but never made a point of bringing to others' attention how much he knew. The judicial assistant handed him a file, and he called out the name and cause number of the next case to be heard. A woman with a child in a baby carriage came forward.

"I know I shouldn't have him here, but my sitter canceled on me at the last minute," she said.

"Things happen," said the commissioner.

"I am really sorry. I've been here so many times, and I keep getting things wrong. I guess that I need to get an order or notice printed in a newspaper." She handed a motion over to publish a notice of her desire to be the guardian of her grandchild.

Madison looked at the file and nodded. "Your grandchild has been living with you for some time."

"Six months," she said with pride. "His mom took off, and I have been looking after him. I need to make it legal so I can take him to the doctor and such. I can't afford a lawyer, and I make mistakes."

"What kind of work do you do?"

"I am a cashier at a pet store and do grooming as well."

"Well, that is good work," said Madison. "I take my dog to a groomer from time to time. You have a tough job. I couldn't do what you do. You are trying to do lawyer work. You can represent yourself, but it's not unusual for someone not trained as a lawyer to make mistakes." Looking over her head at the lawyers, he added, "Even lawyers make mistakes from time to time. We just do the best we can. When I do a home project, it usually takes me three or four trips to the hardware store to get it done. I accept that it will take me longer to do a project than a professional, but I get it done." He signed the order and handed it to the judicial assistant to file. "You did this just fine. Now you need to take a copy of your summons and arrange for its publication in a newspaper. There is a box in the clerk's office where you can drop off the summons."

"A lawyer at the free clinic has been helping me."

"That is great. The boy looks happy to be with you."

"He is," she beamed. "I do the best I can, and we enjoy each other's company."

"That is good," said Madison. "Thank you for bringing him in. It's good to see a happy boy. Best of luck to you."

"Thank you, Your Honor," she said. "Thank you."

While Commissioner Madison was talking to the woman, attorney Alfonso LaFontaine entered. He was a short man who always wore bow ties to court. Alice Medford and Ellen Bowman were behind him. He pointed at a bench for them to sit. He was filling out a form when attorney Ian Edgington arrived, slightly out of breath. As he entered, he patted the top of his head to be sure his comb-over of ginger hair was atop his head and had not fallen to the side, looking like the broken wing of a wounded bird.

Except for these four, the judicial assistant, and Commissioner Madison, the room was empty. Madison motioned for the lawyers to come forward. He looked at the form LaFontaine had handed to the judicial assistant and typed into his computer the cause number of the case. LaFontaine began to speak, but stopped when Madison signaled that he was reading. After he was done reading, Madison said, "For the record, this is in regard to the custody of Emma Kelly. Attorney Alfonso LaFontaine, who represents the petitioner, Alice Medford, is here in the courtroom, as is attorney Ian Edgington, representing Issac Kelly, who, it appears, is not present in the courtroom."

"That is correct, Your Honor. I just received notice of this emergency motion brought by Mr. LaFontaine. I received notice only two hours ago. I advised Mr. Kelly of the motion, but he was at work and not able to be here."

"On the computer screen, I see an ex parte motion was filed, but it is not yet scanned into the computer. There is a motion to be heard in two weeks as to whether your client, Alice Medford, can take her granddaughter to Disneyland."

"That is right. For reasons that elude me, Mr. Kelly has not agreed to let his child go to Disneyland with her grandmother," said LaFontaine.

"There are many reasons why he has concerns. This motion to have temporary custody granted is but an example of why he has concerns about the grandmother seeking extended time with her granddaughter out of state and out of communication with him," said Edgington.

"A trip to Disneyland is not the issue today. What is the issue?" asked Commissioner Madison.

LaFontaine handed the judicial assistant some papers to pass up to the commissioner. "This is what I filed today. My client is very concerned that Mr. Kelly is involved with a young woman who is almost half his age. This woman was in jail for several months and tried for murder."

Madison looked up from the papers. "That was in Hardin County. She was acquitted."

"She was convicted of fourth degree assault for poisoning her father. She later killed her father," LaFontaine enunciated the word 'killed.' "In fact, she cut his throat."

"That was in the news some time ago," said Madison. "She was working with the police, trying to gain a confession from him that he abused her as a child. No charges were brought."

"It was all a lie!" shouted Ellen Bowman, standing up. "She is attractive but coldhearted as a bronze mermaid. She is not to be trusted. My son never abused her. She made it all up. She is a very sick, dangerous person."

"Who are you?" asked the commissioner.

"I am Ellen Bowman."

"Please sit down. You are not a party to this case. Is Alice Medford in the courtroom?"

"I am Alice Medford, the child's grandmother," said Alice, standing up. "After Ellen told me about Amanda Bowman and what she was capable of, I thought it necessary to get her away from my ex-son-in-law who doesn't really know her. I am very grateful to Ellen Bowman who is beside me." She gestured toward Ellen who stood up.

"When I saw my ruthless granddaughter next to Emma in a coffee shop, I knew that I had to alert Alice to the danger her grandchild was in."

"Thank you," said the commissioner, "but let's let the lawyers speak for now."

"Your Honor, my client has been more than kind to Ms. Medford," said Edgington. "He has allowed her extra visitation time when he really doesn't have to give her any visitation time with his daughter. A grandparent may have some visitation with the grandchild, but only if it is in the child's best interest."

"It is in the child's best interest to see her grandmother," interrupted LaFontaine.

"Well, that is to be determined at a later time," said Edgington. "What Mr. LaFontaine is attempting to do is get custody of the child in advance of his motion for Disneyland."

"What is the basis of the motion, Mr. LaFontaine?"

"The child is impressionable. This Amanda Bowman comes to his house when the child is present. She works as a barista and has even named a hot milk drink after her."

"How is that dangerous?" Madison asked.

"It is part of a pattern of conduct intended to unduly influence the child," said LaFontaine. "This woman is clearly unstable and should not be allowed near the child."

"If what you want is a restraining order against Amanda Bowman, you should bring a petition for a restraining order."

"What we want is to protect the child, and for the child's protection, she should reside with my client, Alice Medford. Amanda Bowman poisoned her father and Ian Franklin, and shot Ian Franklin."

"She was acquitted of shooting Franklin and of poisoning him. She was only convicted of a gross misdemeanor in regard to the poisoning," said Edgington. "She is not a psychopath."

"Just because she was not convicted of these crimes does not mean she did not do them. The evidence was overwhelming. The jury simply did not believe her guilt beyond a reasonable doubt," said LaFontaine," and she killed her father."

"Ms. Medford and Ms. Bowman are friends. How did they meet?"asked the commissioner.

"I can tell you," said Alice.

"Please do."

"I often get coffee at a café called Bluebeard. That is where Amanda works. I was going inside one day when Ellen came out. She was in such a state that she knocked over some magazines. She was in tears. Amanda and her boss had mocked Ellen over the death of her son."

"That's right," said Bowman, nodding. "It was disgraceful the way they talked to me. I was in tears. I had just gone in there to say hello to Amanda and tell her I loved her."

Alice picked up from where she had begun. "I saw what a state Ellen was in and tried to comfort her. I am like that. I am a people person and care about people. She was a stranger to me. I had no idea the connection we had. I had no idea that Amanda was having a relationship with my ex-son-in-law. Ellen and I have become friends. We have both lost a child. The loss of a child is something that runs deep in you and only another who has had such a loss can understand. We comfort one another."

"I see," said the commissioner. "But I don't see any reason for an emergency change of placement. Mr. LaFontaine, you can argue for a change of placement on the day of your Disneyland motion, but the child stays with her father, at least until then."

11

Rick was not pleased with Amanda's progress in perfecting her espresso art. Since she started socializing with the old man, as he called Ike, her interest in the craft waned. Fortunately for him, another barista, Shantel, had shown a steady hand in pouring the froth and far more commitment than Amanda. After he gave her a set of tools, he accompanied her to a tattoo artist's studio where she had a colorful butterfly inked onto her shoulder. Both were very attractive. Being young and attractive is an unstated requirement in the espresso business. Since Amanda was letting her talent go fallow, he often asked her to take orders and Shantel to make drinks. Amanda was making change for a customer who had just ordered a drip coffee when Kyle Boardman entered the shop followed by three others.

"Amanda," he called out across the room, "I have returned with others as I said I would."

"Kyle," she said.

"I told you it was her," Kyle said to a light ginger-haired boy with freckles. He had a round face and a wide smile. When he saw Amanda, he smiled.

"Jimmy," she said, and grinned. "You, I recognize."

Next to Jimmy was a girl with long blond hair. She was wearing a junior varsity outfit.

"Let me guess. You must be Erin."

"Yes," beamed the girl. "We never got to thank you for all the juices and cookies you gave us."

"That was my job."

74

"If Dr. 'how do you feel today' Franklin had his way, we would have had only rice cakes and water until we confessed to whatever he wanted," Erin joined in.

Next to her was a teenager in Gothic dark clothes and wearing black lipstick. She glanced at Amanda and then at the floor. Her gaze stayed there.

"You're Mary Dugan," said Amanda.

"Yes, that is me," said the girl, and she said no more.

"We were the first of Dr. Franklin's patients, as he often called us," said Kyle. "I told others about you being here, but these guys were the ones who could come."

"You have all changed so much," said Amanda.

"It's been more than six years since we've seen you. Maybe longer," said Jimmy.

"That's right. It took two years for Franklin to get us to say what he wanted us to say. Then another year of coaching before the prosecutor charged poor Mr. Shipman and his wife," said Erin.

"Then the court took forever before the case was dismissed. A year and a half, if not two years. Then the appeal of the dismissal took another year."

"The law moves slowly. I can vouch for that," said Amanda.

"What does it matter? We are all going to die anyway," said Mary.

"It's the living before then that matters," said Amanda.

"Did you really get away with shooting Franklin? We were all rooting for you," said Kyle.

"I was accused and acquitted, and that is all I can say about it."

Behind them the line was growing. "Did you want anything?"

"A selfie with you would be great," said Jimmy.

"I have work to do. Take a table and I'll come over when I have a break."

"I want a mango juice," said Jimmy.

"Me too," said Erin.

"Me three," said Kyle.

"Water is fine for me," said Mary.

"Excellent," said Amanda.

12

The arraignment docket in Hardin County District Court One began at 1:30 in the afternoon. In the front row of the crowded courtroom, Commissioner Julia Carpenter sat waiting for the judge to appear. She did not turn around for fear that she might make eye contact with a person she had presided over. Next to her sat Vince Jordan, a well-known criminal lawyer, who did not involve himself in family law or landlord tenant matters. Jordan was recommended to her as an aggressive lawyer who always dressed impeccably. Today was no exception. He was wearing a suit and a dress shirt with French cuffs. His initials were embroidered on the left cuff. None of the other lawyers came close to his sense of fashion.

A District Court is a court of limited jurisdiction, where misdemeanor and gross misdemeanor crimes, not felonies, are adjudicated. Crimes for which the sentence is more than 364 days are felonies and are charged in Superior Court. In both District and Superior Courts, a judge can order any number of treatment programs designed to improve the offender's conduct. If nothing else, it provides income for a large number of counselors and therapists who, without the threat of incarceration hanging over the heads of their clients, would be penniless.

A conviction for driving under the influence, or reckless driving, comes with a mandatory loss of driving privileges, higher insurance premiums, and for many, a mandatory breath interlock device installed in their car. The interlock device must be activated before starting a car, and every so often to insure that the driver has not consumed alcohol. With each   legislative year passing, the number of restrictions, penalties, and ramifications for crimes increase. For some, the consequence of a conviction can result in a loss of employment.

When Carpenter received the summons to appear and answer for the charge of reckless driving, she was astonished, then enraged that the deputy sheriff had disregarded what she told him. She served at the pleasure of the judges, many of whom she trained when they were lawyers. A conviction for reckless driving or a lesser offense such as negligent driving, or even a continuance without findings and then a dismissal, did not necessarily mean she would be forced to resign, but it was a possibility.

Commissioner Goldman explained to her one day that lots of lawyers who were their friends wanted to be commissioners. When suggesting that she hire Jordan to defend her, he said that commissioners, like Caesar's wife, must be above reproach.

"He is very expensive," she said.

"So is losing your pension," Goldman replied. She hired him the next day.

"All rise," said the judicial assistant.

A trim woman in her forties quickly sat down in the judicial chair. She had shoulder-length brown hair with a patch of white hair on the right side of her head. It was so white it looked as if someone might have dropped a can of bleach on that side of her head.

"Please sit down," she said with a welcoming smile. "My name is Florence Monroe. I am a judge for the District Court in Salish County. Judge Loomis and I traded dockets for the afternoon. He will be back tomorrow. The first case I will hear is the *State v. Julia Carpenter*. Is Ms. Carpenter in the courtroom?"

"Yes, Your Honor," burst out Jordan, standing up. "She is right here." He pointed to Carpenter.

"Please come forward," said the judge.

Jordan and Carpenter sat to the left of a young prosecutor at the same table. The prosecutor recited the name of the case and introduced himself.

"For the record, my name is Vincent Jordan," began Jordan. "My client is to my left. Before we proceed to her arraignment, I have a preliminary matter to address."

"What is that?" asked the judge with a slight cock of her head.

"I have an affidavit of prejudice to file."

"We've never met; you've never appeared before me."

"An affidavit of prejudice requires no explanation except when a defendant declares, under oath, that he or she cannot receive a fair trial from a judge. No reason must be given," responded Jordan. He motioned as if he were going to hand the document to the JA for filing.

"Well, it is certainly your client's right to do so. I have driven a couple of hours specifically to take her plea. I assume it will be 'not guilty' to the charge of reckless driving."

"What my client intends to do is of no concern of yours once the affidavit of prejudice is filed," retorted Jordan.

"True, very true," said Monroe. "I am here today because no judge in your county wants to preside over a criminally involved judicial officer of this county. I think that is understandable. A person can only affidavit one judge in a case. If you hand that document forward, then my trip here will have been wasted and you will have needlessly wasted an affidavit."

"How so, Your Honor?" asked Jordan.

"As you know, once a judge makes a discretionary ruling in a case, he or she cannot be disqualified from the case by an affidavit of prejudice. Even though taking a plea, fixing bail, and conditions of release may include some actions of discretion, such as the amount of bail and scheduling the next hearing date, they are considered ministerial acts by statute."

"What are you suggesting, Your Honor?"

"I am suggesting we take your client's plea and set a date for the next hearing. If you decide to affidavit me, you have ten days from today's hearing to do that. If, on the other hand, you exercise your right of affidavit, then I may decide or not decide to take the plea and set the next hearing date. In any event, I would not be the judge at the next hearing, but whoever the judge is would know that you have wasted your option of an affidavit."

"I would like to enter my plea today and move on," spoke up Carpenter.

"Is that what you want?" asked Jordan.

"Let's just move this along," said Carpenter. "I am innocent and should never have been charged."

"We hear that a lot. But you have been charged, and so you are here," said the young prosecutor, who seemed to have taken umbrage at not having been included in the conversation. "The police report sets out very clearly that the defendant was driving at a high speed, went into a culvert, came out of the culvert at such a high speed that her car flipped over on its top, and skidded for almost a hundred yards. She tested for alcohol at a hospital and her blood level exceeded the legal limit."

"The housewife at the farmhouse where she went gave her coffee fortified with shots of whiskey," blurted out Jordan.

"But for that, she would be charged with driving under the influence. Maybe she really didn't know how much she drank before the housewife gave her fortified coffee," said the prosecutor.

Carpenter spoke out, "I hadn't drunk anything. I was coming home when I was chased by a crazy woman in a black van. I told the police who the woman was, and they did nothing."

"No one has seen that black van," shot back the prosecutor. He glanced down at his file and then said, "You demanded a forensic accident report, and the report found no trace of another car."

"Are you Julia Carpenter?" asked the judge.

"I am," said Carpenter.

"How do you plead to the charge of reckless driving?"

"Not guilty," she said.

"A plea of not guilty will be entered."

"Mr. Prosecutor, do you have a recommendation for bail?"

"Personal recognizance, Your Honor, but we would like the standard conditions of release for a case like this. Law abiding behavior and no consumption of alcohol."

Jordan retorted, "That seems unnecessary, Your Honor. She is not charged with an alcohol related offense."

"It is a standard condition of release for a charge of reckless driving," said the prosecutor.

"Does your client have a drinking problem?" asked the judge. "Either way, no consumption of alcohol should be imposed," said the judge. "The last thing we want is for there to be an appearance of favoritism."

"The deputy did the exact opposite of favoritism and recommended reckless driving. He targeted her because she is a court commissioner," replied Jordan.

"This is not the time or place for such accusations," said the judge. She then asked the judicial assistant for the next hearing date.

"My client will waive her right to a speedy trial to accommodate the scheduling problems for a listing judge."

"Thank you, Mr. Jordan," said the judge.

When Jordan and Carpenter were waiting for the elevator, Ellen Bowman approached them. She introduced herself as Amanda Bowman's grandmother.

"I could not help hearing you mention a black van."

"Yes, what of it?" snapped Jordan.

"My son, Stephen, had a black van. Amanda killed him, you know."

"Yes, I know," said Jordan.

"I am the administrator of my son's estate, and I don't know where the van is. Perhaps Amanda took it."

13

Contrary to the law of physics that no two bodies can occupy the same space at the same time, court clerks schedule multiple cases to be heard at the same time in the same place, resulting in delay and frustration, and many billable hours for the lawyers who have to stand or sit and wait to be heard.

On the day set for the motion of Alice Medford to take Emma to Disneyland and out of her father's custody, several cases were scheduled ahead of her motion.

In the gallery she sat ramrod straight, listening to the arguments of counsel deciding who should win and who should lose. For the most part, her opinion was the same as Commissioner Carpenter's. She thought this was a good sign. As a man and a woman walked up to stand before the bench, LaFontaine told her they were next up, and this should be an interesting case.

"Why is that?" she asked.

"Carpenter does not like it when people represent themselves, especially when they have issues outside of the ordinary," he replied with a knowing wink.

Carpenter called out the names of the parties. They approached from opposite sides of the courtroom. Both were wearing dresses. The one approaching from the right side of the courtroom was wearing hoop earrings, once popular in the year 2000, and she was walking awkwardly on three-inch heels. Around her neck she wore a string of pearls. Approaching from the left was a much smaller woman wearing tennis shoes, jeans, and a cashmere pullover sweater. When standing next to each other, the one on the right towered over the one from the left. They were in their early forties.

Carpenter asked them each to raise their right hand, and she swore them in. "This matter comes on for temporary orders regarding who can live in the family home, pending the divorce and use of vehicles."

"She can live in the house, and we each have a vehicle to drive," said the taller one. "We have agreed on most things, but she wants support from me, and she wants me to pay bills that I think are hers to pay."

"I don't have a job," said the shorter woman. "How can I pay bills if I don't have a job?"

"You'll get your chance to speak," said Carpenter.

"What really angers me is that she refused to use my preferred pronouns," said the giant on the right.

"Your what?"

"She should use my preferred pronouns. I want to be called she or her, but she continues to refer to me with the masculine pronouns."

Pointing to a multicolored sign, the giant read, "This court is respectful of all genders and gender identities. Please feel free to introduce yourself and your gender pronouns to our staff. Anyone disrespecting you will be reprimanded by the Court."

"That is true. This court, and all of the courts of Hardin County, are dedicated to administering justice fairly and impartially without regard to race or gender identification."

"We are still living in the same house. I saw him in the bathroom. He hasn't transitioned all the way yet, if you know what I mean."

"I know what you mean."

"Just because margarine wants to be called butter, it is still margarine. He will always be a man pretending to be a woman, whether he has surgery or not."

"That is just hurtful," said the giant, tapping her or his chest lightly in a dandy fashion.

"While you are here, call the petitioner, 'the petitioner.'"

"It's hard isn't it? He was a Marine when we married. I told him that I would support him and that he could still stay married. He told me he didn't want to be a lesbian. I have not purposely insulted him."

"Her, I am a her," said the giant.

"It is just hard getting used to what has happened. I thought we would be married forever."

"I want a restraining order requiring her to use my preferred pronouns whenever speaking or writing about me."

Far in the back of the courtroom, Edgington and LaFontaine exchanged glances indicating that each was expecting Carpenter to erupt in rage at the back-and-forth argument of the litigants. They were certain that the request for a restraining order on the use of pronouns would send her into a black hole of rage, but it did not.

"I appreciate how difficult it is to feel wrong and how difficult it is to be wrongly accused of a crime or misconduct. I can order that the two of you stay five hundred feet away from each other, but I can't issue a prior restraining order on speech. The law of free speech sometimes allows me to punish someone for what they say, but not to prevent them from speaking. Some courts issue gag orders in limited circumstances, but this is not such a circumstance. I wish you both the best, and we are done," Carpenter said.

"Who is this person? Has an alien taken over Carpenter's body?" said LaFontaine to Edgington. Exchanging smiles, they walked forward to stand before the court bar. Once there, they distanced themselves as if they were enemies who suspected one another of concealing a samurai sword. On LaFontaine's left side, Alice Medford stood quietly. Ike Kelly stood on Edgington's right side. Both were careful not to look at the other just as their lawyers had advised.

To LaFontaine, Carpenter said, "As I understand, your client wishes to take her granddaughter to Disneyland for a week, and she will cover all the expenses."

"That is correct, Your Honor," began LaFontaine, but he became silent when Carpenter raised her hand.

"I understand the joys of Disneyland. Mr. Edgington, why is your client opposed to the trip?"

"He is not opposed to Disneyland."

"I didn't think so," said Carpenter.

"What he is opposed to is Alice Medford continuing to try and undermine his parenting. She comes to his home unexpectedly, promising the child treats and dinner at McDonald's. He is the father and has a right to determine when it is appropriate for the child to go to Disneyland, as well as when the child will spend time with her grandmother. He is concerned that Ms. Medford is undermining his parenting and speaking badly of him to the extent that she is seeking custody of the child."

"I could order that she not discuss with the child her desire to have custody of her."

"You could. I hope you do, but such orders are hard to enforce, especially when one adult is telling the child to keep secrets from the father. The law presumes that a parent knows what is best for his child."

LaFontaine interrupted, "The child's mother is dead, and the father has moved a woman almost half his age into his house. This woman was recently accused of attempting to murder her father and upon acquittal of the charge, she actually killed him."

"Has she been charged with murder?"

"No, but I do not understand why not. Everyone knows she killed him and wanted him dead."

"She was defending herself. The father abused her for years. No charges were brought against her. She is living in the home of Mr. Kelly because she is the child's nanny."

"Is that what they are calling it?"sneered LaFontaine.

"Objection," burst out Edgington. "Baseless innuendoes should have no part in this proceeding."

"For the record, what is the nanny's name?" asked Carpenter.

"Amanda Bowman," said LaFontaine. "She was charged with trying to kill Ian Franklin and her father, Stephen Bowman. She was convicted of a misdemeanor assault charge and killed her father."

"No charges were filed in the father's death," said Edgington.

"I know who she is," said Carpenter. "She is not a party to this lawsuit and not on trial."

"My client is concerned that her granddaughter is with this woman many times unsupervised."

Carpenter studied her computer screen for a few minutes. Finally, she said, "Other than what you told me, there is nothing. She has nothing pending and no criminal history of convictions except for the one mentioned."

"Nevertheless, my client is concerned about her being near her granddaughter and the wisdom of the father leaving the child with her," pressed LaFontaine.

"You want four things, Mr. LaFontaine. You want your client to take the child to Disneyland; you want your client to have custody; you want Amanda Bowman to have no contact with the minor child; and you would like to have a parenting investigator appointed to investigate what is in the best interest of the child."

"That is correct," said LaFontaine.

"Mr. Edgington, your client is opposed to all of those requests?"

"Yes, Your Honor."

She raised the palm of her hand toward him, and he stopped talking. "Do either of you object to me asking your clients some questions?"

Both said no. Carpenter asked each to raise his or her hand and swear to tell the truth. They each said "yes," as if there was any other possible answer to give.

"Mr. Kelly, why do you not want your child to go to Disneyland? Disneyland is a place where many parents and grandparents take children."

"I am not opposed to a trip to Disneyland. I am opposed to the trip being forced upon me, and the way Alice – I mean Ms. Medford – told Emma about the trip before consulting with me. I dislike her coming over to the house unannounced. I have told my attorney that. Next thing I know we are in a court battle, and she wants custody."

"Anything else, Mr. Kelly?" asked Carpenter in a gentle voice.

"I want her to stop bad mouthing me and other things. The first thing out of Emma's mouth when she comes back from time with Alice is that she needs more vegetables; I am not home enough; and her grandmother already misses her. My lawyer said if we agree to Disneyland, it is just the toehold she wants for custody."

Carpenter nodded that she understood and asked, "Ms. Medford, what is it that you really want? You are closing in on seventy. Do you really want full-time custody? Children Emma's age demand a lot."

"I want to be able to take Emma to Disneyland. I want to be a part of her life and not shut out. I love her, and she is the only living connection I have to my daughter.

"I don't say bad things about Mr. Kelly. They should eat more vegetables, and I tell her that I already miss her when I take her back to her father."

"I am ready to rule, unless anyone has something else to say," said Carpenter as if daring either lawyer to say more. Neither rose to that proffered poison bait. "Ms. Medford, you can take the child to Disneyland, but you must tell Mr. Kelly where you are staying, and you must bring Emma back. If you do not, then you could be charged with kidnapping. Neither of you are to speak about this lawsuit in the presence of the child, and neither is to speak ill of the other in the presence of the child. I will not appoint a parenting investigator. Nothing warrants an investigation. Not agreeing to a trip to Disneyland is a parent's prerogative. As to his association with Ms. Amanda Bowman, I am not going to speculate. There is no legal basis to prohibit her from seeing the child. No award of attorney's fees. I want a written order completed before either lawyer leaves the courtroom. You can use blank order forms if neither of you has an order that can be interlined to match what I have ordered."

"Thank you, Your Honor," mumbled each lawyer in a tone usually reserved for a curse.

In the hallway outside the courtroom, while waiting for Ike, Amanda was reading a biography of Frederick Douglass. In high school, she was an indifferent student, but she found that she enjoyed reading. Not so she sounded witty around her café friends, but because she liked to learn things. She had never known the fact that Douglass' mother was black and his father white. She thought it interesting and disturbing that he spent much of his life trying to find out who his father was, and she had spent much of her life trying not to know her mother.

"We have to talk now," said Edgington.

"Fine," replied Ike.

"Not here. There is a conference room in the library where we can talk." Edgington pointed the way. His gesture was sharp as if cracking an imaginary whip.

"Ok," said Ike.

Amanda stood up to join them.

"Not her. She stays here," commanded Edgington. His face and neck were flushed.

"She can hear what you have to say," said Ike.

"Fine," said Edgington, stomping away from them.

Once the conference door was closed, Edgington began in a loud voice, "You embarrassed

90

me in the courtroom and weakened your case. Don't you understand that once your child goes on the trip to Disneyland, they will cook up an excuse not to bring her back?"

"The court order expressly states when she is to come back," replied Ike.

"That is what it says, but I know LaFontaine. While on the trip, they will claim Emma told them that you lied, and you are sleeping with Amanda."

"We don't sleep together. She has her own room. I have mine."

"No one believes that. Even if it is true, having her in your house is a liability. She killed her father. She is a danger."

"I am not a danger to Ike or Emma. They have not harmed me."

"Sweet cakes, family law is all about impressions and suspicions, not about truth. You killed your father. Everyone knows that."

"It was self-defense. He tried to rape me like he had for years, and I overreacted."

"You slit his throat and stabbed him in the eye."

"Like I said, I overreacted."

"What if Emma does something you don't like? Will you overreact then? That is what LaFontaine wanted to say. While on the trip, they will make up a lie that you harmed her."

"Is that what you would do if you were LaFontaine?"

Edgington gulped twice for air and said, "No, but it could happen."

"Alice sounded sincere to me. Maybe I misjudged her. She is pushy, but she was a part of Emma's life. You told me to limit her visits. Maybe I shouldn't have listened to you," Ike said.

"I am an experienced family law lawyer. I have done this for over thirty years. I know what I am doing. In front of the Court, you made it sound like I manipulated you. You made it sound like I was creating disagreement. You came to me. If you are not willing to follow my advice, I don't think I can help you. And if I cannot help you, no one can."

"My lawyer helped me when I was told no one could help me," said Amanda.

"John Abel?" Edgington exclaimed with the greatest disdain his little soul could muster. "He doesn't know family law."

"He knows respect," said Amanda.

14

Captain Elizabeth Knight's office was in the corner of the first floor of the Harbor City Police Station. It had a view of a shopping mall, an Islamic Center, a Yellow Cab parking lot, and an ever-growing homeless encampment. She was not where she wanted to be, but far from the rookie cop she once was. She was always on the lookout for a better place. In a few minutes, Laconia Jones and Steve McCoy would be in her office, as she had directed them. She liked that no matter what a cop may think of her, they never kept her waiting.

The police station was in a remodeled Costco building that had won awards for its environmental innovations, but not for interior design. It was a functional building, similar to a World War II British air shelter, uninviting and sterile. It was functional, not to be admired for its aesthetic qualities, but to be used and then dismissed when a better version came along, much like she thought the senior officers ahead of her should be.

During the Pandemic, the public front door was locked to avoid the spread of the virus. Now that the Pandemic had passed, the public door remained locked at her command. This eliminated the need for a lobby desk sergeant who, by tradition, was an older cop hanging on for his pension. Instead, the door was locked, and there was an intercom not far from the door. It was not a system designed to aid a person in immediate danger.

McCoy and Jones did not need to use the public entrance. They arrived in separate cars and each used their own key to enter the building. McCoy was a few years younger than Laconia.

McCoy was a detective sergeant in charge of the Burglary and Theft Unit. Laconia was the detective sergeant of the Homicide Unit. He was the detective sergeant of the unit for several years, having replaced the former head of the unit, Bob Baneman, after he arrested Baneman for murder. McCoy was the last person promoted by Baneman into the unit. Rather than report to Laconia, he became a Hardin County Deputy, then eventually returned to the Harbor City Police. He worked, or if you asked Laconia, 'wormed' his way up to head of the Burglary and Theft Unit. McCoy aspired to become a lieutenant, and he enjoyed the favor and company of Knight. Laconia enjoyed the work he did, as well as being as far away from Knight and her minions as possible.

They arrived at the elevator leading to Knight's office at the same time, each by a very different route from the parking garage. "McCoy, how is the planting of evidence going?"

"Laconia, always good to see you too. Have you let any murderers go free while looking for a warrant?"

Laconia smiled. He was broad-shouldered and more than willing to take a fellow to jail without incident. But if they wanted to fight about it, they still went to jail, sometimes by way of the emergency room. He never used excessive force, but he had a lot of force in reserve when needed. McCoy, not a small fellow himself, never challenged Laconia to more than a verbal exchange of wits, such as he had at his disposal.

"You need to work on your repartee, McCoy. When I arrest a fellow, they don't go free like some of yours do."

"At least I don't have friends like John Abel," McCoy said and added, "Why you are friends with a defense lawyer, I will never know."

"Why you have friends, I will never know," said Laconia.

"I'll be your boss one day."

"How do you figure that?"

"One day, one of the old men above Knight will retire. Then she will be promoted. A lieutenant will take her spot, and I will move into a lieutenant spot. I have friends and am up for promotion. You were a detective sergeant when I met you, and you are still one. You are like a train on a side rail going nowhere. Lieutenant Davidson may take early retirement. His parents in Arizona need him. Maybe I will take his slot. One day I will pass you by."

Laconia said nothing more and knocked on Knight's door.

"Enter," said Knight. But she kept her head down reading a report while McCoy stood before her desk. Laconia, however, was not idle. He walked to the window, looking out on the view of the shops and parking lot of the strip mall.

"On your lunch hour, you can skip over and get just about anything you want from your vacuum repaired to a ham sandwich," he said. "I didn't know they had a Michael's there. Is that where you had your pictures framed?" There were several nature photographs displayed on the walls.

"I didn't summon you to discuss my window view or wall pictures."

"Before we get started, Bob Hoskins says hello," said Laconia.

"Who is that?"

"He was one of the lobby sergeants you replaced with an intercom."

"Is he enjoying his retirement?"

"He was when I last saw him. He was fine, then he blew his brains out about five months ago."

"I am not responsible for that, and you know it," she glared. "Those jobs had to go. They were doing little except sitting behind plexiglass, waiting for people to come in the door."

"People would come in off the street asking for help from time to time."

"From time to time, some came by, but that was not a good enough reason to keep the lobby unlocked. You fight progress whenever you can. Is it because they are my ideas? You were always helpful when I was a rookie. Once I became your superior, though, you became entrenched in your obstructionistic ideas."

"It is not personal. When you were a rookie, I had hopes for you," said Laconia.

Breaking the silence that followed Laconia's remark, McCoy spoke up, "Any trouble in the homeless encampment?"

"Relatively quiet," Knight said, slipping the memorandum she was reading into a drawer. "I want the two of you to interview Amanda Bowman. She may have run Commissioner Carpenter off the road."

"Why us?" asked Laconia. "Before she was charged with murder, I was taken off the investigation of Gary Shipman's murder. You put McCoy in charge of the investigation so you could charge her. You knew that I wanted to investigate further."

"No need to rub my nose in it. That proved to not work out very well," she admitted.

"Not well at all," said Laconia. "She was acquitted of the charges. Rather than leaving her alone, the two of you went to her without talking to her attorney, John Abel, and convinced her to wear a wire."

"We know what we did," said McCoy.

"Some things need repeating," smiled Laconia. "While you recorded their conversation, she slit her father's throat, stabbed him in the eye, and claimed over the wire that she was being attacked."

"No charges were filed. Her claim of self-defense was verified," McCoy reminded him.

"Swept under a gigantic pile of papers is what happened," said Laconia.

"Now is your chance to talk to her again. Her father's death is a cold case. Perhaps the two of you can heat it up. She now lives with Ike Kelly."

"Ike Kelly and his wife, Tiffany, were suspects in Shipman's murder. She drowned either by accident or suicide," McCoy explained.

"You investigated Ike Kelly and determined that he was at home for trick-or-treaters when Shipman was shot," Laconia said to McCoy.

"Steve did a great job," said Knight. "But I have done a little more research." She handed them an aerial photograph of the area between Ike Kelly's house and the Shipman house. They were two blocks apart. "I think it's possible that Kelly could have slipped out of his house, gone undetected to the back of Shipman's house, and shot Shipman."

"Ike Kelly is an experienced marksman," said McCoy.

"Shipman was shot at close range, four times with a Colt .45. Two rounds went into the side of the house. Not really marksman-like work. A marksman or experienced killer would have put one bullet to the head and one in the heart," said Laconia.

"Perhaps he is so good that he knew how to make it look like Shipman was shot by a nervous, inexperienced person," said Knight.

"Ike Kelly had motive because his daughter was one of the children abused by Shipman," McCoy said, as if ending Knight's words for her.

"*Allegedly* abused by Shipman," said Laconia, using an official sounding tone of voice.

"Don't go all defense on me," said Knight. "We had good evidence on Shipman that got thrown out by Judge Albert."

"Very good evidence. I was involved in the investigation from the beginning," said McCoy.

Laconia did his best not to laugh, but a slight smile crossed his lips.

"There is nothing funny about a dozen children being abused at a day care center and us not being able to get one conviction," snapped Knight.

"Nothing at all," replied Laconia. "Why would we interview Amanda Bowman?"

"I think it's possible she was having an affair with Ike Kelly while his wife was alive. Amanda worked as a receptionist for Ian Franklin, the therapist for the children. They may have been in this together," said McCoy.

"She may have driven Commissioner Carpenter off the road," said Knight. "I want you to investigate this case like an attempted assault. I want you to find the car she was driving. We think it was her father's van. We have not been able to locate it."

"So, you want me to pretend I am a traffic cop and interview her?" said Laconia.

"If you don't take this seriously, you may just become a traffic cop," said Captain Knight.

15

Ike Kelly knocked three times on Amanda's bedroom door. "Time to get up," he said. "Morning. Wake up time." Before he could knock on the door again, she opened it. She was already dressed in jeans and a bulky sweatshirt.

"I know and I'm ready, but coach, do I have time for a bowl of cereal?" she grinned.

"It's on the kitchen table next to a glass of OJ."

"You are good, coach," she said and gave him a peck on the cheek.

"I'll double-check and get the shooting bags while you eat."

"Thanks," she said. He headed to the basement where his workroom was located.

Two dark green range bags were side by side on a workbench. One was new; one was well worn around the edges. Next to the bags was a canvas tote with the name New Yorker on it.

Fifty rounds of reloaded .45 ammo, 100 rounds of CCI .22 ammunition, cleaning equipment, ear guards, soft cloths for cleaning ejected shell cases, and a pair of Leupold binoculars were inside the older bag. When it came to shooting gear, Ike didn't pinch pennies. Next to his range bag was a .45 and .22 automatic, both in soft cases. He put them in the bag and zipped it closed. Then he double-checked Amanda's range bag. In it was a box of reloaded .38 ammo and a box of 100 rounds of .22 ammunition. Next to her bag, in separate soft cases, was a Ladysmith 38 special revolver and a three-inch .22 revolver. After several training sessions, he had her focus on practicing with revolvers rather than automatics. They are reliable and better for an inexperienced shooter to carry because they have far fewer moving parts than automatics. Therefore, less things can go wrong if you have to make a quick decision. He put the guns in her case, along with a three-ring binder. In the binder were log sheets to record her shooting progress. They had more than enough ammunition for several training sessions.

When he came upstairs, she was ready to go. With a smile, he handed her the new bag. She had not seen it before. "This is for you. If you're serious about shooting, you might as well have a serious range bag." When they went shooting before, she packed her gear in the canvas tote bag.

"Thank you," she said and gave him a hug, which he awkwardly returned.

"You are serious about shooting, and I appreciate that. I appreciate all you do. Emma couldn't be happier."

"And you?" she asked, still holding him close.

"I am happy too, very happy," he said, and added, "If we hurry, we can avoid a lot of traffic."

"And a lot of talk you don't want to have." She laughed and picked up her new bag. "Thank you," she said, lifting the bag up to eye level.

The shooting range was located near a small town, about an hour's drive from Harbor City. They drove to the interstate and headed south for a few miles. The morning traffic was light. "Today I want you to work on calling your shots right after you shoot. If you think you hit the center X, I want you to call out if it is at twelve o'clock or six o'clock. The aim is to be as precise as possible. No need to rush, but keep a regular pace. Shoot, call your shot, breathe, aim, and fire. No need to rush, but work on developing a rhythm. Understand?"

"I understand."

"I'll write down in the logbook what you think you did, and then we will compare it to what you actually did. Understand? This is the path of improvement."

"Yes, we have done this before. I understand this is the way to become a better marksman. I have been reading about a lot of different things. I recently read about the fear of intimacy. I now understand more about myself. I fear getting close to people because of my father's betrayal. It is triggered by a sense of abandonment."

"It is good to know yourself. Even while warming up with the .22s, we should stick to the routine."

"Rick, the manager at the Bluebeard Café, wants me to get a tattoo for the city championship."

"He just wants to put his mark on you."

"Perhaps. Why do you care?"

"Who said I did?"

"Your tone said it for you. Why would you care? Why are you afraid of intimacy? We are not all that different. I know that we are a few years apart in age, but you are not feeble. I appreciate that you have never tried to push yourself on me."

"I don't want to hurt you, and it is more than a few years."

"You don't want to be hurt."

"What makes you think I have a fear of intimacy? Is this something out of a magazine?"

"You don't share your thoughts or feelings, but rather talk about stuff, like ball games or the burn speed of different kinds of gunpowder."

"That is an important thing to know," he said.

"Maybe so if you want to shoot something, but not if you want to have a relationship with a living person."

"Tiffany used to ask me to share my feelings and thoughts. Honesty didn't really help my marriage with her. When she asked me if I would have married her if she wasn't pregnant, I told her the truth that I would not have, and she never forgave me for my honesty."

"I see your point," chuckled Amanda. "Perhaps that was a time you should have lied."

"I suppose so," said Ike. Exiting off the interstate, they found themselves on a four-lane road enmeshed in slow moving traffic in either lane. "I didn't know why she asked that question. I should have lied. She was dissatisfied with me, and she was always finding things to criticize me about. I put the dishes in the dishwasher the wrong way. I bought the wrong kind of beans, and so on. She was angry with me and would not say why, and I was no better. I felt trapped by her pettiness. When she asked if I married her because she was pregnant, I knew that it would hurt her to the quick to tell her the truth. If she was not pregnant, we would never have married. She knew the truthful answer. I know that she did. She wanted me to lie. She expected me to lie, but I just couldn't. I just couldn't lie anymore, and I told her the truth. They say the truth will set you free. Saying the truth did set me free, but it was a painful freedom with nowhere to go."

The traffic opened up, and he sped around a few cars until they could travel without stop-and-go restrictions.

"Have you always told me the truth?" she asked.

"Tell me why you want to be a marksman, and I will tell you."

"When I was little, my father and Grandmother Bowman would take me to a shooting range. They were both good shots. At least I think they were. They never let me shoot. I was very young. My job was to pick up the brass, wipe it off, and put it in the box. You know how shells bounce about? If I couldn't find a shell, they mocked me until I found them all. 'You have your mother's laziness,' they would say. Anytime I did something they disapproved of, it was because of my mother and the terrible blackness she had passed on to me."

"I had no idea. I'd like to meet your mother."

"Maybe. I am so embarrassed by the thoughts I have had of her that I hardly know what to say to her. I had everything so wrong all these years. I don't know how to make things right."

"Not seeing her is not going to make things right between you."

"You are good at giving advice," she said.

"You are already a good shot. Why do you want to be better?"

"They told me I was never going to be a marksman like them. They said that all I was good for was picking up their brass and nothing more."

"They are not around you now."

"They are forever in my head," she said. "Getting good at what they said I would never be good at is a way of getting them out of my head."

"We each have our own private exorcisms to undergo to make us whole," said Ike.

"Back to the tattoo. Rick wants me to have a tattoo of a cup of coffee on one arm and a tattoo of the Bluebeard logo on the other."

"That's nuts. He just wants you to be a walking billboard for him."

"My body, my choice," she replied. "Again, why would you care? I live with you; I watch over Emma when you are at work. We eat together, but what am I to you? The little sister you never had, the girlfriend in waiting? Am I too young for you? Most older guys dig younger women."

"My AA sponsor said I should never sleep with a woman who has more tattoos than I do. I don't have any. What do you say to that?"

"I say your sponsor doesn't get laid a lot."

"So, you think you have a chance," she said and winked.

"You have been through a lot with your father. I don't want to take advantage of you. I am afraid that if we have sex I will lose you. I know that sounds crazy, but that is how I think."

She put her hand on his shoulder and leaned toward him. "You are not going to lose me by having sex with me. What I was forced to do has nothing to do with what I want to do. Turn the car around and let's go home. Emma is at Disneyland. It is just us in the house for the weekend."

"And you won't get a tattoo?" he laughed.

"Never, ever, if you turn the car around."

He sped up and did a quick turn in front of advancing traffic, reckless as a teenager in love.

16

Before they interviewed Amanda, Laconia wanted to visit the dirt road where Carpenter had flipped her car. He thought it was essential to walk around the crime scene to understand why criminal charges were filed. Rain and wind and countless motor vehicles had changed road conditions since the accident. He had read the forensic report and studied the photographs, but he wanted to walk the area with the deputy who filed the charges. McCoy thought it was a waste of time. The forensic report was all he thought was needed, but if Laconia wanted to walk on a dirt road, he wanted to be there. Deputy Pence was waiting for them when they pulled in behind his car. He tapped his wristwatch when Laconia stepped out of the driver's seat. "You said 8:00am."

"I stopped and got us coffee and some pastries. The drive-through was slower than I anticipated," said Laconia. "You like coffee black? I brought sugar, sweeteners, and cream if you don't." He held up a paper carry tray in one hand and a paper bag in the other.

"Black is good."

"I brought croissants, croissants with chocolate, and lemon pound cake. Which would you like?"

"Lemon pound," replied Pence. He took a bite and with his mouth full, said, "Sergeant, you didn't have to do this."

"That's what I told him," said McCoy.

"We came onto your patch and took you out of your routine. Bringing coffee is the least I could do for you, deputy. Can I call you Leon?"

"You can."

"Then call me Laconia," said Laconia. "Whatever you call McCoy is up to you," he added with a laugh.

McCoy let the invitation to be informal pass by, hoping that it would not return. He started to walk along the road where Carpenter's car had gone.

Leon and Laconia leaned against Leon's squad car, drinking coffee and eating their pastries. McCoy, having declined Laconia's offer of coffee, walked along the culvert that Carpenter had driven into and out of, only to flip her car over. He walked with the heavy steps of a city kid kicking up gravel dust with each step.

Laconia took a last bite of his croissant and tossed a napkin into the bag. "You recommended charging Carpenter with reckless driving. Reckless driving is when a person drives any vehicle in willful or wanton disregard for the safety of persons or property. Negligent driving is when a person operates a motor vehicle in a manner that is both negligent and endangers, or is likely to endanger, any person or property. As I understand it, this accident happened when no one was around. Why go for reckless? Why have a crash specialist come to the scene?"

Pence took a long sip from his cup. "Did you ever work traffic cases?"

"Long ago. Usually just DUI. I had one case where a drunk crossed a road and hit a car head on. Neither were killed, but the woman almost lost her foot."

"I've worked lots of cases. Teenagers get their driver's license and a motorcycle. Springtime is a good time for doctors who want to harvest healthy

107

organs, but a bad time for parents who hoped to see their son graduate."

"She wasn't on a motorcycle or drunk and no one was endangered except her. Why did you call in a crash expert?"

"She insisted on calling one. She claimed she was run off the road."

"You didn't believe her," said McCoy, joining them.

"Her description of what she claimed happened didn't make sense. She turned a corner at a high speed and lost control; that is what happened. She claimed that a black van ran her into the ditch. I looked at the side of her car, both sides of her car," he emphasized. "I did not see any black paint on her car."

Laconia looked up and down the road and toward both sides. It was all soy fields. A couple of farmhouses were set back from the road. "Did you talk to any of the people to see if they saw a black van?"

"You sound like you are working for the defense. Would you do this if she wasn't a court commissioner?" Pence inquired.

"Did you charge her because she was a court commissioner? I checked. You must have known that a criminal charge would destroy her career. A driver goes into a ditch. Not a big thing. You could have passed on charging her and let the insurance company deal with it."

"Is this about city cops protecting one of their own from a big bad rural sheriff?" asked Deputy Pence.

"This is about us finding out if a person who has threatened her drives a black van," said McCoy.

"Really?" deadpanned the deputy. "She tried to high-tone me, and I didn't like it. I think she lied to me. The accident didn't happen the way she claimed.

"Let's walk through the accident," said Laconia.

All traces of the accident were long gone, but the road was more or less the same. At the corner, the deep gravel was pressed down and sprayed away. "She claimed that she was run off the road," said Laconia.

"Which makes no sense because she should have gone into the right lane," said Pence.

"What if she spun out and was on the left side of the road, and the black van came alongside her?"

"That is not what she said happened," said Pence, looking at the incident report.

"True, but what if she was mistaken and went to the left side of the road and then the van came alongside her?"

"That is not what she said happened."

"Eyewitnesses are very unreliable," said Laconia. "I had a witness swear that she saw things that could not have happened unless they had x-ray vision. You have never had a witness give a false statement?"

"I know I have," said McCoy.

"I have, too, but she told me what she told me, and we investigated it. If what she said happened didn't happen, why did she lie?" Pence asked.

"Maybe she just told you what she believed happened. People under stress remember things vividly, but sometimes they are wrong."

"She claimed that she went into the culvert and did not try to speed out of it," said Pence. "That is not consistent with the tire marks. Had she taken her foot off the accelerator, she would have ended up in the ditch."

"Instead, in a panic she tried to drive out of it. When she got onto the road, she was going too fast, and the car flipped over," said Laconia.

"She claimed that the black van was driven alongside her and kept her from getting back onto the road. If that was true, why didn't she collide with it when she got back onto the road?"

"Maybe by then the van was gone," said Laconia. "So why did you charge her?"

"I didn't believe her, and she was rude. She gave me a story that didn't make sense and was indignant that I didn't believe her about a phantom car running her off the road."

"What if she hadn't been rude?" asked Laconia.

"I charged her with what I thought was the right violation. I am not going back on that. And that's that, gentlemen. She drove recklessly, and if I am called to testify, that is what I am going to say. She wanted a forensic investigation, and she got one. She tried to lie about the accident, and she tried to intimidate me because she is a court commissioner. I don't have any reason to change my opinion. She was reckless and could have killed someone the way she was driving. I've got work to do, gentlemen. If you want to play criminal defense, do it without me."

17

At the station, McCoy and Laconia went their separate ways. McCoy went to lunch with Captain Knight at an upscale restaurant, Plumly and Mathews, with a view from a hill that overlooked Harbor City. It was a busy place for taking executives and businesspeople.

Laconia decided to lunch alone in his office and review incident reports from the Shipman murder. McCoy arrived back at the station an hour later than he said he would. At about 3pm, they drove to Ike Kelly's house.

"Did you learn anything from reading and rereading the file?" asked McCoy in a tone that suggested there was nothing more to be found that they did not know.

"Not much, but my belief that you are a lousy detective was reinforced."

"Screw you. Your lack of a future is your own doing. Why do you say that?"

"When you replaced me as the lead detective, there was much more to be done. Instead, you did little and recommended that Amanda Bowman be charged with the murder of Shipman."

"She was caught in the parking garage with the murder weapon right after Franklin was shot in the knee. She was his receptionist, and for months she saw the children and parents come into his office for counseling. She herself was a victim of childhood abuse. It was only logical that she decided to take the law into her own hands and shoot Shipman, once the Court of Appeals had decided that he wouldn't have to stand trial." He rolled down the passenger window and spit. After rolling the window back up, he continued, "The case against her was solid. She couldn't remember where she was when he was killed. She killed him, and I think she is planning to kill again. Did you know that she and Ike Kelly take weekly trips to a shooting range?"

"How do you know that?"

"I have my sources," grinned McCoy.

"After I was replaced, I left a note that the alibi witness for Tiffany Kelly and Joe O'Conner had to be interviewed. That wasn't done."

"I made a command decision that it was not necessary. They were seen by many witnesses taking children around trick-or-treating."

"All the witnesses said identically the same thing. 'We were all together. We were never out of sight of one another. It was a cold night, and we all stayed together.' They all said that. They all used the same words."

"So what? It was a cold night."

"But they used the same language. They had their statements prepared. It sounds to me like the parents of the children Shipman was accused of abusing drew straws. Then the one with the short straw did the killing while the others provided alibis."

"Maybe they do things like that where you are from, but we are talking about people with decent homes and income."

"I was born and raised in Center Point. You think black people in Center Point are more likely to conspire to kill?"

"I didn't say that," said McCoy.

"What did you mean by where I come from?"

"I didn't mean anything. The witnesses had no reason to lie."

"They had every reason to lie, and you did nothing to follow up on the possibility that they were all involved. You focused on Amanda Bowman as the killer and did nothing else."

"The case was strong. It was very strong…" he began to say, but said no more when Laconia shot him a cold glare. Laconia shook his head and pulled into the cul-de-sac where Ike Kelly's home was located.

McCoy had seen Laconia take down men twice his size when action was needed. Once they were at a gang disturbance. The police were blocked by onlookers and hecklers. Laconia took out a nightstick and began slashing it back and forth, clearing himself a path to the combatants with indifference as to who he struck, whether they were civilians, participants, or officers. An enraged Laconia was something no one wanted to see twice. But departmental changes were in motion, and he wanted him to know that.

Laconia parked in front of the house.

"You've run the Homicide Unit for years doing what you want, assigning who you want to cases," said McCoy.

"The system is pretty much what it was when Bob Baneman was in charge. Cases get assigned in rotation. If a detective is on duty when a murder occurs, he or she gets the case when the call comes in."

"Captain Knight is right. People have different skills. The cases should go to the people based on their strengths and the complexity of the cases they are working on," said McCoy.

"Something to think about. But if cases were assigned by skill level, you would never get a case," replied Laconia.

"That is just it. Your attitude is holding the department back," said McCoy. "The captain and I were talking at lunch. She has plans to consolidate the Burglary and Theft Unit, the Homicide Unit, and the Gang Violence Unit into one 'Super Unit' headed by a lieutenant who can better manage the department resources."

"Just what the people need, another bureaucrat behind a desk protecting us. If you are that lieutenant, I fear for all of us." Laconia slammed his car door and headed toward the house.

"Well, get used to the idea of it because that is what will happen," McCoy responded, catching up with him.

"Here, take a breath mint," said Laconia offering him a packet.

"My breath doesn't stink."

"It smells like pussy," said Laconia.

Before he could stop, McCoy cupped his hands over his mouth and nose. "It does not."

Laconia just grinned and rang the doorbell. He rang the bell several times until Ike came to the door. He was wearing sweats, no shoes, and his hair had the look of being swiped into place with his fingers.

"Detectives, how can I help you?" he asked, with the door pulled back, and his shoulders square to the door frame.

"You remember us?" asked Laconia.

"Of course."

"We'd like to talk to you and Amanda. She is here, isn't she?"

"Is there a problem?"

"No, no, just following up on some matters," said Laconia. "May we come in?"

Ike stepped out of the way and gestured for them to enter. In the hallway were the two range bags waiting to be stored away.

"Did we interrupt your plans?" McCoy asked, pointing to the bags.

"No, not in the least," replied Ike. "Why are you here?"

"Is Amanda here?"

"I am here, detectives," said Amanda, coming up behind Ike. Like Ike, she was wearing sweats and no shoes. Unlike Ike, she had delayed her appearance to comb her hair.

"We can talk in the living room," said Ike, pointing toward a large room with a baby grand piano off to one side. On the far side of the room was a formal dining table with a modest, vintage chandelier above it. In the center of the room was a round glass coffee table surrounded by large leather chairs. Ike and Amanda sat in chairs next to each other. "Do either of you want something to drink? Tea, coffee, water?"

Before McCoy could speak, Laconia said, "No, we're fine. We are here about Commissioner Carpenter."

"Ms. Bowman, may I call you Amanda?" interjected McCoy.

"Certainly, that is what you called me when we last spoke. That was when you asked me to help you with the investigation of my father."

"I recall," McCoy muttered, and in a louder voice he asked, "Do you own a black van?"

"No."

"Did your father own a black van?" He glanced down at a notepad. "The license plate number is UBR 952."

"I don't recall the license plate number but, yes, he had a van. Rather old, somewhat scratched up. He used it to haul items and so forth. I haven't seen it for some time."

"Did you ever drive it?"

"Yes, years ago. But I haven't for a long time. Why?"

"I am the one who asks the questions."

"Fine, but I'm the one who can refuse to talk to you if I want. I have that right, do I not?"

"The right to silence is reserved for those who are arrested. You are not under arrest," retorted McCoy. "Do you know where it is?"

"You don't have to talk to us," said Laconia. "But obviously, if you have nothing to hide, it would be best for you to talk to us."

"No, I don't know where it is," she replied.

"It is reported that Commissioner Carpenter was run off the road by a black van," said Laconia. "You were previously in her courtroom, and we wanted to rule out the possibility that you were driving it."

"Well, I wasn't," smiled Amanda.

"Can you tell us where you were when she was run off the road?"

"I have no idea when she was run off the road. Whenever it was, I was elsewhere."

"I can tell you the time and place of the assault."

"Not interested," said Amanda. "I can't recall where I was at all times. I would hate to make a mistake and then be accused of deceit."

"I think she has answered your questions as fully as she can at this time. If there is nothing more to talk about, I suggest you leave," said Ike.

Neither Laconia nor McCoy showed any interest in leaving. Instead, Laconia pressed his back against his chair. "This is a really nice chair," he said. "Leather just has a better feel to it than faux leather."

"When we were investigating the murder of Gary Shipman and the shooting of Ian Franklin, you neglected to tell us that you were a three-gun bull's-eye champion. Why was that?"

"I don't recall ever being asked if I had won any awards for marksmanship. I didn't think it was relevant."

"You never told me that," said Amanda to Ike "What does it mean?"

"It means that in pistol shooting competition, Mr. Kelly was far better than most at scoring with a .22 pistol, a nine-millimeter, and a .45. The type of gun used to kill Shipman and wound Franklin. I did some research and in a competition at fifty yards, you almost had a perfect score. That was holding the gun with only one hand. Right?" Laconia asked.

"That was years ago," said Ike. "Like I said, it was not relevant, and I was never asked."

"Franklin was shot in a parking garage. The shooter was in a stairwell. How difficult would it have been for a shooter of your ability to hit his knee?"

"I am not as good as I used to be. To get to the level that I was, you have to train daily."

"At the level where you were a few years back, could you have made the shot?"

Ike nodded a couple of times. "Yes, I could have made that shot, but I didn't."

"Amanda claimed that she came down the stairwell and saw the shooter looking for something. I think it was the shell casing we found."

"I saw a man in the stairwell, but it wasn't Ike," blurted out Amanda.

Laconia went on as if he had not heard her. "We assumed that the shooter of Shipman was not a skilled shooter because he was shot four times from close range, and two other shots went into the side of the building. Franklin's shooter was skilled."

"Or very lucky," said Amanda. "If Franklin's knee was what he was aiming at."

"If it was one shooter, that would explain why the same gun was used to kill Shipman and wound Franklin," said Laconia.

"Since I was already tried for shooting Franklin and killing Shipman, I could confess now, and you could do nothing because of double jeopardy," offered Amanda.

"Do you love him that much?" asked Laconia.

"It is not a question of love. I am innocent," said Ike, reaching out his hand toward Amanda, who held onto it.

"It makes sense to me that the shooter would kill Shipman, thinking that he had abused his child. Your child was reported abused by Shipman. Your wife, who is now dead, was one of the leaders of the parents who wanted him charged with multiple counts of abuse. It was surely a terrible shock to her when the charges were dismissed. If he abused my child, I would have wanted him dead. On the other hand, if the abuse did not really occur, but by Franklin's manipulation, he convinced my child she was abused, I would want him to suffer. Rather a Dante form of punishment, killing the most guilty one, and just wounding the less guilty one."

"Who is Dante? Is he the guy from Kansas City?" asked McCoy.

"Florentine," said Ike.

"Another possibility you might consider is that Franklin's shooter wanted you to find the gun and point you back to the owner of the gun," said Ike.

"Back to Joe O'Conner," said Laconia.

"You only have his word that the gun was stolen before the shooting of Shipman," said Ike.
"Perhaps the shooter was in an awkward way attempting to get your investigation of the murder of Shipman headed in the right direction," said Amanda.

"Something to consider," said Laconia.

"Something to waste our time on," said McCoy.

Rising to his feet, Ike said, "If that is all the questions and theories you have today, then we are done."

"For today," said Laconia.

18

Laconia was at his desk when McCoy knocked on the door and opened it without waiting for a response. "I'm off to lunch with the captain." Laconia nodded. "We have things to go over. I won't be back for three hours." Again, Laconia only nodded. It was a Wednesday, and Wednesdays were McCoy's and the captain's long lunch day. "If you need me, you can call me on my cell."

"I will do my best to get by. We aren't Starsky and Hutch. I can get by on my own."

"That's a good one. You are showing your age relying on an old cop show. If we were Starsky and Hutch, which one would I be?"

"Which one would I be?"

"Which one was the dumb one?"

"Neither. They were both smart."

"Then I had the wrong cop show in mind," said Laconia. He turned his attention to a stack of papers in front of him.

"Are you usually this pissed off about me opening your door when it's closed?"

"You wanted to announce you were off with the captain. I gave you the opportunity to tell me you were in her favor and I was not. Enjoy your lunch, and don't forget to use a breath mint."

"Enjoy this office while it is yours. When I make lieutenant, I am moving you out."

"Don't forget the breath mint," reminded Laconia as he stood up. "Best not to keep her waiting."

Laconia waited a few minutes. Then he went out to his car so he could keep his appointment with

Sarah Shipman and her lawyer, Calvin Green, at her house.

Sarah Shipman still lived in the house where her husband was shot. It was a large house with a tall cedar fence in front. The day care she ran was in the basement. The entrance to the day care was at the back. Gary Shipman was shot on the back porch, which was above and to the side of the day care entrance. After he was shot, he crawled partway around the house to the front. In her upstairs bedroom, Sarah heard the shots and called 911. Then she waited there for aid to arrive. Laconia wondered if she ever considered selling, or if she stayed in the house in defiance of the killer, who most likely lived in the neighborhood. The day care was a neighborhood day care with most of the parents living within three blocks of it. None of the parents had moved away, and only Tiffany Kelly had passed away since the killing. Perhaps she was involved, but Laconia doubted that if she was, she acted alone.

Laconia was met at the door by Green. "We agreed to meet with you because you wanted to talk about Gary's death. If you try to bring up the child abuse accusations, then the meeting is over," said Green.

"I wasn't involved in the child abuse accusations then, and I am not interested in them now. That is, unless they might help me find the murderer."

"Fair enough," conceded Green.

Sarah was seated at the kitchen table. She was in her fifties, a few years older than when Laconia last spoke to her. She was somehow less fragile than before. It was almost as if the tragedy of her husband's unsolved murder made her more resolute and defiant. At the height of the accusation, she was even afraid to go shopping. She feared that an irate parent would curse and berate her as a child abuser, the same as some of the parents from the day care center had done. Tiffany Kelly was the worst. However, others had harassed her at a grocery store to the point when the store manager suggested that Sarah shop elsewhere.

"Thank you for seeing me," began Laconia.

"Sergeant Jones," responded Sarah. On the table was a plate of shortbread cookies. "I did not expect to see you again. Would you like a cookie? Coffee or tea, perhaps?"

"Coffee and cookies would be nice," said Laconia.

She got a plate for him and poured him some coffee from an automatic coffee maker. "Black or cream and sweetener?"

"Black is fine," he said. "When we met at the hospital on the night your husband was killed, I said I would do all I could to find his killer. I still intend to do that."

She responded with a weak smile. "I've given up on justice for Gary. I make do by living here and seeing the ones who accused us look away when they see me."

"Is that why you stay?"

"This is my home. This was my home before we turned the basement into a day care center. The housing market for places where child abuse is alleged and murder has occurred is down, and it's expected to stay down. Even if I wanted to sell, I could not sell for a suitable price." She paused and took a sip from her coffee cup. "At the hospital you said you were the lead detective and then you were not. You were replaced by McCoy, who made it clear that he thought finding my husband's killer was of little interest to him. It all happened so fast. Amanda Bowman was accused of killing Gary, and my former lawyer, John Abel, was defending her. Why did you abandon me? Why did Abel?"

"I was taken off the case when it was decided to charge Amanda Bowman with the murder of your husband. I didn't abandon you. I was relieved of my duty, so to speak, but now I'm back. I can't speak for Abel, but I suspect he never believed that Amanda killed your husband."

"Did you have anything to do with Abel representing Bowman?" asked Sarah.

"No, Abel knew her mother, and he basically does what he wants when it comes to representing, or not representing, people."

"It always seemed like a betrayal for him to be my lawyer one day, and the next day he was representing the person accused of killing my husband."

"The prosecutor, James Brinkmeyer, tried to have him removed from the case, but the judge did not see it as a conflict of interest," said Green. "So, why are you here, Laconia? When you called, you mentioned something about a detail you wanted to clear up?"

"While reviewing the case file, I saw that you called McCoy. Did he talk to you after you called? The note in the file, written by the person who took your call, marked the message as urgent," Jones said.

"I do remember calling him. After we were done talking, he convinced me that my concerns were addressed," replied Sarah.

"Did he say how?" Laconia asked.

"No," she said, shaking her head. "Perhaps he was right. I might have imagined what I thought that I saw. The problem with trauma is that whatever you think you saw or heard, you are convinced of it. People who witness plane crashes sometimes claim to have seen the passengers beating on the windows. But that is impossible because the windows are tinted or too high up. I have seen a therapist for many years."

"Has it helped?" Laconia asked.

She shrugged. "Sometimes. It's nice to have a person to talk to."

"What did you tell McCoy?" Laconia asked in a follow-up.

"When we met at the hospital, you asked me about people who might have harmed Gary. I told you that Tiffany Kelly had driven past our home the day of the killing. I thought it was strange. Our house was not on her way to anything."

"I remember."

"I had not thought about it, and then one day I realized that Tiffany was not alone in her car. I didn't know who it was at the time, but there was another person with her. I know now that person was Joe O'Conner."

"Are you sure?"

"These days I am not very sure of anything that happened, but yes. She was driving slowly past our house. It was as if she and Joe were casing it."

"You never told me that," Laconia stated.

"No, but when it all came back to me, I called Detective McCoy. He came to the house and we talked. He explained to me that it was perjury to make accusations that were untrue. He told me he had confirmed from several sources that Joe

O'Conner was at work when I said he was in the car with Tiffany."

"There is nothing in the case file about his coming to see you."

"He did come to see me. Of that I am certain," said Sarah. "I may not be sure of many things, but of that I am sure."

"Why didn't you tell me about him when we were in the hospital?"

"I just didn't want to accuse someone wrongly. I was on the second floor looking at the street. He was in the front seat scrunched down, and I saw him. At first, I thought it was a pile of clothes on the seat, then as she drove away, he straightened up."

"I want you to write a statement for me of what you remember from that day, as well as what you told Detective McCoy and what he told you."

"Will I get into trouble?" she asked Calvin.

"Gary was my friend. That is why I took your case," said Calvin. "I think you owe it to him to write down what you remember."

"Thanks," Laconia said to Calvin. To Sarah, he said, "Just write down what you remember. Write two statements concerning what you remember about Tiffany and Joe O'Conner and about contacting McCoy."

19

After Amanda confessed her lack of remorse to Father Martin, she began to sporadically attend Saint Andrews at the Wednesday noon Eucharist service. Over time, her attendance at the service became more regular. She doubted that she could ever come to trust a God that allowed her to suffer as she had. Over time, though, she came to believe that her suffering was not unique, and in time it might be of service to others. Only a few attended the service. After the sermon, all were invited to stand near the altar for communion.

Father Martin's sermons were short and usually about the saint whose day it was. She liked the simplicity of the service and that all the people knew one another. John Abel was often there. If an associate priest was not in attendance, he filled in and offered wine by saying, "The blood of Christ, the cup of salvation." She noticed that Abel and a homeless man who wore a dress never drank wine, but instead drank grape juice. She asked him if he believed that the wine was no longer wine, but the blood of Christ. He simply said it was one of the mysteries of faith he did not question, but he didn't test it either.

A Catholic priest rebuked her for coming to the altar because she was not Catholic, and she was not baptized. Father Martin told her to come and receive the Eucharist and wine or just a blessing, as she thought best. John the Baptist baptized with water, but Christ baptized with the spirit. It was not his place to deny anyone the opportunity to know Christ. Whether some type of mystical transformation of the bread and wine occurred or not, she felt somehow closer to Christ when she received the bread and wine.

She was walking across the church parking lot to her car, thinking that she might start attending Sunday services when her grandmother called out to her from a car parked close by.

"Are you stalking me?" Amanda asked.

"Not at all," replied Ellen. "I was returning from the Riverside Mall and just turned the corner. I saw you, and I wanted to talk to you."

"I know what happened."

"I understand now. When you have children you might understand how difficult it is to believe anything they do is wrong. Please follow me. There is a coffee shop not far from here. Please, you are my granddaughter. I don't want us to be strangers."

Amanda nodded. "I'll follow you."

Ellen led her to the Cosmo Coffee Shop, only a few blocks away. There were several in the Harbor City area. Modeled after Starbucks, the shop had a busy drive-through lane and a decent sized sitting area with tables and lounge stuffed chairs. It was once a popular spot for police officers to meet and chat, until a massacre of four officers at another coffee shop occurred. A directive by Captain Knight that no more than two officers were to meet in a public coffee shop or restaurant while on duty soon followed. It was not a popular order because many thought it meant, in part, that she was condemning the deceased officers for being partially responsible for their own deaths.

Ellen greeted the barista by name who, in turn, greeted Ellen by name. "I'll have the usual, Erin. This is Amanda, my granddaughter."

"She's your granddaughter!" Erin said with the kind of excitement usually reserved for a rock star. She said to Amanda, "I've seen your work at Bluebeard. We only serve coffee in paper cups now, or I'd draw you a latte design. Perhaps when I am at the Bluebeard the next time, you would show me a few tricks?"

"Sure," responded Amanda. She quickly added, "I'll have a small latte."

"That would be great," smiled Erin. "I'll bring your drinks over right away."

"Thanks," said Ellen.

"I have some pictures with me from when you were little," said Ellen, taking a small photo album out of her purse.

"You said that you weren't stalking me. Why do you have those?"

"I carry them around because I have never given up hope we could talk one day, and by chance, today is the day." She placed the picture album on the table. "I know it's old-fashioned not to have pictures on your phone, but these were taken before smartphones were everywhere." She opened the book to photographs of Amanda as an infant being held by her father. He was smiling and so was she. She was wearing a sun hat, and she was laughing.

"This was taken at the family cabin on Pine Lake. The three of us went there when you were very young. It was taken during a weekend after Stephen had not seen you for a while."

"I don't remember that."

"Of course not. You were only two and a few months old. You were always happy and never seemed afraid of Stephen."

"I was two. I was too young to know what to fear and what was right and what was wrong," Amanda retorted. "Are you trying to say because I was happy at two that nothing happened?"

128

"No, no. Not at all."

"Here are your coffees," said Erin, setting them down.

"Thank you," said Ellen.

"It is so good to see the two of you finally getting together," said Erin. "Your grandma talks about you all the time. I had no idea she was talking about you."

Amanda nodded and said, "Thank you." Once Erin was back taking orders, Amanda asked, "What have you told her?"

"Very little, just that we were estranged because of what your father did."

"That is all?"

"Yes, that is all." Ellen reached into her large purse and put a small black photo album the size of a CD carrier on the table. "When you are young, you don't realize how broken the adults are around you. But everyone who lives is bent, twisted, and often shattered by the winds of fate."

"When did you become a poet?" sneered Amanda.

"I am saying this badly. I have thought so much about what I wanted to say to you, but now I am not sure where to begin. When your mother made accusations against Stevie, I was hurt and angry and did not believe her. Stevie denied that he had done anything, and he said your mother was trying to keep you from him, me, and all of our family.

"He showed me articles and books about parental alienation. There are four criteria for detecting parental alienation. I remember them well because he told me about them over and over again. A parent actively trying to block access to a child was the first one. Your mom did that and got restraining orders against us. The second one is making unfounded abuse allegations. You accused Stevie of abusing you, but when I asked, you denied that you were abused."

Amanda responded, "You asked me, but you asked me over and over if he had touched me. I said he had, then you told me that it was when he bathed me and nothing happened. You convinced me, a child, that nothing happened."

"I know now that I should never have talked to you or questioned you the way I did. I was leading you to the answer I wanted. I know that now. The third criteria is that the relationship deteriorates. Since the separation, the accusations between your dad and your mother got worse and worse."

"That's because she knew that he was abusing me," Amanda explained.

"She suspected it. She never saw the abuse. She even said he mentally abused her. I never believed that. The fourth criteria is intense fear by the child of a parent. I never saw you fearful of my son. But as you got older, I saw you more and more not wanting to visit your mother."

"I was manipulated."

"Stevie was very young when his father and I separated. I wanted to be the perfect mom and for him to be the perfect son. I wanted to show his father that he was not needed. But the flaws in me and the flaws in Stevie, I did not see. He was so much like his father. So clever and deceitful. I, too, was manipulated." Ellen slapped her hand on the table. She flipped open a couple pages of the album and stopped at a photograph of Amanda in a school play dressed as a fairy princess. On either side of her was Ellen and her father. This formation was repeated often in photographs up to her graduation from high school. In between these photographs were others of Amanda and her father doing various things, such as shopping, fishing, and standing near a roller coaster at the state fair.

"Why are you showing me these photographs? They don't tell the story of what went on when there was no one to photograph what he did to me."

"I understand that now," said Ellen. "I should have been more vigilant, but what I saw was what was in the photographs. That is what I am trying to say. I understand now that what you say happened is actually what happened to you. When I confronted you at the Bluebeard Café, I did not believe my son was capable of what you said he did. You killed my only son, and I was in denial that he did anything wrong."

"And now?"

"In going through his effects, I found a diary, a secret journal. He wrote about his desire to possess you as a wife. It was not pornographic, but it was disconcerting."

"You make it sound Victorian."

"It was disgusting, but it made me realize that what you said was true." Ellen fidgeted with her hands and wiped her eyes.

"I have always thought you must have known. That you turned a blind eye to what he was doing."

"I just thought he loved you in the normal way that a father loves his daughter."

"Why did you call my mother a liar?"

"Because I thought she was. I thought she was making up things, and I wanted to protect you from her lies."

131

"Can we be friends again?" Ellen asked. "You used to come over to my house often after school. You never told me any of what was happening."

"I thought you knew."

"No, no." said Ellen, shaking her head from side to side. "I wasted so much time not seeing things and not appreciating the gifts of life right in front of me. Please don't shut me out."

"I need to think about these things," said Amanda as she stood up. Before she could clear the table of her coffee cup, Ellen took it and held it next to her cup.

"Mothers," Ellen observed. "We are always cleaning up things. Can we at least talk some more?"

"Yes. Give me your number."

Ellen quickly wrote it on a notepad and stood up. They were near the counter, and Erin was happy to see them together.

"Do you know where the black van is?" asked Ellen.

"The black van? I am not sure. I haven't seen it for years. I thought he sold it," replied Amanda.

"No, I found the title to the van in his papers, but I am not sure where it could be," she said. "Perhaps it is at the Pine Lake cabin."

They parted with tentative hugs. Behind Amanda's back, Ellen gave a thumb's up to Erin, who reciprocated the sign with one of her own.

20

Ron McBride enjoyed sitting on his porch watching the sun rise up over Mount Rainier. The cars on the interstate, the ships in the harbor, were all cast for a few brief moments in the red rays of the rising sun. He enjoyed the ever-changing vista. His house was the highest in the Center Point area of Harbor City. Crime had decreased since he sobered up over twenty years ago, but it was still an area that unarmed white folk and honest black folk avoided after dark.

He had already been up for hours. In the backyard were three large grills filled with charcoal still too hot to put his marinated ribs on. Once a hustler, always a hustler. When he sobered up, he transferred his marketing skills into many endeavors. Some were for profit and some were because he felt a debt to the community he had terrorized for many years. Even the L.A. gangs that came to Harbor City in the eighties quickly learned to avoid him.

He was known as the Pope of Center Point. With his large hands, he brought many a man to his knees begging for mercy. Crime for him, aside from an addiction that had brought him to his knees, was profitable. The street to the side of his house sloped quickly downward. Across from his home was an apartment complex that he owned through a company that was a subsidiary of another company, whose true ownership was concealed by another company.

Born a hustler, he could not be idle. In the summer, he organized a picnic for the Pride Festival in Center Point, and he printed and sold T-shirts with that logo. On weekends, he sold barbeque rib dinners. During the week, he gave away food to children who were in need. He went to AA meetings daily. He was a hustler for AA. When people saw how it changed his life, they understood the power possible to change their own lives with faith in a Higher Power. He was where he began life, but he was changed from the life he had led. He was even awarded two Urban League Legend Awards for his community service. He was an avid photographer, and he was often asked to photograph weddings and Center Point events. Once he sobered up, he discovered that he had many hidden talents.

For twenty years, he was relatively crime-free. Still, when he saw Laconia park in front of his house, his first thought was that old endeavors might have come home to roost. When he saw that Laconia was alone, he knew that couldn't be the reason for the morning visit. As rock solid as Laconia was, he was not foolish enough to try and arrest him on his own. Laconia's destructive powers, when he was enraged, were legendary in Center Point, but so were McBride's. If they ever came to blows, it would have been like a tornado taking on a hurricane. Before Laconia reached the steps to his porch, McBride asked, "Care for some lemonade, my friend?"

"Lemonade would be fine." Laconia sat in the wooden Adirondack chair next to McBride's. Both were secured to the porch by bolts and chains. Center Point was not the kind of area to leave things unattached, no matter the reputation of the owner.

"You don't seem surprised to see me. Should I be worried?" asked Laconia.

McBride smiled and shook his head. "Those days are far behind me, as I am sure our mutual friend would tell you."

"Abel never betrays a trust, but I have a favor to ask of you."

"It must be a serious favor to bring you out at such an early hour."

"Do you know Steve McCoy?"

"Everyone in Center Point knows who McCoy is, but I have not had the personal pleasure. My nephew, Tyke, the car mechanic, knows him. Before Tyke stopped boosting cars, McCoy arrested him. Took him down to the ground and put a knee into his back just to let him know who was in charge. Needless. Tyke had complied. "All my nephews have received the lecture from me and their mothers and fathers. When the man stops you, comply, and keep your mouth shut. No need to argue your innocence with a cop. You are going to jail if they want you in jail."

"I know that lecture. My mama gave it to me, but I didn't need it."

"Nobody thinks they need it until they need it, and then in anger many forget it."

"I am not here to argue or defend the injustices of the police," said Laconia.

"You were always fair. When Baneman raided my house on that trumped up drug charge, you being there made him less violent. He only tore up half my house looking for the drugs that the snitch planted."

"How did you know to find it before the raid?"

"Instinct, my friend. After the snitch left, I looked and searched the house like my life

135

depended upon it. As it did," he chuckled. "What about McCoy?"

"On Wednesdays, Captain Knight and McCoy have a standing long lunch. I would like to know where it is and when they part."

McBride took a long sip of lemonade. "Not like you to pry into the affairs of your fellow man unless crime is involved, and if crime is involved, shouldn't you consider involving Internal Affairs?"

"Do you still have a niece that works at Plumly and Matthews?"

"I have family all over Harbor City, as you well know. She greets people during the day shift and seats them, but I think you may already know this."

Laconia nodded that he did and took a long sip of lemonade. Out in the harbor, a grain ship was headed out to sea. The sun had risen high enough that the morning cast of red had faded away. In every negotiation, silence is broken by the one needing agreement more. "What do you need to know?" Laconia asked.

"I don't need to know why, but I need to know that you will have my back and my relatives' backs if it goes south. If snooping on a captain and sergeant in the police force gets found out, it will not go well."

"I won't let things go bad," said Laconia.

McBride cocked his chin down and raised his eyes like a maiden aunt looking over her spectacles. "Things can go bad," he intoned.

"I will never not take responsibility. I want to know when they part. What they are doing is not important to me. I am doing some work and don't want to be interrupted."

"Laconia, my brother, I appreciate the trust. But even trust has a price. We have not discussed remuneration. This sounds like private investigator work. You know that in order to do P.I. work, you're required to have a license, don't you?"

"What are you suggesting? Be fair."

"We can discuss the particulars another time, but assistance in my meals for kids project is always appreciated, as is the purchase of T-shirts for the Center Point Reunion."

21

The murder case file for the death of Gary Shipman was several hundred pages in length. The hard copy of the investigation reports, witness interviews, ballistic report, photographs, and medical records were contained in several three-ring binders. One binder labeled "Work Product" consisted of pages of copied field notes, internal correspondence between police officers, emails, and text messages exchanged between the police and the prosecutor. Each page was stamped at the top in red capital letters "WORK PRODUCT."

These were documents not to be shared with the public or defense attorneys. Within these pages, the police might voice a concern that a witness seemed unreliable, but in the incident report, that concern would not appear. A prosecutor might send out a message about a gap in a time that needed to be filled in to establish or destroy an alibi defense, and comments about the lack of a defense lawyer's skills.

Near the end of the documents, Laconia saw an email he sent to McCoy and prosecutor Brinkmeyer, suggesting they arrange to interview the children who went trick-or-treating with their parents. The parents were quite deft at giving each other alibis, but no one interviewed the children. At the time of the shooting, they ranged in ages from five to nine. Perhaps the children had different recollections of the night Shipman died. As he read through the various emails, the urge to crumple them surged once again through his veins.

All Laconia wanted to do was find out who killed Shipman. But Brinkmeyer was more concerned about not traumatizing the children by evoking unpleasant memories. He thought it odd then, and he thought it odd now. Brinkmeyer thought nothing about interviewing them countless times about the allegation of abuse. However, asking them what they were doing blocks away from the shooting was somehow unhealthy for the children.

First, the parents were contacted who, in turn, contacted their therapists, who, in turn, wrote letters suggesting that their children were too young to question. Others asked to have a list of the questions provided so they could ask the children the questions. Then he was off the case, and McCoy was in charge. Amanda was arraigned for having killed Shipman, and he was ordered to leave the investigation to McCoy.

Laconia was in his office. Even though his door was slightly open, it was customary, no matter what one's rank, to knock on the door before entering. Except custom and courtesy were not traits that Captain Knight held in high regard. "Laconia, Harbor City has plenty of recently dead people. Why do you keep going back to that?" she demanded, pointing to the file. "I told you to focus on the recently dead, not dwell on a cold case."

"We arrested two Pleasmont brothers early this morning for a drive-by shooting and a couple of assaults. I expect a lull in crime for a day or two," replied Laconia.

"I told you to leave the Shipman murder alone," Knight said. "That was an order, not a suggestion."

"His murder was never solved."

"Yes, it was solved. We were just not able to get a conviction. Your friend, John Abel, saw to that. The jury was fooled by Amanda Bowman's youth and good looks," Knight pressed.

"She never testified," replied Laconia.

"With good reason. If she testified, Brinkmeyer would have shredded her on the witness stand."

"It's a cold case, and I am troubled by there being no resolution," Laconia said. Without a conviction, it is an open case. That is protocol. Simply declaring an unsolved case closed is contrary to written policy."

"The resolution was that a guilty person fooled a jury. It is not a cold case. You really need to update your understanding of police procedure. A cold case is an unsolved case until a suspect has been identified, charged, and tried for the crime. This case went to trial, and the suspect was found 'not guilty.' Ergo, it is no longer a cold case. If the case had gone to trial and not resulted in a verdict of 'not guilty,' then you could look for new evidence. It might be reopened, but that is not the situation here."

"If the killer wasn't Amanda Bowman, then the case is not solved."

Knight shook her head. "I tell you that the case is closed. It is not a cold case. John Wilkes Booth never got tried for Lincoln's murder, but that is no reason to look for another killer. You are just clinging to some idea that McCoy messed up. Well, he didn't. I worked with him and double-checked his work. It was a good call to charge Bowman. Brinkmeyer simply did not do his job, and she walked."

"Amanda Bowman lives with Ike Kelly, one of the parents. His wife is deceased. Bowman may be connected to the attack on Commissioner Carpenter."

"Tiffany Kelly drowned herself," Knight said. "What of it?"

"I am not sure, but by going back over the Shipman case, I may find something relevant to the Carpenter case," conceded Laconia. "There are gaps in the investigation that need filled in."

"Gaps in your head, not in the case. You are looking for an excuse to reopen the Shipman murder," snapped Knight. "I am having these files gathered up and archived. I don't want to see you near them again."

"Very well," said Laconia, looking at his wristwatch. "Have a nice lunch."

"What is that supposed to mean?"

"Nothing," said Laconia.

"I am writing up a directive that the Shipman files stay in archives," Knight said as she turned quickly toward the door.

"I understand," said Laconia, thinking how glad he was to have the files on a thumb drive.

Only a few moments passed before a secretary knocked on Laconia's door and said she was sent by Captain Knight to pick up files for archives. Laconia smiled. He saw no reason to take out his frustration on the secretary, who was already nervous about being sent to retrieve some files. He pointed to the one on his desk and to four others on a shelf.

"If you need more time with them, I can come back," said the secretary.

"No problem," he said, putting on a worn tweed blazer and holstering his CZ 75 SP-01, a full-sized handgun. It was his pistol. He thought it was much more accurate than the department issued Glock. He wore the holster behind his hip to keep it out of sight, but with a slightly forward cant. The forward tilt of the holster, sometimes called an FBI tilt, made a quicker draw than if the holster was angled straight up in the zero position.

"I'll be out for a while."

"Roger that," said the secretary.

At the Center Point barbecue joint, Laconia ordered a half rack of ribs, baked beans, coleslaw, and a Coca-Cola. While he ate, he received a text that McCoy and Knight were at Plumly and Matthews, and they had just ordered a bottle of wine. He wiped his fingers with a wet napkin and drove to Stadium High School. Construction on the school began in 1880. It was intended to be a luxury hotel resembling a French château, but the panic of 1883 ended the project. In 1906, fire gutted the building, so the Harbor City School Board bought it and turned it into a high school. Since then, several reconstructions and additions took place, but the original turrets overlooking Destiny Bay remained. Despite its elegant appearance, it had the same problems of the less glamorous high schools of Harbor City.

Like other schools, police officers were assigned to remain near Stadium High School during morning hours and dismissal hours. These were peak times for fights and bullying between students and for students from rival schools to come looking for a fight. A squad car parked in front of the school reduced the number of skirmishes on school grounds.

Laconia parked next to a squad car and introduced himself to the rookie beat-cop in the driver's seat, showing him a year-old photograph of a boy with short-cropped hair, wearing a tie. "He should be out in a few minutes," said the officer with a chuckle. True to his prediction, in less than ten minutes, Kyle Boardman walked out the front door.

"That's him," said the officer, pointing to a boy wearing combat boots and a spiked mohawk with red highlights. "Kyle, a word," said the officer waving him over. Kyle Boardman strolled toward the squad car with an artless swagger and bent down to look the officer in the eye. His backpack was suitable for a week in the woods.

"This is Sergeant Jones. He has a few questions for you."

Boardman looked away, spit on the ground, and then he glanced back at the two officers. "You can't talk to me unless a parent is present."

"You're not under arrest or a suspect. I want to talk to you about Gary Shipman," said Laconia.

"He's dead."

"Very dead for a long time," said Laconia.

"Why would you want to talk to me now? No one talked to me when he was killed."

"That's why I want to talk to you now," smiled Laconia. "Could we go someplace and talk? I'm in the mood for a huckleberry malt."

"I'm in the mood for a milkshake, a double cheeseburger, and fries," said Kyle.

"That can be arranged too. My car is there." Laconia said, pointing at a dark red four-door sedan.

"The Goldfish Inn near the zoo makes great burgers," said Kyle.

"Sounds good. Very good, " said Laconia. Where they were going was far away from the Plumly and Matthews restaurant.

It was a clear day. The five-mile drive to the Goldfish took them along Destiny Bay where people were out in mass, rollerblading and walking dogs.

The Goldfish was once a tavern, but after a shooting, it changed hands. The new owners refined the menu and redecorated the place to make it more family friendly. They retained the wooden high-back booths along the walls from when it was once a tavern.

By habit, Laconia chose a booth far from the front door and the side where he could see whoever entered.

The waitress came over with menus, but before she could put them on the table, Laconia and Boardman gave her their orders.

"I should call my mom. I won't tell her I'm with you."

"Why not?"

"Because if you wanted her to know, you would have come to my house. I'll tell her I'm going to the library. You can take me there, right?"

Laconia nodded.

"Great! That way I am not lying, and she is not worried. What do you think of my mohawk?"

Laconia rubbed his bald dome.

"Not my style."

Kyle grinned. "Not my dad's either. You came to our house a couple of times after Shipman was killed. My dad didn't like you, and that made me a fan. Any enemy of my enemy."

Laconia nodded. "Why didn't your dad like me?"

"He didn't say, but let me tell you why I have a mohawk, and maybe then you will understand. When they started taking me to see Ian Franklin, the child counselor, they wanted me to tell him I

144

was abused. Those meetings went on and on. My dad used to cut my hair on Sunday night. If I was a good boy, he gave me a number two buzz cut. But if I had gotten a bad grade or a teacher had complained, I got a number one buzz. A one-buzz cut is about a millimeter above bald. You could hardly see any hair. Sometimes, I think he set the shaver at one-half. Not bald like you, but very close. When I went to school the Monday after a number one cut, the boys would laugh and rub their heads. Franklin kept pressuring me to say Shipman or his wife had touched my privates. Sometimes he pressured me to say that I saw others touched. Finally, he told me that others said they saw Shipman with his hand down my pants. I panicked. I wondered if I was a liar. Eventually, I said yes, I was abused. That led to Franklin asking me for details. When I couldn't think of anything, he made suggestions. If I said yes, he was happy; my mom was happy; then my dad was happy; and I got a number two haircut."

"That is in the court record," said Laconia.

"I suppose some of it is." Kyle took a large bite of his cheeseburger. After only a few bites, it was gone.

"When I was in court and the judge put me on his knee and ordered my parents out of the courtroom, he asked if Shipman had ever harmed me. I said no. He asked me why I lied. I said my mother and father told me to lie. The case was dismissed, and I got a year of number one haircuts. My dad was furious. He was especially furious when a lawyer came and told us that he was dropping the lawsuit against the Shipmans and the State. 'You cost us a million bucks, you dumb kid,' my dad often said."

"You told the truth."

"Did I? I wonder sometimes if I really was abused and just didn't know how to speak about it. I was so angry at my parents for making me talk. I just couldn't continue to say what they wanted me to say."

"I'm not here to reopen the case of abuse against you. I'm here about the night Shipman was murdered."

"My parents divorced about a year after he was killed. After he was killed, they just seemed to stop talking to each other or to me. They would look at me as if I had ruined their lives. Maybe I did. They wanted millions from the State, and I blew their chance."

"They may have had other problems."

Kyle shrugged. "After the divorce, dad continued to cut my hair every other Sunday. He was supposed to come over on Wednesdays and take me to dinner, but he seldom did. It got so I was surprised when he showed up. It was just too painful to expect him and not to have him show up."

"My parents were separated. My dad solved the problem by never coming around," said Laconia.

The irony of his remark eluded Kyle.

"One weekend, my dad was drunk all day and night. He was angry about work, about a ballgame, about a woman he was seeing who told him she didn't want to see him, and he was angry at me. He wanted me to play football. I told him I had no interest. He said I was big enough. I said that I didn't care. When he went to cut my hair, he was vicious. He nicked my ears and gouged my scalp. Mom got a restraining order to stop him from ever cutting my hair again." Kyle ran the palm of a hand along the side of his head. "I still go over every weekend. He looks at me and says I look like a freak. I tell him the apple doesn't fall far from the tree. I'm just more visible than him. Clever, huh?"

"I guess."

"I may get it cut shorter just to show them I can do what I want."

"Tell me what you remember from the night Shipman was killed."

"I remember no one ever asked me what I saw."

"Why do you remember that?"

"Because each time you came over, my father told me not to speak unless I was spoken to. Then I heard him tell you and another cop that he didn't want me bothered. I remember that well."

"Now I'm asking. What do you remember?"

"Well, it was a dark and stormy night," Kyle paused. "Well, not that stormy, but it did rain some, and it was dark when we finished making the rounds. There were six cars hauling us around. We worked one block, then we went to another location. Some of the parents went out earlier in the week and knew where people put up decorations. Those were the houses with the most loot."

"Do you remember where you went?" Laconia asked.

"For the most part."

Laconia spread a map of the area on the table. "Can you point out where you went?"

"Sort of. The parents came to our house first. It was about 4:30 when we started, still light out. The parents drove us to different spots farther and farther away." He pointed to an area not on the map. "At about 7:30 we were at a community center that's not on this map. When we left, we were more jammed together in my parents' car."

"Why was that?"

"That was because Mrs. Kelly and Mr. O'Conner were no longer with us, and the kids in their car had to pile into the other cars."

"Are you sure Kelly and O'Conner were gone?"

"I'm sure Kelly and O'Conner were gone. Kelly left her car in the parking lot, and I saw it as we drove off. You can ask the other kids who were with me. It was a secret we were not supposed to tell."

"Ok, go on," Laconia encouraged Kyle.

"They were gone for maybe forty-five minutes. We went around for about two blocks and when we got back to the parking lot, O'Conner and Kelly were waiting for us. I think my dad knew that because he was on his cell phone. Then midway down a street, he told us to turn around. It was not the pattern we were following before that."

"You remember all this?"

"Ask the other kids. We were not alone."

"How did Kelly and O'Conner act?"

"O'Conner seemed to go out of his way to tell jokes and make us laugh. Ms. Kelly was not like that at all. She seemed eager to get going. She said she left her husband at home doing all the doorbell answering and felt she should get back. We broke up in the parking lot. We didn't hit any more houses."

"You remember anything else?"

"That is what I remember today. Why are you interested in this? Did some new evidence turn up? Why are you talking to me now?"

"Like self-pity, there is no statute of limitations on murder. Let's get you to the library."

"Sure," said Kyle, drawing the last of his milkshake with a straw from a steel container. "But maybe you could help me."

"How so?"

"I have to go back to the counselor for anger management or get suspended from school."

"What did you do?"

"I punched the star quarterback. He missed a game, and everyone was upset until his substitute won the game. Now he is the only one still angry. He may ride the bench for the rest of the year. I did the school a favor, but I still have to go to anger management."

"You punched him, and he missed a game? You must have some punch."

"I suppose the bicycle chain I wrapped around my fist may have helped."

"You just happened to have a bicycle chain?"

"I rode my bike to school and was locking it up. Then he came along, all letter jacket like, calling me a punk. He said that I was riding my bike to school like I was a junior high kid. His friends joined in. You know how it is if you let a bully own you; he owns you forever. So, I punched him with the chain in my hand. The lock hit him in the eye. His friends started to hit and kick me, but the school cop broke it up. I got suspended for a week. So did his jock friends, as well as the jock. He got a pass but couldn't play anyway."

"Sounds like anger management might be a good idea. But if you can stay away from collecting felonies, there might be a place for you in law enforcement."

"Really?"

"Better to have you on our side than not. But you will have to cut your hair."

"A gun for short hair? I can do that. Would you like to talk to the other kids without their parents finding out? I could help with that."

"You are detective material," said Laconia.

22

Assistant Chief of Police, Alan Merwin, reviewed the performance evaluation of Laconia that Knight submitted for his approval. He had to agree that Laconia could at times seem insolent to those with thin skin, and he was never good at paperwork.

Merwin sighed, pushed his reading glasses up, rubbed the sides of his nose with a thumb and forefinger, and then stared at the pictures on the far wall of his office. There were several. One of them was him standing next to Laconia after he received the Medal of Valor. Another one was him, Laconia, and several other law enforcement officers taken right after they defeated a law enforcement team from a larger city north of Harbor City. The game was called the Bacon Bowl. The game proceeds were donated to the children's hospitals of each city. He was the team's quarterback, and Laconia was the running back. Laconia was new to the force at the time, and Merwin was a lieutenant.

Merwin was a backup quarterback at Princeton. After he graduated, he went to the University of Iowa where he obtained a Ph.D. in Criminology and a law degree. He was promoted quickly from patrol duty, but he thought the time on the street invaluable for making decisions in administration. He seldom mentioned his education unless he was accused by the unwary of just being a dumb cop.

In the first half of the Bacon Bowl, Laconia was a beast behind good blockers. Baneman was the running back in other years, but Laconia was younger and stronger. So, Merwin decided to play

Baneman sparingly. Within a few steps past the line he was in full stride, knocking down linebackers.

In the second half, things went sour because Baneman and others brought beer for the players. With the guards and tackles stumbling over themselves, hardly sober enough to hold a three-point stance, Laconia was hit behind the line of scrimmage before he could gain speed. Merwin's pocket quickly collapsed whenever he tried to pass. Laconia suggested that he move him to full back and stay in as an extra blocker and put Baneman in as running back. More than once, Laconia stopped a giant defensive end from blindsiding him. Even after Laconia's nose was smashed, he still stayed in the game defending Merwin. It was not the kind of thing you forgot. Nor did either of them forget watching Baneman slammed to the ground because of the ineffective blocking he created by serving beer at half-time. The team survived the second half, mainly because Laconia asked to play defense as well as offense. In the safety spot, he stopped a couple of touchdowns by swatting passes away.

Merwin liked Laconia far more than just for the time they played football together. Laconia received the Medal of Valor for entering a house and saving a woman and her small daughter from the estranged husband who was threatening to kill her and himself. The obviously drunk husband answered the door. After a few obscenities, Laconia whispered for backup into his shoulder walkie-talkie. But once the door was slammed shut, he did not hesitate. The wife was upstairs, drenched in gasoline and tied to a bedpost; the little girl was next to her mother. Laconia talked to the man before he could reach the second landing. Then he bravely subdued the husband after he slashed Laconia a few times with a curved fishing knife.

Laconia requested that Merwin pin the medal on his uniform. A few months later when he requested a transfer into the Homicide Unit, Merwin made sure it happened over the objection of Baneman, the sergeant of the unit.

Merwin glanced back at the performance review. Overall, Knight rated Laconia's performance as below average. In her notes, she suggested that a once exemplary officer was experiencing burnout from years of dedicated service, and she felt perhaps he was in need of a less strenuous position. In contrast, McCoy's performance review was glowing. Knight described him as energetic and willing to learn new things. She described McCoy as possessing leadership qualities and wrote that he was respected by his fellow officers.

For each of her promotions: from patrol officer to sergeant, to shift sergeant, to lieutenant, and finally to captain, Merwin supported her. Not because he expected anything in return, but because he believed her devotion to service and the community was in line with his beliefs and goals.

When the Pandemic struck, the front door to the police station was closed. Long-term officers no longer fit for street work were pensioned off short of their full-service hours. Merwin strongly opposed it. Knight, however, in an alliance with Budget and Finance and Human Resources, convinced the chief to keep the lobby closed. Merwin thought it was a mistake, and he wrote many memos and argued in meetings to keep the lobby open, all to no avail. Knight said the numbers simply did not work out, and the chief listened silently, finally agreeing with her.

The issue was personal, but Merwin never told them why it was so personal to him. When he was six, his mother had hurried him into the family car and driven to the sheriff's station. It was late at night. They lived in a small town. The sheriff's office and jail were on the first floor, while the sheriff's home was on the second floor. Young Merwin and his mother had just gotten inside the station when their father pulled up out front in a pickup truck. Drunk as usual, he was yelling and cursing her. The sheriff, a large man who was a Marine in World War II, stood between them. The sheriff gave his father two choices: go to jail or home. His father chose home. Days later Merwin and his mom returned home, and things went well for a while. Then the cycle of abuse, shouting, and slapping began again.

When he was seventeen, Merwin moved out and slept in a 1956 Chevy during his entire senior year, and he then went on to Princeton. If he and his mom in Harbor City got stuck outside the station trying to talk into an intercom like the one installed near the front door of the police station, he didn't think they would have survived. His father was swinging a hatchet when his mother gathered him up and drove him to the sheriff's station. The sheriff knew his father, and when he spoke to him, his father calmed down because they knew each other.

This was not a past he told others, but it was infused in every decision and recommendation he made supporting more officers on the street and in the schools talking to students. Merwin knew that he would never be a police chief. That opportunity passed him by when the City Council decided to do a nationwide search for a new chief, rather than hire from within. Merwin had reached as high a rank in the department as he could, but he had no desire to look for work in another city.

Merwin wanted to be sure that in the Harbor City Police Department, statistics would serve the needs of the people and not the needs and calculations of Budget and Finance. Listening to Knight extol her budget saving suggestions made him question her judgment. Perhaps she aspired to his job or higher, he didn't know. He didn't want to know, but that her judgment was flawed in one area made him question her judgment in the performance evaluations.

Merwin shook his head. He had known both Laconia and McCoy for many years. What Knight described was not the men he knew. The opinion of a supervisor over those they supervise is seldom questioned. The phrase "approved by" really meant rubber-stamped. His pen hovered above the signature line, but he did not touch the page. He placed the performance reviews in his desk drawer and locked it.

23

Knight ignored the new sign on the door requesting that a person knock if the door was closed. She had read in a leadership manual that superior officers should always show they are in charge. She wanted it known that a sign posted by a subordinate would not stop her. She turned the doorknob to Laconia's office and began to barge in. But for a chain lock Laconia had installed, she would have quickly entered the room and assumed a command position. Instead, she banged her head on the door and screamed, "What the fuck!" Following close behind her was McCoy, who collided with her, causing her to bump her head and yell again, "What the fuck!"

"Captain, is that you?" asked Laconia through a grin he could not totally suppress. His tone was as sweet and solicitous as he could make it without breaking into laughter.

"What the… Laconia!"

"I'll take that as a yes," Laconia said. After removing a thumb drive from his computer, he undid the lock.

Rubbing her forehead, Knight asked, "Who gave you permission to put a lock on your door?"

"Who said you could put a lock on your door?" echoed McCoy. "I don't have a lock on my door."

"It's in the rules and procedures manual. Sergeants and above are entitled to their privacy."

"Where?" snapped Knight.

"I'm not sure," responded Laconia. "If you find where it is forbidden for me to have a lock, let me know. Why are you here?"

"I ordered you to return the Shipman files to archives."

"That is where they are, unless someone else checked them out."

"Then why did you interview Kyle Boardman? I was on the phone for over an hour with his mother. She was in tears, saying that she suffered PTSD from the abuse her son suffered. Your questioning him brought it all back to her. She threatened to sue and said she was calling her lawyer, Vince Jordan." To emphasize her point, she gestured toward his cheek with her forefinger with each word, "The case is closed."

"I don't recall you telling me that I could not continue my investigation."

"I most certainly did," Knight said.

"Not my recollection. Perhaps you should put that in a memo to me for the case file and distribute it to the department."

"You have no authority to tell me how to do my job."

Laconia handed her an incident report from his office printer.

"This is my summary of my interview with Kyle. His recollection of the night Shipman was killed is very different from the version provided by the adults McCoy interviewed. He says that Tiffany Kelly and Joe O'Conner drove off and were not with the other parents at the time when Shipman was shot."

"What are you going to do with that report?"

"Send it to archives to be added to the Shipman file."

"After I told you to leave the case alone?"

"Not my recollection, captain. Put it in writing, and I will sign off that you want the investigation to end, even though a new discrepancy has recently come to light."

Laconia put on his tweed jacket and holstered his CZ 75.

"Where are you going?" Knight demanded.

"I'm going to interview Joe O'Conner."

"You are so insolent. After I tell you not to investigate the Shipman murder, you're just going to go interview him?"

"McCoy and I are both assigned to investigate Commissioner Carpenter's claim that she was run off the road. She was going home from the MAACO shop when the accident occurred. If she was followed home, then she might have been followed from the MAACO shop."

"You think they would remember that?" scoffed McCoy.

"Perhaps, and it is possible that the black van, if it exists, might show up on CCTV."

"Steve will go with you," said Knight and added, "Keep your questions to the black van."

The MAACO shop was only two interstate exits and a few blocks from the police station. When traffic was light, it was only twenty minutes away; when heavy, about forty minutes. The post office was on the left, a block up from the MAACO entrance. Laconia parked in front of the office. As they walked in, a customer was walking out.

"Sergeant McCoy," Maggie said, as she nodded to Laconia. McCoy was the lead detective investigating Shipman. Early on, he met with a group of parents. He suggested that their children continue seeing Ian Franklin. The expectation was that in the course of counseling, more information would be revealed about the abuse by the Shipmans. Laconia and she had only met a couple of times.

"Maggie, how are you?" McCoy asked.

"Fine. Have there been developments? Is Sarah going to be charged?"

"No such luck," said McCoy. He explained that they were interested in possible CCTV footage from the date of Carpenter's accident. "Even if you had surveillance footage, I suppose you copied over it."

"No, we keep surveillance video for at least three years. That is how long a person has to file a civil claim. It's not like the old days when we used VHS and copied over tapes. Now it is all computerized."

"Do you have any video of the entrance?" asked Laconia.

Maggie nodded and motioned toward the back-room area. On the wall were several screens. "You would be surprised how often people complain their vehicle was damaged while with us. These tapes have ended a lot of claims dead in their tracks."

"I spoke to a witness who remembers the night Shipman was killed. Your husband and Tiffany Kelly left the group during the time he was shot," said Laconia.

"Kyle Boardman has had a lot of problems. His mother called me to say someone talked to him without her permission."

"That was me," said Laconia. "Do you and Ms. Boardman often talk?"

"No, but she found it troubling that someone talked to her son without her permission. She wanted me to know. I have a child, Randy, who was abused by Shipman. Are you talking to all the children?"

159

"Was Randy trick-or-treating with Kyle on the night of the shooting? I am trying to find out what happened."

"I am trying to protect my son. You cannot talk to him unless you get a court order. My lawyer, Vince Jordan, says if you want more information on that night, you should arrange any interviews with him. Is that clear?" McCoy asked.

"Very," said Laconia.

"Sergeant Jones was acting on his own when he contacted Kyle," said McCoy. "I am sure it is very clear that neither Kyle nor his mother will be bothered anymore."

"My vision is quite clear," said Laconia. "Stop the reel," he commanded. On the screen a black van passed by the entrance.

As she searched on her computer, Maggie spoke. "The poor boy has had a lot of problems since his mother and father divorced, trouble in school. He seems to cry out for attention in the most inappropriate ways. Have you seen his hair? He wears a mohawk with red highlights. He is not always honest; he likes to make things up and get his father or mother in trouble. He made unfounded accusations to a school counselor, claiming he was forced to lie about being abused. He nearly blinded a football player with a bicycle chain. Here we are," she said, pointing at the screen. "What time of day are you interested in?"

McCoy answered, and she started the video again. She fast-forwarded the recording, then stopped it at the point when Carpenter's vehicle was shown entering the lot.

"Let it run longer," said Laconia. After a couple of cars passed, the black van appeared.

"Can you make a clip of Carpenter entering your lot up to this van passing?" McCoy asked.

"Sure, I can email it to you."

"Move the video forward to when Carpenter left the lot," said Laconia.

Maggie fast-forwarded the recording quickly. On the screen they saw Carpenter wait and then turn left back toward the interstate. The far side of the street was not within range of the surveillance camera. "We want a clip of her leaving," said Laconia.

When they left the MAACO shop, rather than head to the interstate, Laconia circled around the post office block. Behind the post office was a street lined with campers and worn cars. On the other side of the street with the parked cars were trees and open areas, with tents and shopping carts stuffed with old suitcases and sleeping bags. The street itself was home to many backpacks and other debris indicative of long-term homelessness. He drove around the block a couple more times. Finally, he parked near the intersection that was behind the post office which had a view of the entrance to the MAACO shop.

"This is where I would park and wait for Carpenter to leave the MAACO shop. If she was headed to the interstate toward her home, she would go by here," said Laconia.

"Do you think the homeless would remember the van? For a bottle of wine, most of them would say they did," McCoy responded.

Laconia pointed at a camera mounted high on a post near the post office's property line. It was pointed toward where they were parked.

Despite three clerks at the front counter, the line for postal service was long. "We need to talk to the manager," McCoy announced in a loud voice.

"We don't have one," said a tall clerk through a smile.

Holding up his badge, McCoy said in a louder voice than before, "This is police business."

"Someone will be with you in a moment," replied the clerk. He pointed to the line of customers. 'I will be with you soon."

"I need some stamps anyway," said Laconia, smiling back at the clerk who was unimpressed with McCoy's demeanor or official status. The clerk had thick arms and a smile for every customer. When they got to the clerk's counter, Laconia bought a sheet of forever stamps honoring August Wilson.

"Good choice," said the clerk. "What was that about wanting to see a manager?"

"I am Detective Sergeant Laconia Jones. This is Detective Sergeant Steve McCoy. We would like to see the Postal Inspector or whoever is in charge of the shift," said Laconia.

"Helps to know who you are asking for. I'm the Postal Inspector. I am Inspector Levi Orgel. How can I help you?"

"Best if we talk in your office, sir," said Laconia.

"We are short-handed. A clerk called in sick, and I couldn't get a replacement."

"It is important to me," said Laconia. "We will be quick."

"Very well." With a nod to the clerk near him, Orgel placed a closed sign on his counter.

Orgel led them to his office, passing several workers who he greeted by name and who all smiled back at him.

His office was small, made even smaller by two large filing cabinets. He stood behind his desk and asked, "So what brings you here other than stamps?" Orgel asked, while looking directly at Laconia, to the irritation of McCoy.

"We are interested in your CCTV at the back of the lot," said McCoy.

"The courts have decided that the good citizens of the homeless encampment have the constitutional right of privacy to litter, urinate, defecate, shoot up, and fornicate in public. Unless you have a warrant, I can't help you. If you get a warrant, you should know that none of the cameras show any area of the encampment. We went up to the Court of Appeals on this, and I can't help you. I understand the police might come in and move them out and put up a fence, but that is just a rumor you might know more about than me. Anything else?" he asked, looking at Laconia.

"The encampment doesn't interest us. We saw that you have a camera near the intersection with 38th Street. We're interested in knowing if a certain van was parked there at about 5:30pm."

"Why?"

"This is a police investigation; we are not at liberty to say," said McCoy.

Laconia rolled his eyes, then said, "What he means, whether he knows it or not, is that officially we are not at liberty to say. But between us, we are interested in knowing if a black van was parked there on a particular date because the driver may have been stalking a certain person who was later run off the road."

"We keep footage back pretty far. Come with me." He led them into a room with monitors. "If

163

the van was parked near the intersection on the date you are interested in, it would show up on this screen." The image went to the far side of the road. "We have had some thefts, so the court said we could leave the camera in place that displays on this monitor in the off-chance that thieves go this way."

He asked for the day and time they were interested in and pushed a few buttons on a screen that moments before were blank. The traffic on the back street was light, but constant.

Orgel explained, "People who come here for the drive-through at the side of the building often use this street if they are headed to the mall, rather than turn onto the main street in front of the building. Whether it's quicker, I have my doubts, but the side street gets a fair amount of use."

"A testament to the desire of people to use shortcuts whether they save time or not," said Laconia.

"Precisely," said Orgel with a chuckle.

Laconia pointed to the screen when the van appeared and jotted down the time.

The side windows of the van were tinted, and they could not see the driver.

"Waste of time coming here," said McCoy.

"We know that the van was here. That's a lot," said Laconia. "But yet there's more, " he added, mimicking a TV show on late night-advertising. "The window is moving."

For only an instant, they had a glimpse of the driver whose profile looked like a female. Her hair was dark like Amanda's, and the profile similar to Amanda's. The interior of the van was visible, but the driver's face was obscured by cigarette smoke. After a few puffs, the butt was thrown out onto the street, and the window was rolled back up.

Moments later, Carpenter's car passed by on the main street, and the black van followed after it.

"Can you provide me with this footage?"

"Of course. Send me a formal Public Disclosure Request or a warrant. I recommend that you go the warrant route. Public Disclosure Requests go to Washington, D.C., and linger there longer than some Congressmen stay in office."

24

Carpenter stepped out into the cold northwest fog and stood next to the door of the gym, letting her eyes adjust to the darkness, clutching her car fob and a pepper spray keychain. The lights of the parking lot were frosted globes, illuminating little. Her hair was damp from an hour's workout of stationary bike, quick light-weight repetitions, and a half hour of dance workout. Her car was not far away, but she wanted to watch car headlights illuminate the lot before she ventured away from the gym lights.

McCoy advised that she change her routine, but she liked having routines in her life. *Go to lunch at different times*, he suggested, but she was a court commissioner. She had hours to keep and litigants to see at set times during the day. Her work life was public knowledge. *Take different routes home*, he also suggested, but what did that matter if the person knew where she lived and where she worked? *Park in lighted areas.* All the better to be seen by someone watching. *Have you considered carrying a gun or pepper spray?* was another suggestion. "How would that stop me from getting run over?" she retorted. The idea of carrying a gun revolted her. Through a smile, he suggested wearing glasses with little mirrors on the side like cyclists wear to see if they are followed. "I am not paranoid," she said and ordered him to leave her office. As he left, he said that he didn't think she was paranoid, but he also didn't think she was sideswiped into the ditch.

Why she lied about that, he simply didn't know. The crash site review did not support her version of events. There was no paint on her car.

She traveled several yards along the edge of the culvert before rising up to the road and her car flipping over. What she said was not true. He knew it was false when she said it. But he did not know why she lied.

The fact that she was followed was the truth. It was true that as she rode along in the culvert, Amanda passed her in a black van. That image was embedded in her memory.

Why did she embellish the facts? She asked herself over and over. She sensed that the deputy did not believe her. The more he questioned her, the more she felt compelled to demand an investigation at the scene of the accident. The end result was a charge of reckless driving, and she was possibly in danger of dismissal as a court commissioner.

As a commissioner, she often wondered why a person would stick to an obvious lie. Now, she understood. It was just too painful to admit a lie and suffer the consequences. It wasn't as if not admitting the lie made it any less of a lie.

She did not vary her route from the courthouse to the shopping mall. It seemed stupid to do that. The route from the judicial parking garage was simple. Once out of the garage, she traveled west on Eleventh Street that with a slight bend became Twelfth Street until she reached the Pine Street intersection. She then turned left and followed the street south until she came to the strip mall. There she had three choices. She could take a left onto a side street behind the mall past a homeless encampment, and then turn left into the mall. Another option was turning onto a back street along the back of the mall. The third option was traveling past the police station, taking a right and then a left into the main mall entrance. For some reason, she always took the route past the police station and into the mall. She drove past the brightly lit Burger King, but when leaving the mall, she varied her exit route. Each route, once chosen, was fixed without variation.

She took different on-ramps to the interstate. What difference it made, she was not certain, but somehow she felt more in control by altering her routes. No matter what, the end point was always the same. Either she believed that she could alter her destiny by small changes, or nothing she did mattered because she was no longer being stalked, or maybe Amanda was simply too clever for her. She was convinced Amanda followed her. Perhaps that was it. She had had her vengeance and moved on. She was tired of waiting for one cosmic footfall that would never happen. Behind her, the lights of the gym went dark, and the owner appeared beside her as she was locking the door.

Young, trim, and forever moving quickly to wherever she was going, the owner said, "Julia, are you okay?"

"Fine, never better."

"Is your car over there?" the woman asked, pointing to the vague dark outline of a car.

Carpenter nodded with a shiver. The cold fog made everything seem ten degrees colder than an impartial temperature reading.

"I will walk with you."

"You don't need to."

"Not a problem. I've complained to the mall security that better lighting is needed."

"There is mall security?"

"Not really." She pointed to a tall pole in the distant center of the parking lot. In the distance, there was a row of small shops still open for business. "There are security cameras, but the personnel are far away in the closed mall several blocks away." Carpenter nodded and looked up. "Not a real comfort."

"No time like the present," said the owner, and she accompanied Carpenter to her car. She waited until the engine responded to the touch of the start button.

The owner glanced about the parking lot. What few cars left were far away. "Looks all clear."

"Thanks for coming with me. Do you want a ride to your car?"

"No, I'll be fine. My car is not far away. See you Friday?"

Near a wall at the far edge of the lot, a black van was parked in darkness. In the driver's hand was a small pocket spiral notebook. On the pages were written the dates Carpenter attended her gym and the routes she took. What Carpenter thought were random routes were noted. The days she exited the parking lot directly to 38th Street, Monday, when the traffic was light. The exit was not controlled by a light, and crossing the intersection to go left was not convenient. So, she seldom took that route. Some days she would go to the left from the gym, circle around the mall, and exit onto Pine Street, about a block from the police station. On the days when she exited from the mall to the west onto a side street, she had two choices. If she went left, she had a short drive to 38th Street where the intersection was controlled by traffic lights that made turning left easy. If she went right, she would have to travel three blocks past a Yellow Cab dispatch center and then take a right past an area that was a homeless encampment. It was the least direct route for her to the intersection, but she predictably always alternated going left and right whenever she took that exit.

The driver of the black van watched as she pulled out of the parking space and headed toward the west exit. She double-checked her notebook and confirmed that Carpenter would soon be taking the street past the homeless encampment. The driver left the parking lot by way of the back route. At Pine Street she did not hesitate and pulled into the far lane, forcing drivers in both directions to slam on their brakes. More than one sounded a horn of disgust. She did not care. She turned onto the street headed to where Carpenter would soon arrive and parked with the motor running. On the passenger seat, covered by a towel, was a .38 revolver. In the back seat was a shotgun. She retrieved the shotgun as Carpenter rounded the corner and headed toward her.

The driver accelerated the van across Carpenter's path, forcing Carpenter to slam on her brakes. From the driver's side window, she fired the shotgun into Carpenter's windshield. The blast terrified Carpenter. She fired the .38 into the sides of the front and rear passenger side tires.

Screaming, Carpenter scrambled out of her car and ran toward the homeless tents. She was across the street when the second shotgun blast erupted. Carpenter felt the blast and the sting of several pellets hitting her back and the backs of her arms and legs. It was like a swarm of bees surging at her. She heard two more shots, and then there was silence. She knew that she was screaming because she could hear herself. She raced into the encampment and saw a man at the edge of it sitting in a lounge chair in front of a tent. He seemed interested, but unaffected by the gunfire.

"Help me! Help me!" Carpenter pleaded.

"Help you what?" the man asked. He was a giant of a man, well over six feet, with broad shoulders and a thick red beard. Before she came running, stumbling into his light, he was reading by the light of a Coleman lantern.

"I can't hear you," she screamed, gasping for breath. "Hide me! She is after me!"

"Get in the tent and be quiet," the man said.

Pointing to her ears, she indicated that she could not hear.

He explained with exaggerated gestures to hide in his tent. It was a well-worn tent, capable of sleeping three people cramped very close together. Once she was inside, he motioned for her to be quiet and stay inside until he told her to leave. She did as he directed. Once in the tent, she kept her breaths shallow and covered her nose. Whoever the man was, he hadn't washed his clothes or bathed for some time. She didn't care; she burrowed deep into what clothing and blankets she could find. She did not know how long she stayed frozen, but the more she became accustomed to her cramped position, the more she wanted to look out. *Why had she trusted the man, why? Why had he not seemed concerned about the gunfire?*

She felt around for her cell phone, then remembered it was in her purse in her car. Why she even thought for a moment that her cell phone would be with her, she did not know. Parts of the camp were lit by fires in large metal drums. Through the thin tent fabric, silhouettes appeared like demons from another world. She was afraid that if she spoke, she would be swallowed into the darkness surrounding her and never be seen again.

The man stuck his head into the tent. "Can you hear me?"

"Barely," she responded. "Can you speak louder?"

"Any louder and everyone will know where you are," said the man.

"Can I come out?"

He leaned forward and cupped a hand over one of her ears like a megaphone. "Yes. I scouted our area. No one I don't know is anywhere near."

"Can I go to my car?"

"All four of your tires are flat. You must have left the door open."

"Why do you say that?"

"The alarm did not go off and the door was open."

"Is my purse inside?"

The man shook his head. "I didn't see it."

"Will the police be here soon?"

"No idea. I don't have a phone. This is not the kind of place where the police are invited."

"You don't need to yell. My hearing is coming back."

"Good. Most people don't realize how loud gunfire is. What you hear in movies is really muffled compared to the real thing."

"I don't understand why she wants to kill me. I may have made a mistake, but I was working on the information I knew."

"I don't understand."

"It is a long, long story. No need to go into it."

"Fair enough. The good news is, I don't think whoever shot at you wanted to kill you."

"Why do you say that?"

172

He reached over and brushed her shoulder. "Your back is covered in rock salt. The front window is peppered in rock salt. A shotgun blast of rock salt is not intended to kill. I learned about it when I was a teenager stealing pumpkins." The man laughed and added. "We are only a few blocks from the police station. We should go there."

"You'll walk with me?"

"Of course," he said.

"I appreciate it because she may still be nearby."

"All the more reason for me to walk with you."

"But why? Why help me?"

"Because you need help from someone. I've been living rough for some time since my wife tossed me out. It feels good to be of help to someone. If you can walk, let's go."

She nodded, crawled out of the tent, stood up, and staggered to regain her balance. "I am weaker than I realized."

"Whenever anyone in my platoon said that gunfire didn't bother them, I knew they were lying either to me or to themselves."

"You don't seem afraid of gunfire."

"Appearances are deceptive. I have learned not to care about gunfire. Take a few breaths and then we can take off."

"Why are you living in a tent?"

"Halfway houses have rules against fighting and drinking."

"Are you drunk now?"

"You're in luck. You caught me between binges. Whoever was shooting at you wanted to drive you into the encampment. We should move on."

"Why do you say that?"

"The ambush was in front of the encampment. On the other side of the road."

He reached into the tent and grabbed a blanket and a stocking cap. He jammed the cap on her head and put the blanket around her shoulders. "Best to not be too much of an obvious target."

"What about you?"

"No one I know of on this continent wants me dead."

As they walked, they talked and his eyes never stopped scanning for danger. The side road was dark. "You were in the military?"

"Army. I retired. I was a master sergeant."

"So why live in a tent?"

"My ex-wife gets half my pension. I am not bitter. In dark days, I think of suicide to ruin her retirement plans, but she was right to divorce me. I was not home all that much. I was deployed often and, when not in the field, I was seldom at home. When at home, my head was elsewhere."

"I don't even know your name."

"My name is Ed Robinson."

"My name is Julia Carpenter, and I think your wife made a big mistake."

"She knows me better than you do."

Once they got to Pine Street, they crossed the street to the police station. The lights of passing cars illuminated the worn path near the edge of the street, but Robinson told her to walk farther away from the street. At all times, he made sure that he was between her and the street. The police compound was large. When they got to the door of the police garage, the path became a wide sidewalk, but Robinson motioned for them to walk near the edge of the building, which was separated from the sidewalk by small trees. A steep berm connecting

174

the wall of the building to the sidewalk made walking difficult. He directed her to walk near the edge of the building.

"Why?" she asked.

"Going to the police station is the reasonable thing to do. If the shooter wanted to terrorize you one last time, it would happen in the last fifty yards to the door. That is when the shooter expects us to think we are safe and let down our guard."

"Is that what you would do?"

He nodded.

The parking garage was separated on the ground level from the police station but connected with a sky bridge two stories above. The entrance to the parking area was illuminated with floodlights. He signaled for her to stop with a raised fist. After he stood still for a moment, he motioned for her to move quickly with him to the edge of the station where there was darkness. The entrance area to the garage was well illuminated. He gestured for them to leave the darkness of the sidewalk near the street and run past the illuminated vehicle entrance to the side of the building.

At the edge of the building, before the main doors was a floodlight. They waited, watching the cars go by. "The plan is simple. Once we are out of the shadows, we move quickly and open the door. Once we are inside, we will be safe. I was here a year ago. There is a lobby and a desk sergeant on duty 24/7 at the end of the lobby. Don't stop until you are next to the sergeant. I will hang back and watch the door. Understand?"

She nodded.

"On the count of three, we go."

"If she used rock salt, why are we so careful?"

"She used another gun to shoot out the tires. One, two, three," he said and then ran.

The door was only fifteen feet away. In front of the entryway to the station was a thin blue line, separating the station from the public walkway. Once there, he yanked on the door, but it didn't budge. Next to the door was an intercom and a sign: "Press one for ordinary service. In an emergency, call 911. Use the phone in the kiosk behind you."

Cursing, he told her to keep pressing the intercom. "Whoever heard of a police station being closed?" He yelled and cursed some more. "Where is the phone?" he said, looking around.

The sign referred to a phone attached to a short pedestal. On the pedestal was a list of services and shelters.

"You keep pressing the intercom. I'll call 911," said Ed, bending down to speak into the phone. He was yelling at the 911 dispatch operator that he was outside a locked police station when the black van pulled up next to him. He straightened up, and the driver shot him in the head.

25

Laconia was at the coast with his friend, Mandy, when Raymond Knott, the lead police technician, called to inform him of the assault on Carpenter and death of a veteran seeking refuge at the police station.

"This is my weekend off," Laconia said. He had just stepped out of a shower with Mandy and was wearing only a towel. "Gather evidence as only you can do and we will talk on Monday."

"McCoy is in charge."

"He is fairly competent."

"He wants to lead a nighttime raid into the home of Amanda Bowman."

"When I said fairly competent I was being more generous than I realized. Nighttime raids are restricted to emergency exigent circumstances associated with the immediate threat to the well-being of innocent parties," said Laconia, quoting from memory the manual that he helped update after the death of an officer in a raid that went bad. "Is she holding someone hostage?"

Knott responded, "My job is to collect evidence and make sure the others collect evidence correctly. What I know is that Bowman was identified as the shooter by Carpenter, and McCoy has requested that a SWAT team be on standby."

"She lives in a house with a small child and a man who owns guns, a lot of guns, and he is a marksman," Laconia informed him.

"You were the one who said McCoy was fairly competent. Still want to stand on that?" Knott asked.

"As I said, I was being overly generous. I'm at the coast. It's two hours away."

"Make it an hour and a half. I can dawdle on the evidence collection. I've got two crime scenes to process. I doubt he will submit the declaration for a search warrant without at least a preliminary report from me. The data is confusing. I could buy you some time by claiming it is very confusing."

As they talked, Laconia began to get dressed by putting on his pants with one hand, while holding his cell phone with the other.

Mandy and Laconia were lovers for many years, and this was not the first time a getaway was interrupted. She held out the arms of his shirt for him to slip into, smiling as he tried to keep his balance when a toe refused to emerge from a pant leg. They had first made love twenty years ago, and since fallen into the routine of not seeing each other for weeks at a time because of work and other activities. He liked to ride his motorcycle. She was a single mother raising children. She had a family that disapproved of him being black. Neither expected the other to be monogamous, but they were because neither wanted to disrupt the balance of love and affection they had for each other.

"Confusing in what way?" Laconia asked.

"Carpenter was ambushed not far from the homeless encampment. The shooter used a shotgun loaded with rock salt."

"Makes you think murder was not intended."

"The veteran was killed with a shot in the head in front of the police station."

"Possibly more than one shooter."

"That I don't know. I was just a level one forensic technician when Tommy Sanchez was killed in a raid. That was years ago. He was a good officer, and he was killed in a nighttime raid that never should have happened."

"You stall, and I will hurry," said Laconia.

Laconia was using the speaker on his phone.

"Tell McCoy the intended victim might have been the veteran," Mandy shouted.

"McCoy will never believe it," said Laconia.

"But it may slow him up," said Knott with a laugh. "Thanks, Mandy."

"Sorry to leave like this," said Laconia at the door.

"Duty calls," she said. "Luckily duty didn't call two hours ago, or I would be really pissed – frustrated and pissed."

"Thanks," he said. "Are you taking off?" They came in separate cars.

"I have an ocean view to wake up to and a complimentary continental breakfast to look forward to."

Laconia made the drive in an hour and a half. When he got to the police station, the SWAT team leader had a blueprint of Ike's house on a whiteboard and was reviewing entry points with the team.

"Have you got the house under surveillance?" Laconia asked.

"All quiet and no lights on, no one coming in or going out since we set up surveillance," said the team leader.

He knocked on McCoy's office door and entered. McCoy was drafting a search warrant declaration. "Why are you here?"

"I heard about the shooting over a police scanner."

"Everything is under control. I am just waiting for Knott to finish his preliminary report. It's obvious that Amanda Bowman attacked Carpenter and killed a man by mistake, but Knott says he needs to do some more measurements. Ridiculous delay."

"Technicians. You can't live with them, and you can't live without them. Where is Carpenter?"

"I have her statement here," said McCoy, holding up several sheets of paper.

"Where is she?"

"In the second-floor conference room. She is pretty shaken up. You shouldn't bother her," said McCoy.

"I'll just pop in to give her an encouraging word."

"She signed her statement."

"I'll take it with me. See if there are any holes that need filling."

"There are no holes. I know my job. Bowman was driving the same black van that she ran Carpenter off the road with."

"I know your work. Any idea where the van is?"

"Not yet."

I'll just pop in and say hello," Laconia said. He picked up Carpenter's statement and took it with him.

Carpenter was not alone. A department crime victim advocate was with her. They were drinking tea. The advocate quickly made introductions. "Has Bowman been arrested?" asked Carpenter.

"No, not yet," said Laconia.

"She has to be arrested," Carpenter emphasized.

"I'm sure she will be, but I have a couple of questions." Laconia held up Carpenter's statement.

"You say the van pulled in front of you, forcing you to stop?"

"Yes, that is what happened."

"Are you sure the lights of the van were on?"

"Absolutely."

"The glare of the headlights must have been intense."

"Not so intense that I could not see that it was her."

"What was she wearing?"

"She was dressed in black. She had a hood over her head, but I could see that it was her. I know her."

"You saw the shotgun?"

"My eyes were focused on it. She shot at my windshield, and I dove out of the car. She shot me in the back as I ran. I got to the encampment, and a man saved me."

"If your eyes were focused on the shotgun, how did you see her?"

"I just knew it was her. I recognized the van."

"I see. Perhaps we need to rewrite your statement a bit," Laconia suggested. An hour later the SWAT team leader met Laconia in the library and said his men were restless. Laconia gave him a hundred-dollar bill and suggested the team have coffee at an all-night truck stop. "Just a few points to clarify." He hesitated and pulled out another hundred. "Maybe more than a few. Donuts are on me. If they want breakfast, they are on their own."

Back in the conference room, Laconia addressed Carpenter again. "In your declaration you say that you saw Amanda Bowman point a gun before she shot Mr. Robinson."

"Yes, that's right."

"Was she alone?"

"Yes."

"So, she fired from across the street?"

"No, she pulled alongside. The passenger window went down, and she fired."

"Was the light on in the cab of the van?"

"No."

"Did the driver move over to the passenger's seat behind the windshield?"

"No, she fired from the driver's side through the passenger window that was down."

"If the van's overhead light was not on, how could you see the shooter? Wasn't there glare from your headlights reflecting on the van and the van's headlights in your eyes? You didn't see the shooter, did you? Did you see her, did you? Laconia asked in a gentle tone of voice, as if the two of them were confidants for a long time.

"Well, I didn't really see her. I knew it was her. Sergeant McCoy said it was okay to say I saw her if I was sure it was her."

"The devil you say." Laconia shook his head sadly. "You need to be accurate. A defense lawyer might tear your statement apart." He handed her a pen and a fresh witness statement to write. "You are a court commissioner. You don't want to be caught in a lie."

Barging into the conference room, McCoy shouted, "The SWAT team has gone out for coffee and donuts. What is the delay?"

"Just a few things to clear up," Laconia said.

"Captain Knight has approved the raid and the arrest."

"We won't be long."

"A judge is on the phone waiting to have the declaration read to him."

"I suggest he make himself a pot of coffee."

A couple of hours after sunrise, a judge approved the arrest of Amanda Bowman and a search of her residence. As McCoy was shouting commands, organizing the search and SWAT teams, Laconia went to the front door and knocked. He overruled McCoy's command that the SWAT team break down the door. On the third knock, Ike answered.

"I have two warrants. One to search your house and the other to arrest Amanda Bowman. Is she at home?"

"In the kitchen with my daughter, Emma. We were having breakfast. This must be a mistake."

"Come with me," Laconia said, motioning for the officers to take up positions by exit points at corridors and windows.

Close on his heels, McCoy followed. Before Laconia could say anything, McCoy loudly announced to Amanda that she was, "under arrest for assaulting Commissioner Carpenter and for murder."

"Amanda was here all night," said Ike.

"I didn't assault or kill anyone. When was I supposed to have done these things?" asked Amanda.

"As if you didn't know," said McCoy, cuffing her hands behind her back.

McCoy read her Miranda Rights to her and asked her to nod if she understood them. "Innocent people always say they are innocent."

"Doesn't seem to make much difference," said Amanda, adding that she wanted her lawyer, John Abel.

"I would like him here while you search the house," said Ike.

"We normally don't invite lawyers to a search," said McCoy with a huff.

"People normally don't ask for one," said Laconia. "If he can come quickly, you can have him here."

"You can start the search," McCoy commanded the officers.

"You can wait a half-hour,' Laconia said to the search and SWAT teams. "You waited all night; you might as well wait a bit more."

"I said we can start the search now," said McCoy.

"And I say that is not going to happen unless you walk through me," said Laconia. All the officers nodded in agreement that they preferred to wait, and McCoy went to his car in disgust.

When called, Abel came quickly.

26

Assistant Chief Merwin arrived for what he thought would be a normal, unremarkable day of paper shuffling, but it wasn't. The front door to the police station was barricaded with yellow and black tape. In the parking lot, several mobile television vans were parked. In the conference room Commissioner Carpenter alternated between hysterical tears and repeating over and over to a crime victim advocate, "The door was locked. We thought we would be safe. Why was the door locked? Why didn't anyone answer the door?"

Merwin went to his office. He began making phone calls, returning calls, reviewing incident reports related to the shooting and to the arrest of Amanda. He reviewed the minutes of many meetings leading up to the decision to keep the public entrance to the police station closed 24/7.

It was a budget saving measure that Merwin opposed from the beginning. He took no satisfaction in having the folly proved by the death of a man who had gone to extraordinary lengths to save a complete stranger.

Amanda Bowman was the suspected shooter. He recognized her name. He was aware that she was previously charged with two counts of attempted murder.

Merwin believed that a hands-off approach to management was best. Looking at the chaos, he began to wonder if that was the best approach to management, after all. Why put people in positions of authority only to micromanage their work? Knight's decision to replace Laconia with McCoy as the lead investigator, and the sudden decision to charge Amanda Bowman, gave him pause to ponder his faith in Knight's good judgment and his desire not to intrude into the day-to-day activities of the department.

During Amanda Bowman's trial, she rolled up her sleeves and showed the scars on her arms to the jury. She had cut herself on her arms in an attempt to forget the pain of her father's abuse. Revenge is not a legal defense, but it can be a powerful incentive for juries to find reasonable doubt if they think the accused is a victim. This defense had caught McCoy, Knight, and the prosecution by surprise.

Not long after the trial, Amanda killed her father, but no charges were filed because of evidence of self-defense. Or was it more a case of self-preservation than self-defense? Knight, McCoy, and prosecutor Brinkmeyer, after her acquittal, asked Bowman to wear a wire and gather evidence against her father. At their request, she went to her father's house, and then she claimed self-defense. It sounded sort of like self-defense on the wire, but it could have just been Amanda pretending to be in danger. After a cursory review based upon the statements of Knight, McCoy, and Brinkmeyer, the county prosecutor decided not to press charges. *Very convenient*, thought Merwin. *One less sex offender, and the misuse of a victim to entrap an offender swept under the rug, all at one time.*

The death of Ed Robinson at the front door of the police station was unrelated to Amanda Bowman. On the other hand, though, it was a logical conclusion to a string of failures in Captain Knight's judgment, which made Merwin question his own judgment and trust in her, even though he supported her rise through the ranks.

186

At 3:00pm, Knight received an email asking her to meet Merwin in his office at 4:30. The email did not suggest an alternative time, which meant it was an order, not a request.

A secretary, shared by Merwin with another assistant chief, announced Knight's arrival and told her to head on in. Merwin's office was one floor above Knight's, but on the opposite side of the station, which gave it a view of a large mountain that was always snow-covered. "Liz, good of you to come," he said, as if she had a choice.

"It's been a busy, busy day as you can imagine, sir."

"Please sit down. What can you tell me about these dreadful events? We've never had a killing at our front door," Merwin said, disregarding Knight's unspoken suggestion that when he demanded she report to him, it was an inconvenient and needless waste of her time.

"He was a veteran. A decorated veteran of the Iraq and Afghanistan conflicts."

"Did he know the commissioner?" asked Merwin.

"No. He didn't know her."

"He died a soldier's death," said Merwin.

"How so?"

"Every day all across the world, soldiers die protecting people they do not know. 'What God abandoned, these defended, and saved the sum of things for pay.' That is from 'Epitaph on an Army of Mercenaries,' a poem by A.E. Housman, an English poet."

"I don't read poetry. I've never heard of Housman," said Knight, who let her irritation at being recited poetry at the end of a busy day tinge the tone of her voice.

"Have you ever heard these lines? 'Those that I fight I do not hate, Those that I guard I do not love;….' Those are lines from a poem, 'An Irish Airman foresees his Death,' by W.B. Yeats."

"No, No. I studied sociology with an emphasis on law enforcement when I was in college," Knight said with exasperation. She added, "We arrested the shooter."

"Amanda Bowman?" Merwin probed.

"That's right. Commissioner Carpenter identified her as the shooter. At least initially identified her until Sergeant Jones interviewed her and interfered in the investigation. Now she has some doubts, but it is almost certain that Bowman was the shooter. She attempted to run Carpenter off the road only a few weeks ago."

"How did Sergeant Jones interfere?" Merwin asked.

"I am not certain, but when McCoy interviewed her, she was certain it was Bowman who shot at her. Then when Jones re-interviewed her, she changed her statement and was less certain," said Knight, and added, "He caused her to doubt what she saw, when with McCoy she was certain."

"Even with the changes, you obtained search and arrest warrants?"

"The search was delayed by several hours because of Laconia's intervention. Valuable time when evidence may have been lost. The shotgun was not recovered. Several firearms are being tested, so we may have recovered the gun that killed the veteran."

"It is speculative that Sergeant Jones caused a loss of evidence. I understand that the house was under surveillance for several hours before the warrant was executed," said Merwin.

"It is not speculative that we don't have the gun, and the van has not been found. The delay doubtless gave Bowman time to conceal it."

"Perhaps, but there is no record of anyone leaving or entering the house after the surveillance was set up."

"What is most troubling to me is that Sergeant Jones returned from the coast and undermined Sergeant McCoy in front of officers. If Jones was concerned about McCoy's work, it should have been handled in private, sergeant-to-sergeant. Have you signed off on his performance review yet?"

"No, not yet. It's not due for a few days."

"There has been friction between McCoy and Jones for some time. Jones simply cannot resist making life difficult for McCoy. He undermines him at every opportunity, and I have counseled him about it more than once. With him coming back and undermining McCoy, it is just too much to overlook. I've written up a supplemental report to add to his performance review. His poor performance these past few months cannot be overlooked." She placed the supplement on his desk, then another document. Tapping the new documents, she said, "I did a full performance review as well that includes the new information. You have sat on the reviews for a while, and I want to make it simple for you."

"How thoughtful and energetic of you."

"Sir?"

"To give me options on how to sign off on the time to review how it was that a man died in front of the police station because the main entrance door to the station was locked."

"If you want, you could sign off now, and I will take it to HR."

"I will review it," Merwin said, slipping the documents into a desk drawer.

"It is due Friday."

"Because you made changes, I have more time to review it. It's in the manuals. I read them, as well as poetry."

"Of course you do, sir. I don't mean to rush you."

"Or suggest I was a rubber stamp?"

"Of course not," she said.

"A decorated veteran died at the front of the police station because the door was locked."

"I have investigated the matter. It was a breakdown in protocol by the night sergeant. At night, all calls from the front door go to his station. He was away from his post without arranging coverage."

"Why was that?"

"Because of the dispatch calls about a shooting in the area. He was in the break room getting people out on the street."

"That sounds like a very sensible thing to do."

"If he had arranged to have a person at his desk, yes, that would have been reasonable. But he did not," explained Knight.

"You think he's responsible that a man died at the front door?"

"There are no other reasons, and I have drafted up a letter of reprimand to go in his file," she replied.

"Have you now? Do you have it?"

"Not with me. I reviewed it with HR, and it was approved."

"Has he been served with it?"

"No, not yet. I was going to have him come in tomorrow. He asked to have his union representative with him when we meet."

"I want to review the letter before you meet with him," said Merwin.

"It's not necessary. A letter of admonishment does not need your approval."

"Are you disobeying a direct order, captain?"

After a long pause, and then with a voice as cold as an iceberg, she said, "No, of course not."

"Good to hear, captain."

"I know how strongly you opposed locking the front door. I know you were disappointed when the chief approved of keeping the door locked, but this was an avoidable consequence of budget cuts. If only the night sergeant followed policy, this would not have happened."

"Send me the letter to review and do nothing until I give you permission to act on it. You seem to have spent the day covering your ass and protecting McCoy's ass, as well. That is not what I call good leadership. Good day. You are dismissed, captain."

27

When you are young, it is fun and exciting not to know where or with whom you will wake up, but Billie and John Abel were married for many years, and they both enjoyed the routine of their lives. Few words were spoken. Both preferred the silence of long-term companionship over chitchat. As usual, Abel was the first one to rise from the bed.

Abel emerged from the master bathroom wearing slacks, a dress shirt, and a sport coat. Common lawyer attire, but unusual because he seldom went to court and usually wore jeans and canvas or flannel shirts. Billie was still in bed reading the news on her iPad. Also on the bed were three dogs, a great Pyrenees and two shepherd mixes. At the side of the bed with a red ball next to his nose lay Barney. "Well, look at you," drawled Billie. "You almost look like a lawyer."

"Thank you."

"Real lawyers wear ties."

"That sounds sexist. Besides, I have one in my coat pocket," he said, patting his chest.

"What's the occasion?"

"Amanda's arraignment is this afternoon."

"You're taking her case? I thought you said after she killed her father that you were done representing her," Billie said.

"You thought I said that."

With a dramatic tilt downward of her head, she peered over her reading glasses and said, "I know you said that. I also know you said that you were going to retire, and you were tired of trials," Billie said.

"Did I say that? I doubt it."

"A dementia defense is a bad defense, especially for a lawyer. You are not going to win friends at the courthouse by defending a person accused of shooting at a court commissioner."

"All the more reason for me to take the case. Not many lawyers want to represent her."

Billie shook her head. "You'll do what you want. Don't complain to me about being tired."

"My asthma is doing better."

"And what about your Graves' disease?"

"I have medication for all my ills," he replied.

"I worry about you. You forget things and are not always as sharp as you should be. If you go to trial, the judge won't quit early so you can take a nap. If something is worth doing, it is worth doing right."

"I have always thought that philosophy leads to unnecessary anxiety," replied Abel.

Barney dropped a red ball at Abel's feet. From head to tail, the dog quivered with anticipation. Two years ago, a vet told them he had two to eighteen months to live because of a genetic condition, but they gave the dog daily medication and prescription food. Except for being slightly underweight, he looked good. As if Barney knew that he was on borrowed time, he packed as much life as he could into the time he had left. With his nose, Barney nudged the ball and pawed at Abel's shoe.

"Duty calls," Abel said with a laugh.

"You indulge that dog."

"As if you don't," Abel said with a chuckle, walking away. Behind him, the other dogs followed, jostling for position to be first out the door to the back yard.

After a few tosses, Abel left the shepherd mixes, Henry and Atticus, to play with Barney. At the same time along the fence, Sophie pranced, protecting the property from all animals, humans, dogs, or others. She took her guard dog lineage seriously.

With the door open, Abel prepared a breakfast of granola and yogurt, staying alert in case the dogs began barking in chorus at a passing stroller. Animal Control had already received one complaint. Billie was afraid of another complaint. Abel wanted to know who complained. Both were indignant that the unknown neighbor did not speak to them first. Abel was soon lost in thought about Amanda and her history, the problems of proof in primal cases.

After Amanda killed her father, Abel said he would not represent her if she were charged. He spent weeks in trial, successfully defending her against charges of attempting to kill her father and Ian Franklin, only to have her stab and slit her father's throat with a kitchen knife.

If he knew she was going to quickly take another run at murder, he would not have wasted his time. But she convinced him that if McCoy and Knight had not induced her to wear a wire and try to talk her father into admitting that he abused her as a child, she would never have seen her father again. Except for their prodding, she would have moved on with her life. When her father touched her, rage took over, and she defended herself. Was that entirely true? Abel was not sure. Perhaps she took advantage of the situation by acting under police quasi-direction to exact her revenge. Perhaps she planned to kill her father from the minute she entered his house, and she simply waited for the right moment to yell into the police microphone that he was attacking her.

Whodunit mysteries are satisfying because at the end you know who the villain is and why. But in real life, most of the mysteries end in who-may-have-done-it. Sometimes it is not even clear, as with the death of Amanda's father, whether the murder was justified or not. In fiction, the murderer usually confesses either out of guilt or because they think they have the upper hand and are about to get away with the crime.

In life, many recant their confession, if one was made, and persist in their innocence, even when the evidence against them consists of fingerprints, DNA evidence, video, or whether sober eyewitnesses exist. When Adam attempted to avoid responsibility for the apple munching and said the woman beguiled him, he was merely the first in a long and never-ending line of defendants, hoping that by denial the ax might not fall.

"Barney, Sophie, Henry, Atticus," Billie began yelling out the door. Abel had no idea how she got there or why she was yelling.

"Didn't you hear them?"

"No," he said. "They must have just started."

"Get in here," she shouted. Stepping onto the back deck, she called their names until they came running. The last to arrive was Sophie.

"I didn't hear them," Abel said.

"Pay attention," she snapped at him and began handing out treats to the dogs.

"That reminds me. I have been looking for a book I can't find."

"What was it?"

"*The Splendid and the Vile* by Erik Larson. It was on my desk. I was going to loan it to a friend. "

"That is not where it was supposed to be. I put it up."

"It was where I wanted it. I suspected your hand was in this."

"It was in my way of dusting. So, I put it on the bookshelf by the door to your office."

"That's where I put poetry books."

"There are other books on the shelf. If you put things away, you wouldn't lose them."

"If you didn't rearrange my books, I would know where they are."

She smiled. "I'll get the book. You should hurry. Murderers and judges hate to be kept waiting."

"Thanks for the tip."

28

When Ian Franklin was shot in the knee, he was slightly overweight. Now there was no doubt that he was corpulent. His blue blazer, stretched taut across his shoulders and protruding, announced there was no hope of buttoning the jacket. Unable to button the top button of his shirt, he wore his tie loose around his neck in what he thought was both casual and stylish. The elevator opened. He let the other occupants exit, then he stepped forward toward the door and popped a mint in his mouth. Previously, he almost died from ingesting antifreeze. Fortunately, alcohol is an antidote to antifreeze, and his alcoholic ways saved his life.

He stepped into the lobby. In his left hand, he carried a silver-topped Italian walking stick. Carved into the curved top was psi, the symbol for psychology. He purchased the cane out of funds he received from the State Crime Victims' Fund. He was a double-dipper into the fund. Not only had he received funds as a victim, but he also received compensation from the fund for counseling victims of crimes. In counseling sessions, he often told clients that the psi was the Greek symbol for soul, and once their souls were free of the resentments and wounds they suffered, they would again be free.

Such was his hope, for that is how it had worked for him who was himself a victim of a crime. In addition to counseling victims of crimes, he also counseled parents of children swept up in the dependency court system. The State Attorneys considered him a preferred provider. Often, they requested the courts to order the parents accused of negligent behavior or drug abuse to see him. If a

State Attorney wanted the parents reunited with their children, he would recommend it. But, if a State Attorney wanted the child adopted by a foster family of their choosing, Franklin prolonged their treatments. He expressed concern about their lack of advancement in counseling until the parents gave up in frustration and relapsed on drugs. Then he got their parental rights dissolved in the best interests of the children, resulting in their placement for adoption.

At the door of the elevator, he looked both ways and then walked quickly toward the courtroom where Amanda's arraignment was going to take place. As he hurried, his cane barely brushed the floor until he saw a person walking towards him. Then he slowed his pace and leaned on the cane, sometimes clicking it on the floor for effect.

The arraignment courtroom was divided into two large sections, separated by a wall with a door and large windows of bulletproof plexiglass. The public section was divided by a middle aisle with rows of benches on either side. The benches were hard and straight-backed, indicating that the occupants were not expected to enjoy their brief stay in the criminal court. Franklin wanted a front row seat so that Amanda would see him as she came out of the prisoners' door. He nudged a person over, pointing to his leg and saying he needed an aisle seat so he could stretch it out. Reluctantly, a large man with tattoos on his knuckles moved over. He had not missed anything. The judge was not yet on the bench.

On the other side of the glass, a young prosecutor announced she was going to read the docket. When a person's name was called, they were instructed to announce their presence and not leave the courtroom. She warned them if they left, a warrant could be issued if they were absent when their case was called. Her tone was indifferent, suggesting that if more warrants were issued, her afternoon workload would be lighter.

On the other side, sitting in the aisle seat, was Alice Medford. Next to her was Ellen Bowman. Alfonso LaFontaine sat behind them, clutching some papers. Each time the door opened, LaFontaine turned to see who entered.

"Ms. Medford, what a surprise. I didn't expect to see you here," said Franklin. He met her previously when he was counseling Emma. After Alice's daughter died, Ike took Emma out of counseling against Franklin's advice.

"Dr. Franklin, how good to see you," Medford replied.

"I hope you are not here for a loved one."

"Hardly," she replied. "Amanda Bowman is on the docket, charged with murder. She is the one who shot that poor veteran."

"I am here for her as well. I wanted to see her in custody. You know our history."

"I do indeed. I can't understand why she was not convicted last time, but this time she won't get away."

"We can only hope," he replied.

"This is Amanda's grandmother," Alice said, gesturing toward Ellen who smiled back at Franklin.

"You are friends with Ms. Bowman?"

"Call me Ellen."

"Thank you. Please call me Ian. Friends united against a common enemy." He cocked his head in exaggerated dismay. "Are you here to support your granddaughter?"

"Hardly. I am convinced she killed my son in cold blood." Looking to the back row, where Kathy Washington sat, she said, "Amanda's mother thinks she is innocent, but really, how likely is that? She tried to poison you with antifreeze and then shot you in the knee. What else does the court need to know to keep her locked up?"

"Sadly, she was acquitted," said Franklin with downcast eyes. "I'm here to support keeping her in jail without bail."

"Dr. Franklin, would you be willing to counsel Emma again?" asked LaFontaine.

"Her father took her out of counseling. I doubt he will let her return because he had rather harsh words for me."

"He may have less to say about that than he thinks. I am serving him with an order giving Alice temporary custody."

"Amanda and Ike were living together while she planned her attack on a court commissioner. Hard to imagine he did not know what was going on. The house was full of guns."

"My card. The courts respect my judgment," said Franklin, handing her a business card and giving the tips of her fingers a sympathetic squeeze. He added, "I accept all major credit cards if there happens to be a co-pay required. Often there is not with most insurance companies."

"Speak of the Devil," said LaFontaine, standing up to deliver the court order to Ike, who just entered the courtroom and sat down next to Kathy Washington.

On the other side of the plexiglass, attorneys entered from a side door, and Judge Albert entered from the back door. He was a large man with snow-white hair. His movements seemed slow, but powerful like an iceberg. The Judicial Assistant (JA) banged her gavel. Before she said, "All rise," everyone had begun to rise.

"Be seated," said the judge while some stragglers were still rising.

The young prosecutor called out a few case names and handed forward agreed orders of continuance. They noticed that the defendants and lawyers had signed off on the orders, and the judge barely glanced at the papers before affixing his signature.

James Brinkmeyer appeared from the side door, followed by Abel. Brinkmeyer was a small man who always wore the same suit and smirk of arrogance. He touched the young prosecutor on the shoulder, and she stepped away from the bench. Brinkmeyer announced that the next case was *State v. Amanda Bowman*. When he spoke to the judge, his smirk evaporated.

Amanda was called into the courtroom, and she sat down at a table as directed by a guard.

"Is your name Amanda Bowman?" asked the judge.

She began to stand up, but before a guard could tap her shoulder, the judge told her to sit down.

"I appreciate the courtesy," said the judge. "But the guards get nervous when an inmate tries to get a head start on them."

Brinkmeyer began to speak, but the judge silenced him with a wave of his hand. The judge's fingers were as large as Cuban cigars.

"Mr. Abel, good afternoon."

"Good afternoon, Your Honor," said Abel, standing next to Amanda. "This is my client, Amanda Bowman."

"Is that your name?" the judge asked.

"Yes, Your Honor. My name is Amanda Bowman."

"You were starting to speak," the judge said to Brinkmeyer. "Now you can."

Brinkmeyer announced the charges of murder in the second degree, assault in the first degree, unlawful discharge of a firearm, and unlawful possession of a firearm. After each charge was announced, Amanda said she was not guilty.

"Pleas of not guilty will be entered into the court file. Give me a moment to read the declaration of probable cause in support of the charges." The judge turned his attention to a computer screen. Since the Pandemic, actual court files were seldom seen in courtrooms unless especially requested by a judge. A declaration of probable cause is a declaration signed by a prosecutor based upon their review of the police reports.

The judge read slowly, occasionally glancing at Amanda. She returned his glances with the demure smile of an innocent person, not a maniacal murderer who had fired a shotgun and stalked a court commissioner. "There does seem to be probable cause. Mr. Abel, do you wish to argue probable cause at this time?"

"No, I'll reserve. But I would note there is a discrepancy between the   declaration of probable cause and what the complaining witness said."

"How so?" asked the judge.

"The declaration states that the complaining witness, Commissioner Carpenter, positively identified my client as shooting at her."

"That is what the incident report says," interrupted Brinkmeyer.

"I don't have the incident report, but I have the statement signed by Commissioner Carpenter." Abel held up the statement. "It was filed with the affidavit of a search warrant in a separate court file. I found it by...well, never mind. I know how to find things," Abel said, handing the statement forward.

"Yes, you do," said the judge, taking a copy.

Abel continued. "In the declaration signed by Mr. Brinkmeyer, he says Carpenter positively identified my client as the shooter. But in her statement, she says that she did not see the shooter, who was not visible."

"I see that," said the judge. "Mr. Brinkmeyer, can you explain this?"

"I have not seen that statement. I relied upon the police report provided by Sergeant McCoy."

"McCoy, you say?" asked the judge.

"Yes," said Brinkmeyer.

"Even with the discrepancies, there seems to be enough to move forward. What is the State's position on bail?"

"The charges are second-degree murder and the stalking of a judicial officer. The State requests no bail."

Abel rose to respond. "Your Honor, the State claims that my client had a shotgun and a handgun, and she shot at the commissioner and killed a man. The police raided her home and found no gun or shotgun that relates to this crime. She is accused of shooting a man with a .38 revolver, but that weapon has not been located. The claim is that she drove a black van. No van has been recovered."

"Objection. The issue is bail, not the State's case," said Brinkmeyer.

"That is true. Weak as the State's case is, that is not the issue. If it was, I would point out that the shooter was alleged to be driving a large black van, and no one seems to know where it is located. It was certainly not at the home of my client, who was at home when she was arrested," rejoined Abel. "This is not a capital case, that is to say execution is not an option for second-degree murder. Therefore, the defendant is entitled to reasonable bail. The bail and conditions of release should not be greater than to assure public safety and her attendance in court. She is employed and has a home and ties to the community."

Abel gestured to the public gallery. On cue, Ike and Amanda's mother stood up. "I recommend release on personal recognizance with an ankle monitor, assuring that she is at home except for work or trips to the grocery store."

"This is a murder charge. Requesting personal recognizance is an outrage," insisted Brinkmeyer.

"What is an outrage is you providing the court with a declaration of probable cause with so many errors. Bail is set at one hundred thousand dollars, cash or bond, and the defendant must wear an ankle monitor," the judge ordered.

29

Carpenter looked at the clock on the wall and at her wristwatch. They were in sync and each confirmed that it was 1:30 in the afternoon. Judge Florence Monroe from Salish County was not on the bench where she was supposed to be and, judging by the silence in chambers, she was not even in the courthouse.

"I'm supposed to be downstairs in Room 100," Carpenter whispered to her lawyer. "Can't this be done without me?"

"Judge Flo, as she likes to be called off the bench, is a stickler for details. Having a criminal defendant in the courtroom is one of those details she is fond of," Jordan explained.

"But it has all been arranged and agreed upon."

"She has driven a long way from Salish County to see you."

"You are enjoying this, aren't you?" asked Carpenter.

"I am often required to be in two courtrooms at the same time. I always let the courtroom know where I am. Just last week you admonished an associate for being late."

"So, this is what it's about. He didn't let the clerk know he would be late."

"I've told him he was in error," smiled Jordan.

"All rise," said the judicial assistant as Judge Flo rushed up and took her perch.

"Please be seated," she said and added, "Traffic on the bridge was delayed because of a jumper. Mr. Prosecutor, are there any agreed matters?"

"The first is *State v. Carpenter*," said the prosecutor. Carpenter pushed Jordan aside and quickly stood behind the counsel table staring at the judge.

"We have agreed to dismiss the charges," said the prosecutor.

"What is the agreement? This case was already continued several times. I remember you and Mr. Jordan sparring over the strength of the State's case. You were adamant that it was a strong case and now the State says, in effect, *we have an agreement, never mind.* Why is that?"

Jordan, seeing that the young prosecutor was unsure of what to say, most likely never having been confronted by a judge who questioned the wisdom of his superiors, breached the silence.

"My client, Commissioner Carpenter, has long maintained that she was a victim of harassment and that her car was forced into the ditch. The vehicle that forced her car into the ditch was a black van that she maintained was driven by Amanda Bowman, a troubled woman."

With a snap of his wrist, he produced the charging documents from Superior Court and gave them to the judicial assistant to hand to the judge. She glanced at them quickly and looked up for Jordan to continue.

"As you can see, the State now believes that my client was a victim of Amanda Bowman. To continue to prosecute her when the State has now charged Ms. Bowman is simply untenable. Recognizing this, the State has agreed to dismiss the charges," Jordan concluded with a slight smile of satisfaction.

"Sounds like the State has decided to overlook a lesser crime in hopes of convicting someone of a greater crime," said the judge.

"Are such things not done in Salish County?" asked Jordan.

"Not involving judicial officers," said Judge Flo. "For a judicial officer, you lead an interesting life," she said to Carpenter.

"Not of my own choosing," replied Carpenter. "If you don't accept the dismissal, then we should have a trial. I want a trial."

"Clients often say the strangest things," said Jordan. "We want a dismissal, and so does the State. Please, Your Honor."

With broad hard strokes, the judge signed the order and waved them away.

While they waited for an elevator, Ellen Bowman caught up with them. "Congratulations. The case should never have been brought."

"I'm taking the stairs," said Carpenter, rushing away.

"I agree," said Jordan. "Why are you interested in this case?"

"My granddaughter has accused my son of molesting her. I know it is not true."

"How do you know that?"

"A mother knows such things. We did our best to protect her from her mother and the poisonous lies she spread about my son. We gave her love and affection, but her mother taught her how to hate and how to lie."

"I still do not understand why you are here."

"I told you about the black van."

Jordan nodded. "It has not been found," he said.

"I may know where she hid it. My son has a cabin near Pine Lake. She may have stored it there."

"Why are you telling me this and not the police?"

"I am Amanda's grandmother. It might sound vindictive if I told the police. I want to stay out of the limelight. I thought you could tell them and not reveal your source. You do criminal law. Having the police in your debt may be of benefit to you someday."

"Where is this cabin?"

"It is tucked away on a back road near a spillway, and I have written down directions for you," she said, and she handed him an envelope.

30

To get good at something, you first have to not be ashamed of being bad at it. Until he became a lawyer, Abel did not understand that basic principle of learning, or the second one, don't take yourself too seriously, but be serious about what you do for others.

Had Abel realized that he would be expected to argue politely with others, he might have reconsidered his choice of profession. He was thirty-seven when he became a lawyer, and he was running out of options of other things to do with his life, having spent his twenties inebriated, hung over or on his way to being inebriated. Three months before he got his license to practice law, he quit drinking. But there was much more to quitting drinking than quitting drinking. He had to learn how to be humble and laugh at himself. That lesson had come to him quickly.

Before his first time arguing in court, a seasoned lawyer advised Abel to take a piss before any proceeding started because you never know how long you will be in the courtroom. He had done that. He could not remember if he had won or not, but what he did remember from that first day was that as he walked out of the courtroom, he realized that his fly was open. Rather than drink, which was what he would normally do when embarrassed or angry with himself or another person, he went to an AA meeting and listened to others share laughs about their foibles. He realized that he wasted too much of his life on vanities and insecurities, and he had to worry less about looking good and more on doing good work. But he still always glanced down before entering a courtroom, whether he went to the restroom or not. He preferred to be underestimated, but he did not want to be thought of as senile.

Abel glanced down and entered Room 100 where Amanda and Ike were already seated. They were a couple of rows back in the public gallery. They were seated neither close together like young lovers nor distant like strangers or angry spouses. Alice was seated on the other side of the courtroom, looking straight ahead. From time to time, she looked sideways at Ike and Amanda. She was sitting ramrod straight in perfect alignment with the wooden bench she sat upon. Next to her was Ellen Bowman. LaFontaine was on the other side of a swinging gate in the lawyer area, strutting about like a rooster. He considered family law courtrooms his domain, and he wanted everyone to know it.

God save us from the self-assured, who know little but convinces others of much, thought Abel. "Where's Emma?" he asked.

"She is at school. We haven't told her about this hearing, but we mentioned that Grandma Alice might pick her up after school. She wanted to know why, and I just told her Grandma wants to spend time with her."

"That is an understatement. Sort of like saying Putin wants Ukraine to live in his house," replied Abel. To Amanda he said, "You shouldn't be here."

"The terms of my release are that I am to stay away from Carpenter and not be in the courthouse unless my presence is required for a hearing or the trial."

"Only for a court proceeding involving you," Abel clarified.

"My name sure came up a lot when they said Ike was negligent, and Emma was in danger."

"You are still not a party to this action. Your name is not on the title."

"She came with me," interjected Ike.

"Stay close together," directed Abel.

"I thought that I was being fair, letting her have time with Emma. Now she makes it sound like she takes care of Emma more than I do. That's just not true. She asks to see Emma and I let her, but she is with us most of the time. There is nothing in any of her paperwork that Amanda has ever hurt Emma, but they make it sound like she is a walking time bomb."

Abel nodded. "Ike, family law is more about who can defame the other the most than who has done what. It's sort of like politics, I suppose."

"I thought my grandmother wanted to reconcile with me, but now I see that I was wrong. She never believed that my father was who I said he was," said Amanda.

"Court is in session, all rise," said the JA as Commissioner Goldman appeared from chambers and quickly stepped to the bench. The first case Goldman called was *In re the Custody of Emma Kelly.* LaFontaine quickly stood in front of the bench, and Alice hurried to stand at his side. Abel and Ike arrived after them.

According to custom established long ago, perhaps at the trial of Socrates, the lawyers introduced themselves and their clients.

"As I understand it, I have three issues before me. One, is there probable cause to allow the petition to go to trial? Two, if I find there is PC for further proceedings, should I grant temporary custody of the minor child to the petitioner, Ms.

211

Alice Bowman? Third, should I appoint a guardian ad litem to investigate the allegations of neglect and determine whether the home environment of Ike Kelly is detrimental for the child? Is that all correct?"

The lawyers agreed everything was correct, and Goldman asked LaFontaine to briefly proceed.

"Mr. Kelly resides with a much younger woman who is charged with the assault of a court commissioner and the murder of a veteran. I have provided the Court with the charging documents. Mr. Kelly has allowed the child to travel with my client to Disneyland and allowed her several weekend visits. Clearly, she is well known to the child, and Mr. Kelly has had no problem in allowing my client to take on parenting functions. She has picked her up at school on more than one occasion. What is important to consider is the safety of the child. At the time of the search of the home, there were numerous firearms recovered."

"Where were they stored?" asked the commissioner.

"The point is that there are many guns in the house. What need does a person have for so many guns? They are a danger to the child."

"They are in a safe in the basement in a locked room or in a bedroom safe," interjected Abel, adding, "No one disputes that the guns are stored in a proper manner, or Mr. Kelly has a right to possess the guns."

"The Court was talking to me," said LaFontaine with a huff.

"Just trying to help," said Abel.

"I do not see any allegations of abuse or neglect of the child," said Commissioner Goldman.

"How are guns locked away in a safe a danger to a child?"

"Safes have doors," said LaFontaine.

"They lock and are made of steel," said Abel.

"I get the point," said Goldman. "Proceed, Mr. LaFontaine."

"A woman accused of murder is residing in the home, and Mr. Kelly has taken no measures to prohibit their contact with one another. This is not the first time Amanda Bowman was accused of a crime. A little over a year ago, she was acquitted of poisoning her father and Ian Franklin. She was also accused of shooting Dr. Franklin," LaFontaine informed the Court.

"She was acquitted of those crimes, wasn't she?" asked the commissioner.

"The standard of proof in a criminal case is very high," responded LaFontaine.

"In answer to your question, she was acquitted of the charged crimes," said Abel.

"It is my turn to speak," snapped LaFontaine.

"Just trying to help," Abel said with a slight smile.

"If every time a person was charged with a crime, and the courts started granting custody to non-parents, there would be chaos," said Goldman. "In this case the father is not even charged with a crime." Pausing, Goldman searched for what he wanted to say next, finally saying, "His friend is."

"Your Honor, you should find probable cause. Even if you do not find enough to warrant changing custody, you should find PC and order a parenting investigator appointed to investigate the best interests of the child."

"What do you say to that, Mr. Abel?"

213

"There is no probable cause for a finding that the child is not well taken care of. So, no finding of probable cause should be found and no fishing expedition allowed."

"Is that all you have to say?" asked Goldman.

"They have not proven their case, so there is nothing more to say," said Abel.

"It does sound like you want an investigation conducted because right now you have nothing," Goldman said to LaFontaine. "Your motions are denied, and the petition dismissed without prejudice. If more information is gathered, your client can file another petition."

Once outside the courtroom, Medford asked, "Can Emma spend the weekend with me? I'll pick her up after school."

"What, what?" questioned Ike. The exasperation on his face said a lot more. "After saying I am a bad father, you want to pretend that nothing has happened?"

"The attorney wrote the declaration. I just signed it," said Alice.

"But you signed it," said Amanda. "Didn't you read it? Didn't you agree with it?"

"Now is not a good time to discuss unscheduled visitation," said Abel.

From behind him, McCoy appeared and pushed Abel aside to get close to Amanda. With him were two uniformed officers for backup.

"Hands behind your back; you are under arrest."

"What for?" asked Abel.

"For one, violation of the terms of her release."

"Your client was not supposed to be near Commissioner Carpenter."

"She is twelve miles away at the state mental hospital. She is doing civil commitments today."

"It doesn't matter. Bowman is not supposed to be near the commissioner's place of work. The courthouse is her place of work," replied McCoy.

"How did you know she was here?" asked Abel.

"I called him," said LaFontaine and smirked. "As an officer of the court I thought it my duty."

"You are an officer of the court and a royal dickhead," said Abel.

"Keep that up, and I will arrest you for obstruction of a police officer," said McCoy. "We found the van, and your client's fingerprints are all over it."

"I haven't seen that van for years," exclaimed Amanda.

"Put your hands behind your back," McCoy ordered. Amanda complied with no resistance.

"Violating conditions of release and new evidence of guilt are things the Court should know about. Don't you agree, counselor?"

Abel did not reply.

"Perhaps no bail will be ordered," pressed McCoy. "Nothing to say, counselor?"

"I only try cases in the courtroom," said Abel.

31

The trial was more than a month away. Abel and Brinkmeyer agreed that the Court should decide whether to admit or exclude the black van as a trial exhibit. Brinkmeyer thought it was an obvious and crucial piece of evidence against Amanda. Abel agreed that it was crucial evidence, but thought it more prejudicial than probative of Amanda's guilt. Therefore, it should not be allowed in as evidence against his client.

The courtroom doors opened a half-hour before the hearing was to begin. On one side of the public gallery sat Amanda and her mother, Kathy. On the other side sat Ellen and Alice. "I always think her Negroid features seem more obvious when she is next to her mother," mused Ellen.

"What?" asked Alice. "What are you saying?"

"What I am saying is what I think," replied Ellen. "Amanda by herself has a nice exotic look. As if she were perhaps from Persia. Sitting next to her mother, you realize that the dark hair is not smooth like one from the Levant, but more like one from the sub-Sahara."

"I hadn't thought about it."

"Of course you hadn't. You're a liberal, and liberals don't see color except when it comes to who they live next to."

"This is not a conversation I am comfortable with," said Alice.

"I am just making an observation about my own granddaughter," said Ellen. "When she was young, I often gave her baths and cared for her. When I washed her hair, I was amazed that it was so black and not kinky yet. I did some research. Do you know what an allele is?" She did not wait for an answer. "An allele is one of two or more alternative forms of a gene that arise by mutation and are found at the same place on a chromosome.

"What we are is merely a series of choices and selections and dominance by one part of ourselves over another. If a person has a single black hair allele, their hair will be black. Amanda has black hair like her mother, not brown hair like my Stephen did. Curly is dominant over straight hair. Amanda has straight hair, which means she did not get a curly hair gene from her mother. However, her mother passed on a gene from her mother, Bridget, who is from Germany."

"Why are you telling me this?"

"We have some time before court, that's all. I used to wash Amanda's hair thinking that I could make it straight. I was afraid that it would suddenly become kinky and expose who she was to all the world."

"Expose that she was mixed race?"

"Exactly. I was concerned not because I am a racist, but because I am a realist. We are a long way from a color-blind society. It pays to be white or be taught white. When Amanda was with her mother, who is obviously black, people thought she was black. When she was with me, she was white with some color in her cheeks. The more I tried to help her be with her father and me, the more her mother made wild and unsubstantiated accusations against my son. She claimed that Stephen was molesting Amanda. Over time, poor Amanda came to believe those accusations. Proof that the dark side of life will always pull down its better half."

"Those accusations were not true?"

217

"Of course not. I spoke to my son at length and questioned him many times, and I saw them together. Amanda could be provocative at times. I could see she was enticing him into a licentious relationship with her, and he always rebuked her in no uncertain terms. Amanda created for herself a delusional world of abuse. I fear that she will do the same with Ike and that Emma might be…" Her voice trailed off.

"Might be what?"

"Well, if she comes to see Emma as a rival for the affection of Ike, then who knows what she will do? Hopefully, the Court will see that she is a troubled woman and the jury will put her away for the murder of the veteran and the assault upon the commissioner. None of these would have happened if she were locked up for murdering my son."

"I was surprised that the judge did not lock her up for violating her conditions of release when he had the chance."

"I was, too, but the judge thought her appearance in the courtroom a minor violation because she was always with Ike. She was also referred to several times in my motion for custody. Her lawyer, John Abel, argued that she was there to testify if needed."

"Clever dodge of a bullet," sneered Ellen. "I worry for you. If they have a child or more than one, will they want to move you out of the picture? If you are ever allowed to see Emma again, will they expect you to take the other children along?"

"He is much older than Amanda. Do you think they will have children?"

"It's not unusual for an older man to impregnate a younger woman, or at least think he has," replied Ellen.

"I should have left things as they were and not gone for custody," said Alice. "I relied on your advice and the advice of LaFontaine. You both said getting custody would be simple."

"I think we both said there are no guarantees in litigation," responded Ellen. "I was thinking only of your and Emma's welfare."

"What I know is that it is not in Emma's best interest not to have me in her life." Alice walked over to Amanda. "I know you have no reason to trust me, but I just want to see Emma and be a part of your life."

Amanda said, "We have not tried to exclude you, but you make it difficult to trust you. If she goes to see you, how will we know she is coming back as you agreed?"

"I miss her so. Being away from her is like having Tiffany die all over again. Please talk to Ike."

"We will talk."

Abel entered with Brinkmeyer and the conversation ended. As Abel was spreading out notebooks and papers, Amanda joined him at the defense table. In quick succession, the court reporter and the judicial assistant entered the courtroom.

"All rise," said the JA as Judge Albert stepped to his chair.

"Please be seated," said the judge, eyeing the courtroom to be sure all had complied with court protocol and stood up. "I have two motions noted for today's docket. One is a motion by the State to admit any statements made by the defendant after she was arrested. The second motion is a defense motion to exclude a black van allegedly driven by the defendant at the time of the shooting."

"That is correct," said Brinkmeyer. "The State, however, withdraws its motion to admit custodial statements by the defendant."

"Why is that?" asked Judge Albert.

"Because she didn't say anything," mumbled Brinkmeyer.

"You brought a motion that was meaningless?"

"It was filed by an intern. Usually there are statements, but she was previously Mr. Abel's client and invoked her right to silence immediately."

"I am not certain if that was said in praise or insult," rejoined Abel.

"I doubt it was praise," said the judge. "I am not certain that I understand your motion, Mr. Abel. Commissioner Carpenter stated that she was pursued and shot at by a person driving a black van. She stated that the person was your client. The black van was recovered near Pine Lake in a garage formerly owned by the now deceased father of the defendant. What am I missing? A failure to get the license plate of the van while being shot at?"

"I think you understand the motion quite well," said Brinkmeyer. "It has no merit."

Sitting beside Brinkmeyer was now Detective McCoy who nodded in agreement.

"When I need your help, I will ask for it," said the judge. "Mr. Abel, the floor is yours."

"I appreciate your comments, Your Honor. I do not dispute that the vehicle used to shoot at Commissioner Carpenter, and kill another individual, is similar to the one owned by the late Stephen Bowman, but similar is not enough. If a yellow bus strikes a pedestrian in a crosswalk, are all yellow buses subject to seizure? Previously, Commissioner Carpenter was a criminal defendant herself. She claimed that Amanda was driving a black van that sideswiped her into a ditch. There is no evidence this van was ever involved in a collision with Commissioner Carpenter's car."

"The State has dismissed the District Court charges against the commissioner," piped up Brinkmeyer.

"That is correct. At one time they did not believe Commissioner Carpenter was run off the road as she claimed. In fact, they disbelieved her so much that she was charged with reckless driving, and now the charges are dismissed. I can't help but suspect this was done to encourage her testimony against my client."

"We reevaluated the case and decided to dismiss the charges. At first, the commissioner's version of facts sounded implausible. Now, not so much. The defendant's fingerprints were found in the van," said Brinkmeyer.

Not letting him continue, Abel said, "The fingerprints were found on the passenger's side of the van. The fingerprints were of indeterminate age. Certainly not new prints because the oil that transferred at the time of impression had long since evaporated. The defendant does not deny that she rode as a passenger in her father's van, but she did not know where the vehicle was for a long time. She had not ridden in it for years. There were no fingerprints found on the steering wheel or on any part of the driver's side of the vehicle. It seems suspicious that the driver's side was wiped down, and the passenger side was not."

"Suspicious or perhaps just careless," interjected Brinkmeyer. "A paper coffee cup was found in the van. The lab analyzed it for fingerprints or DNA, and a partial print consistent with Amanda Bowman's right thumbprint was found. If called upon, Ellen Bowman, the executor of the estate of her son, Stephen Bowman, will testify that she was unable to locate the van. The coffee cup has the logo of the Cosmo Coffee Shop. It has only been in business for the past year. So, the cup was left in the past year, which is after his death."

"The coffee cup could have been placed in the van by anyone who had coffee with my client."

"Who?" demanded Brinkmeyer.

"We will get to that," said Abel.

"I am not certain how any of this supports your motion to exclude the van as evidence in this case," said the judge.

"I call Detective McCoy to the stand."

"For what purpose?" demanded Brinkmeyer.

"For the purpose of hearing his testimony," responded Abel.

"Step forward, detective. Counsel, keep it short and to the point. I don't want an aimless fishing expedition," said the judge.

"Sir, you are lead detective in the investigation of Edward Robinson's death and Commissioner Carpenter's shooting, is that correct?" Abel began after a few preliminary questions about McCoy's length of service.

"That is correct," McCoy said and added, "as you well know."

"The shooting occurred at the front of the police station. Were you there at that time?"

"I was at home when the call came in that there was a shooting. I arrived within forty-five minutes and began assembling a team to investigate and search for evidence."

"The timeline is rather important."

"I am not required to be at the station 24/7."

"I understand that. I was not suggesting you were derelict in having some time off from work. But as you have gathered evidence, what have you learned as to when events unfolded?"

"Commissioner Carpenter was at an exercise class and left there shortly before eight. Upon leaving class, she saw a black van driven by your client parked on a side street."

"You mean allegedly," Abel interceded, getting to his feet.

"Whatever," said McCoy.

"This is my courtroom. Both of you will show respect. There is no jury to impress," said the judge.

"The driver of the van shot up the commissioner's car while the commissioner fled to a nearby homeless encampment. She hid in Edward Robinson's tent for some time, most likely over two hours. He then accompanied her to the police station. They were in front of the police station when the driver of the black van pulled up and fired a couple of shots. One of the shots struck Mr. Robinson in the head, killing him. The time that this occurred was 11:17pm. I got to the station and began assigning duties to the officers and technicians. Then I conducted an interview of Commissioner Carpenter. She was shaken up, but then she calmed down enough to give an accurate account of the events. It took a little while for her to settle down and for me to conduct the interview. The statement she gave me was accurate."

"Objection," said Abel rising to his feet. "If he was not there, how would he know it was accurate? Objection to his giving unsubstantiated opinion."

"Sustained," said the judge.

"You were aware of the prior allegations that my client sideswiped Commissioner Carpenter's car some time ago?" asked Abel.

"Yes."

"You were also aware of where my client lives."

"Yes."

"So, you sent officers to keep her house under surveillance?"

"Yes," said McCoy.

"You did this within an hour of arriving at the police station, did you not? I have the call log if it will help."

"I have it as well. I sent Officer Glover and Officer Dahlstrom to her residence. They arrived at fifteen minutes past 1am."

"And they stayed there?"

"That is my understanding. That was my expectation, and there is no report by either that they left their surveillance position."

"And you have no reason to assume they did not stay on watch?"

"None whatsoever."

"Where is this going, counsel?"

"We are almost there, Your Honor. I have just a few more questions."

A loud sigh was heard coming from the prosecutor's table.

"Based on your interview of Commissioner Carpenter and your work, you obtained a search warrant for Amanda Bowman's residence, as well as an arrest warrant for her?"

"Yes. The warrant was executed at nine o'clock in the morning. Your client was there, and she was taken into custody without incident or comment from her. Normally, innocent people have something to say, but she remained silent."

"Just answer the questions and try not to score points; there is no jury present," said the judge.

"It was important to you to find the black van?" asked Abel.

"Of course."

"You searched the garage and had the area surrounding the house searched to see if it was abandoned on a side road and so on?"

"We looked for it, and it was not in the area."

"Based on what we know from the report of Officers Glover and Dahlstrom, my client was in the house when they set up their stakeout?"

"From what we know."

"There was no hidden tunnel discovered into the house by which she could have snuck in?"

"No," said McCoy, rolling his eyes.

"Sometime later, you decided to search a cabin and the surrounding area near Pine Lake and found the van in a garage on the property owned by Stephen Bowman?"

"That's right. It was in the garage under a tarp."

"You received a tip that it might be there?"

"During the investigation, I searched for the van. Then I realized that a records search might give me insight into where it was possibly located. That is how I found it."

Abel produced a map of the area from a briefcase. Shown in one corner was Ike Kelly's home, and the cabin was shown in the other corner. He placed the map on an overhead projector. "This shows where Ike Kelly's house is and where the cabin near Pine Lake is located. Do you agree?"

McCoy took his time and finally said, "Yes. Looks like something from Google maps."

"It is," said Abel. "You have driven to the cabin, haven't you?"

"Of course."

"It is located in the foothills of the Cascades. The only way to get there by car is on a narrow road?"

"Yes."

"The drive to the cabin takes about an hour and a half, and that much time back?"

"Give or take," conceded McCoy.

"How do you explain that the van was involved in a shooting at 11:17pm, and my client was under surveillance two hours later? How could she drive the van to the cabin and return home before the surveillance was set up?"

After a long pause, McCoy said, "Maybe she didn't take it to the garage, but hid it somewhere else in the interim."

"Any idea where? You looked for it?"

"I couldn't find it."

"A team of officers searching the area could not find it?"

"True."

"The team of trained officers knew what they were looking for, and they could not find it?"

"That doesn't mean she didn't hide it well."

Abel cocked his head and raised an eyebrow, letting McCoy's remark dangle in a prolonged silence, before speaking. "And yet I found some CCTV footage of the street in front of the post office." Abel held up a disk. "I have the footage here from the night of the shooting. I think you may have it as well. It just wasn't produced in discovery by the State. I do my own investigation."

"What does it show?" Judge Albert asked.

"It shows a black or dark colored van heading toward the interstate about five minutes after the shooting. It is going the opposite direction of Ike Kelly's home."

"Show me."

"Your Honor, I object to this evidence. It was not shown to me previously," interrupted Brinkmeyer.

"We can watch it together," said the judge.

This is an ambush, wailed Brinkmeyer, or at least he would have wailed, if not for years of sucking up to authority and backstabbing that prevented him from doing so. Instead, he simply said, "Objection."

"This is not a trial but a preliminary proceeding. I will allow," said the judge.

The footage showed what Abel said it would. McCoy and Brinkmeyer watched it in angry silence.

"So, my motion is simple. The van may have belonged to my client's father. However, the evidence is that if it was involved in the crime, my client was not driving it. Therefore, it should not be used as evidence against her."

"That footage only shows the van headed past the post office," said McCoy. "The interstate entrance is not shown. Your client could have gone straight past the entrance and taken any number of routes back to her home. She might have hidden the van in a garage. We checked the side streets, as well as behind a vacant house and near a school yard. However, she could easily drive past the entrance and reach home before surveillance was in place." When he finished, McCoy slapped a palm on the small shelf in front of him.

"But you agree that if she turned onto the interstate headed south, it was impossible for her to arrive at home before surveillance was set up?" asked Abel.

Shaking his head from side to side, McCoy said, "No, I do not agree with that. There is a 56th Street exit and a 72nd Street exit that she could have easily taken. Maybe even taking the 512 exit would have gotten her back well before surveillance was set up."

"Who is to say she didn't go past the south exit and then take the entrance north?" asked Abel.

"That's right. She might have taken the north entrance and then taken another exit that would put her near Ike Kelly's home. Your post office footage proves little."

"But if she headed south as far as the military bases, getting over to the north side of Harbor City unnoticed is impossible. Even before surveillance was in place, officers were searching for the van."

"Difficult, not impossible," said McCoy.

"After CCTV was checked, the van was not seen on any streets in Harbor City after the shooting. That is true, isn't it?" asked Abel. His tone was solicitous as if he expected little to be gained by further questioning.

"Yes, that is true."

"I have another video to show you," said Abel, pulling another CD sleeve out of his briefcase with the flair of a magician pulling a rabbit out of his hat.

"What is that?" asked the judge.

"This is CCTV footage taken from the Freedom Bridge of traffic headed south. It was taken at the time of the shooting and twenty minutes after."

"Objection," said Brinkmeyer, standing up quickly. "Lack of foundation."

"I got it through a Public Disclosure Request to the Department of Transportation."

"Your objection is noted," said the judge. "There is no jury here, and you can review it if you want should you think that worthwhile. But I want to see it. Why don't you?"

"I do," said Brinkmeyer, collapsing back into his chair like a punctured balloon losing air. The southbound traffic was medium, as was the mist on the windshields of the vehicles. Twenty minutes after the death of Ed Robinson, a black van passed under the Freedom Bridge. The mist obscured the driver's face, but she had black hair like Amanda. The driver looked similar to her as the van sped under the bridge.

"I had a still photograph made," said Abel. He put the photograph on the overhead screen. The resemblance to Amanda was striking. "One might think that was Amanda," said Abel. "But thanks to the zealousness of Detective McCoy, it was shown that Amanda was not the person driving the van. So, the question would be: What person wanted to frame Amanda for the harassment of Commission Carpenter that later resulted in the death of a decorated Army veteran?"

"Did you check the traffic going north? You said nothing about the traffic going north," half-shouted Brinkmeyer. "She could have gone north, taken the next exit, then driven the spur around the city, and arrived at home in plenty of time. She may have a garage in the area we don't know about."

"I did," said Abel. "I have additional footage of the response I received from the Department of Transportation. I made copies for you of both north and south traffic. No vans of any color matching the description of the van from which shots were fired is shown going north. Unlike Detective McCoy, who only wanted evidence of my client's guilt, I wanted to know all of the truth."

"No need to lay it on too thick," said the judge.

"Yes, Your Honor," said Abel. He continued, "It's here. During the time shown, the only person with a deep hatred of Amanda is her grandmother, Ellen Bowman. Ms. Bowman believes Amanda murdered her son and wrongfully accused him of abusing her as a child. Ellen Bowman, as the executor of her son's estate, had access to the black van. If the conditions were right, such as in a speeding vehicle, with the aid of a black wig, Ellen Bowman could easily be mistaken for Amanda."

"Is there a question in our future?" asked Brinkmeyer.

"Were any black fibers found in the van? " Abel asked McCoy.

"Not that I am aware of," muttered McCoy.

"You are not aware of every detail in the forensic report," exclaimed Abel.

"I have more than one case I am investigating," replied McCoy.

"There were fibers found in the van. Black fibers were found on the floorboard. Perhaps you missed the forensic report."

"As I said, I am not familiar with every detail," said McCoy.

"Ms. Bowman is in the courtroom. Let's ask her if she impersonated Amanda," said Abel.

He pointed to where Ellen Bowman was seated earlier, but she was gone.

32

The following day, Amanda's shift at the Bluebeard ended at 3pm. Rick wanted her to compete in the city barista tournament, but she could not. Until Abel's cross-examination of McCoy and her grandmother's disappearance, she did not realize how emotionally draining the allegations against her were.

After the arraignment, Ike bailed her out. She had, for the most part, tried not to make plans for the future, or dreamed that one day she, Ike, and Emma might have a normal life, whatever that was. Going from one simple task to another and keeping fixed routines without deviations was comforting. The idea of competing against strangers and answering questions from reporters about her plans if she won the tournament was something she preferred not to do. Shantel, on the other hand, was looking forward to the tournament, and she was focused on making more and more intricate designs in latte cups.

So much depended upon the trial and its outcome. If Amanda won the city barista tournament or placed second, she would be eligible for the state tournament. If she placed first or second in the state tournament, she would be eligible for the national championship held in San Francisco. Her life was on hold until the trial was over, perhaps for much longer. She was pleased with the cross-examination of McCoy, but Brinkmeyer had laughed at the idea of dismissing the charges.

Abel's cross-examination of McCoy was powerful, but insufficient to convince the judge that the black van should not be admitted into evidence.

"The jury can decide if your client was the driver, but I can't deny them their right to decide if she was," the judge said.

After the judge left the bench, Abel and Brinkmeyer talked. Amanda hoped that Brinkmeyer would admit he made a mistake, but he would not. He believed that Carpenter had seen her in the black van. Abel could try to convince a jury that she was not guilty, but Brinkmeyer was not convinced by Abel's argument. Amanda was dismayed that her grandmother's disappearance from the courtroom was not enough for the prosecutor to reconsider his case. Abel's response was that it was often more difficult to convince a prosecutor to give up a case than it was to take a rancid bone from a dog. Fortunately, jurors have better noses than prosecutors.

After Amanda's shift ended, she was walking to her car parked on a side street, several blocks from the café. Her hand was on the door handle when she was slammed into the side of her car.

"You think you will get away, don't you?"

"Furthest thing from my mind, grandma," she said.

"Well, you won't," Ellen said, spinning her around and jabbing her in the chest with the end of a gun.

"Grandma, why?"

The answer was another blow to the side of Amanda's head.

"Turn around and put your hands behind your back."

Amanda's hesitation resulted in another whack to her head. Once she was turned around, Ellen tightened flex-cuffs around her wrists. They were very tight, but Amanda did not complain, assuming worse things were soon to come her way. Ellen's car was two spaces away, and when they got there, she shoved Amanda into the trunk.

At first, she tried to remember the turns and stops as if somehow she could find her way back, like she was some lost child in a forest. She knew that she should somehow feel the fear of an abduction, but she didn't. The darkness and the rage of her grandmother took Amanda back in time to when she first displeased her grandmother. "No, honey," Ellen said over and over. "Daddy loves you. They lied to you. Honey, that isn't what happened, " she said over and over. It was a long weekend of treats and fun and always with the reminder that what her black mother told her did not happen. "They lied to you. Have some ice cream. She lied to you, sweetie. Your black mother and her mother want to take you away from us. You know that is bad."

She had no idea how often she heard those words, not only that weekend, but every weekend. "Daddy loves you. You need a bath." Every visit began with him giving her a bath to get rid of the smell of her mother. "You don't want to smell like them, do you? How can you stand the stench of their house?" her father asked. Ellen said, "Be like us." A chorus of shame and praise until she did what they wanted. Then she was living with him half-time. Calculated to the second, her father made sure she was with her mother no more than she was with him.

"Your mother doesn't care about the time so much because she doesn't really want you with her." At night she would wake up crying, and he came to her and held her. "You need to relax," he said. "Lie still." Sometimes she was so restless, he

234

tied her hands to the bed and stroked her until she was calm, like a horse gently led to the auction house. With no one to talk to, she grew numb. To forget, she started cutting her arms instead of having feelings again.

"You are your daddy's girl," Ellen would say. "Look how nice people treat you when you are with us. Much better than when you are with your mother. When you are with her, they stare. They follow you around in department stores. The whispering behind your back follows you. It doesn't happen when you are with us. You are better with us than with her. You should stay with us all the time." They said this over and over again, and Amanda believed them. Her grandmother never believed the nighttime visits occurred.

They stopped when she started middle school. At first, Amanda thought her father was angry with her, that she displeased him, and she wanted him to come and hold her. But he told her that she was too old, and it never happened. She believed him and Ellen, feeling like it was all a bad dream.

When the doctor told her about the scarring, and she had multiple yeast infections, she remembered the baths and the nighttime visits. She knew that he no longer wanted her because she was too old, and she hated him. She hated herself. He used her. He told her that it never happened, and she believed him. It was easier to believe him.

Amanda wondered if Ellen ever knew or suspected what was going on all that time. Was she an unsuspecting accomplice, or did she know what was happening? Did she suspect but refuse to believe what she knew was really going on? So many ways to deny the truth if, in the core of your being, you don't want to know the truth.

Amanda went to the priest, hoping to ask for forgiveness for the numbness inside her, but her prayers did no good. Until she met Ike. The more she cared about Ike and Emma, the more she regretted her past. The more she wanted to live, the more inevitable it seemed that her life would soon end.

The car stopped and then backed up an incline to a level spot. Grabbing Amanda by the shoulder, Ellen pulled her out of the trunk, stumbling backwards as Amanda tumbled onto the wet and mossy ground. It was covered in bluish-green moss. Trees with lichen surrounded the area, an old cemetery with long forgotten tombstones. Whoever had brought flowers to these dead people were now long since dead themselves.

"Stand up! Only a few more steps, and it will all be over. I have a spot already dug for you." Ellen had a gun in one hand and kept her distance.

Rather than comply, Amanda dropped to her knees and looked at her grandmother, daring her to come closer. "I could shoot you here just as easily."

"But then you will never know if your son was a pedophile. Do you want to kill me because I killed him or to hide the truth of who he was?"

"You believed Kathy's lies. He never abused you. You only have memories of abuse because she planted them into your brain. I know about parental alienation."

"I know you do. You even attached your statement to a declaration when he was seeking custody. You accused my mother of telling me lies."

"And she was. We took you to counselors, and they confirmed that she had told you lies."

"Yes, and my father convinced me to tell the counselors the same thing. So, I did."

"I didn't convince you of anything except to tell the truth."

"What is the truth, grandma? That you loved your son so much you could not see how he was grooming us both with lies? You sheltered him so he could do what he wanted with me."

"You killed him."

"I did, but did I kill the son you thought you knew or the man he was?"

"Get up. I want to kill you at a place farther in."

"I like it here." She could hear the voices of golfers in the distance on the other side of a ridge.

"I said move!"

"When I was eighteen, I had a pelvic exam. The doctor found scarring in my vagina. I've had yeast infections all my life. You used to tell me it was a consequence of me playing with myself and sticking blocks where they shouldn't go. Do you remember?"

"I do," said Ellen.

"The doctor thought it possible that I was abused. He thought scarring, such as I had, unlikely from a child playing with plastic blocks. The more I thought about it, the more I remembered, and what I remembered was not pleasant. I devised a plan to poison your son with antifreeze. It is sweet and blends well with orange juice or power drinks. My dad liked those two drinks, and I began to poison him just a few drops at a time. Watching him stagger about and forget things was not enough, so I gave him more and more drops. I don't know if I wanted to kill him or just watch him suffer. Eventually, I suppose, I would have killed him, but he was taken to an ER and a doctor diagnosed poisoning by antifreeze. I ran away before the police

237

questioned me. Eventually, I got a job as a receptionist for Ian Franklin. Franklin supported my father's petition for joint or total custody. I wanted to know why. This led me to start poisoning him too. He is an alcoholic, and excessive alcohol is an antidote to antifreeze poisoning. Being a drunk saved his life."

"Get up!" Ellen demanded.

Amanda remained where she was and ignored the demand. She continued speaking. "When McCoy and Knight recruited me to wear a wire, I did not intend to kill him. At least that is what I told myself. They said if they had a confession, they could charge him with so many counts of rape and abuse that he would go to prison for life. At the beginning, I did not intend to kill him. At least, I thought that I didn't intend to kill him. I was like an alcoholic ordering whiskey and telling himself that he intends to quit. The more I thought about it, the more I remembered the kitchen block and the sharp knives it held. I used to sharpen those knives. There was a knife I particularly liked to use when cutting my arms. Should I tell you more? Do you want to know how he died?"

"If you yell, I will shoot you."

"They will hear the gunshot."

"It will just sound like a car backfiring. They will simply continue playing, and you will be very dead."

"Where you shoot me here or bury me they will find me in day."

"Impossible."

"I have an ankle monitor. Forgot about that, did you?"

"You are just stalling for a few more minutes of life."

"They don't use microphones with wires anymore. That's merely a term. They gave me a microphone that looked like a ballpoint pen. Their plan was that I was to get him to admit he had abused me. My plan was to get him close enough to kill him. I told myself that was not really my plan, and it was just a fantasy. I was being recorded. All that was needed of me was to get him to admit that he abused me. At that point, the police would rush in, arrest him, and the world would know what happened to me. You would have known. I wanted you to know that I hadn't made up the stress or abuse. That my mother was right in saying he was an abuser. The closer he came to me, the more the rage took hold of me. Before I entered the house, I knew it would. Yet I still told myself that it wouldn't, and all I wanted was a confession. But then he came close to me. I knew that he would, and I told myself that I would not react. However, I knew, of course, that I would. As he approached me, my right hand reached back for the knife block. I knew it was there because I had purposefully put myself in front of it. He tried to hold me and tell me that he loved me. Then I attacked, screaming that he was attacking me. You know that he abused me."

"I know no such thing," said Ellen. "You are lying. You were deceived by your mother into thinking he abused you."

"What about his diary when he said that he abused me? You told me about it."

"I lied. He had a diary, but he did not confess to abusing you. On the contrary, he wrote about your lust for him, even when you were a child, climbing all over him, touching him in disgusting ways. He needed to restrain you from your natural impulses. Even as a child, you tried to lure him into sin. But he resisted. Everything is written in his diary."

"He was sicker than I thought. None of that was true. None of it. Your son put a gun to my head when I was little. He told me if I cried or told anyone, he would shoot me. I told people he hurt me, and no one but my mother believed me."

"You made things up. You told me it was a squirt gun."

"I told you it was a squirt gun after you repeated countless times that it was a squirt gun. I just gave in. I believed you more than myself. But it was a gun. It was like the gun in your hand, a .38 revolver. That was dad's gun, wasn't it?"

"Lucky guess."

"Clever, using dad's gun. Was the plan to plant it somewhere? Perhaps in the car? Was the idea that they would think I stole the gun from dad?"

"You are pathetically trying to extend your life with questions when you should pray for mercy."

"You can't give what you don't have. I was a child. The gun was mentioned in a letter written by Dr. Blackridge. It was given to Franklin who did nothing, even though he knew that he made a mistake. You should talk to Ian Franklin, the counselor. He knows that I was abused."

"He supported Stephen. He thought your mother was a liar. He thought your mother was making up stories to keep you from your father."

"He did at one time, but then Franklin read the report from the officers who saw my dad and me in a park. Like you, he refused to believe he was wrong. If you are going to kill me, kill me knowing who I am. Either a child who you refused to help or the granddaughter who killed your son. If you knew that I was justified in killing your son, would you still kill me, or would you embrace me as a fellow victim of your son?"

"I will never embrace you," Ellen said, aiming the gun toward Amanda's heart.

"So easy to deceive yourself. Kill me, and you only affirm what you want to believe. Over time, though, you will start to wonder if I was telling the truth. I know what it is like. I lied to myself for so many years. I lied, saying he loved me, and what we did was normal. Then I lied to myself that I was responsible. I even confessed to a priest, but it did no good. I lied to him as well. I told him that I did not regret killing my father. How can you not regret that? I lied to him that I didn't mean to kill him. The confession did no good."

"Was that to the Episcopalian priest? No matter if it did no good. They are just pretend Catholics."

"No, the confession did not help at all because I was not completely honest. I have proof in my car. I have a copy of the police report and the letter Dr. Blackridge sent to my lawyer, stating that the allegations against my father needed an assessment."

"And why wasn't one done?"

"You need to ask Franklin. Afterward, you will still have enough time to kill me."

241

33

"I'll see you again next week, same time," said Deloris Lessing, a young woman with a nervous laugh that seemed to finish every sentence she uttered. Ian Franklin nodded in agreement and walked her to his office door. He left her in the lobby as she smiled and waved farewell to his receptionist, and she left with the mother who always accompanied her.

At first he thought she was just providing a ride for her daughter. Now, he realized that she never went anywhere without her mother. Some days, standing alone on the deck was an act of bravery beyond her. He sat at his desk and thought of the hopelessness that just walked away. A young, attractive, biracial woman when they had first met, he misunderstood the depth of trauma in her childhood abuse.

She still had the same nervous laughter of their first meeting. There were no new scars on her arms. An accomplishment, perhaps caused more by the medications prescribed by a physician than any revelations or suggestions during her sessions with him. Unexpected smells, actions, or the sight of a man vaguely similar to her father could send her into a panic mode. Unable to move or speak, she often fell into an immobile blackout that left her exhausted and drained for days.

Thirty years ago, with a new doctorate, he thought he could lead people out of the darkness that others had cast upon them. Now, he was aware that he knew little, accomplished little, and was less effective than an anti-aging cream against the ever-expanding erosion of wrinkles. The young woman seemed so trapped in the past that her PTSD felt new every day.

Compared to her, Amanda Bowman was a success story, even if she killed her father. At least her rage and self-hatred did not condemn her to inaction and self-loathing. Now, it appeared that she was in a relationship. Offering his business card to the grandmother was an involuntary act of greed, created by a desire for revenge against Amanda. She tried to poison him and then shot him in the knee. It was foolish to again bring himself to her attention, but he had. Foolish, yet he counseled others to be wise.

What did he practice but a vague form of self-help therapy? If they could help themselves, was he really needed, or was he more of a stumbling block, letting them deceive themselves that help could come from another? Medications seemed to help some, but he was a psychologist and could not prescribe medication.

He doubted that he could do much for Lessing. He could toss her the lifeline of hope, but she was tied down by forces and memories that she could not even articulate. Even if she could, they would only drive her farther away from help. Still, her insurance paid for his time, and he accepted the money. But he did not expect to do her any good. When had he gone from wanting to heal people to being a whore of the courts and the insurance companies? He had no idea. It was an effortless slide. His in-house line buzzed. His next appointment arrived late again as usual, and he was no doubt angry as well.

"Kyle, you need to manage your time better. You're fifteen minutes late."

"My bad, doc. Should I just go home?"

"Nice try, but no," said Franklin. "Shall we?" he said, pointing to the door. With slouching shoulders and sighs that could burst a balloon, Kyle headed into the office.

"I have to leave at five," said the receptionist. "I have a hot yoga class."

Thoughts of her young and lithe body, contorted and sweaty, gave Franklin and Kyle pause.

"Can I come?" asked Kyle.

"Definitely not," said Franklin.

"It might do wonders for my anger. You said I need to learn to relax."

"It might come at the cost of over-stimulation," rejoined Franklin.

"If you are still in session, should I lock the door or leave it unlocked?" asked the receptionist.

"Unlocked," said Franklin. The thought of staying in a locked room with Kyle seemed unwise. He followed Kyle into his office and closed the door.

"So, what are you doing to keep anger at bay since last week?" Their routine was a group session for one week, and the next week was one-on-one. This was their one-on-one week, something neither relished.

"Have you always talked like that?" asked Kyle.

"Like what? Like a psychologist?"

"I mean looking down your nose at everyone. Who says things like 'keep anger at bay?'" He made quotation marks with both hands.

"I didn't talk like a psychologist before I studied psychology, yet even before then, I spoke in complete sentences. If you want to spend this session arguing, at least tell me why."

"Clever, but no thanks," said Kyle. "Why don't you ask what I did to not get angry? Somehow, asking how I kept 'anger at bay' makes me want to punch you."

"So, you get angry when you think someone is talking down to you?"

"Yes, I get angry when someone is talking down to me."

"Did that happen this week?"

"I'm in high school. That involves teachers. What do you think?"

"So, what do you do?"

"I take deep breaths. Lots of them. Ms. Archer, the English teacher, says I take too many loud breaths, but I let that slide."

"Good to hear."

"The QB and I pass in the halls from time to time. I point to my eye, and he steers clear."

"You almost blinded him. Now you threaten him. That is hardly good anger management."

"You told me I should avoid triggers that make me angry. Getting him to stay away from me is one less trigger to worry about." Kyle smiled. "Do you think Yoga Pants would bring us sodas if we asked?"

"We need to work on you, not your desire to ogle my receptionist."

"That is reserved for you?"

"That is none of your business. She is too old for you and too young for me."

"I doubt you really believe that, but it was a very adult thing for you to say, counselor. On a more serious note, I followed some of your advice, and I've taken up journaling."

"Care to share?"

"Not the text at this time, but content may interest you. I was thinking about the times long ago when I was very young, and my mother brought me to see you."

"I warned you about dwelling on the past too much."

"Those were formative days. Mom insisted that I was abused. You asked me over and over if I remembered abuse. Such as my dad giving me buzz cuts upon buzz cuts if I said nothing, and praising me when I finally said that Shipman had touched my privates. I accused a man of molesting me so I could get a decent haircut."

"We just wanted the truth. It was buried so deep inside you."

"I was five. How deep could it go?" Kyle slammed his fist onto his thigh.

"I warned you about outbursts. If I report our sessions failed, you may get expelled."

"Dr. Franklin, our sessions are very successful, but perhaps not in the way you think. Are you familiar with Stockholm Syndrome?"

"Yes, but why are you asking?"

"Because, despite the appearance of my grades, I am quite smart and read a lot. Stockholm Syndrome describes the psychological condition of when a victim identifies with and empathizes with their captor or abuser and their goals. Patty Hearst is an example. She is of your time."

"A bit before my time, but everyone knows about her."

"I was a captive. You, mom, and all the other parents who manipulated us into believing that we were victims of abuse at a day care center."

Franklin quickly responded, "We were after the truth, and I think we found it. The fact that you can't accept what happened to you is part of your

246

problem, Kyle. You are trapped in denying a past you cannot accept."

"The judge threw the case out because you bungled your treatment so badly with suggestions and inferences that confused me and the others."

"I don't agree with that, but even if the case was thrown out, it doesn't mean the abuse did not happen. It just means that it was not proven beyond a reasonable doubt. When you were sent back to me, I looked at it as an opportunity to really resolve the issues plaguing you all these years."

Kyle did a few neck and shoulder rolls and smiled. "Those are supposed to help me relax and take away my anger. Guess what? They don't."

"Whatever happened in the past, you need to let it go and not let it control you now," Franklin insisted.

"That is the best you got? For what? Two hundred an hour?"

From the lobby, the receptionist called, "Please come here."

"Why?"

"Just come. You and Kyle. Just come."

Franklin jerked his door open and froze when he saw Amanda. Behind her, he saw her grandmother holding a revolver.

Still sitting in her chair, the receptionist was holding her head. Some blood was trickling between her fingers. Judging by her tremors, getting to her yoga class on time was no longer a priority.

"She moved too slowly, so I cracked her on the head," Ellen said, and to the receptionist, "Keep your hands in view and move away from the desk. Amanda told me about the alarm button." She motioned with the gun in her hand for the woman to sit on a lobby chair. The receptionist moved quickly, taking a box of tissues along for her head.

"Keep the pressure on," advised Ellen. "Come out into the lobby and take a seat," she ordered Franklin and Kyle.

"Anyone else in there?"

"No," said Franklin. "What do you want? I don't keep cash here."

"It's not cash that I want. I want some answers. You know Amanda?"

"Of course. She worked for me and tried to kill me more than once." On either side of Amanda's forehead were marks similar to those on the receptionist's head. Franklin stared at them and finally said, "I saw Amanda when she was a child. She was a stubborn child."

Ellen ordered Amanda, "Sit with them,"

Amanda moved as ordered. Her hands were bound behind her back with plastic flex-cuffs. Ellen pulled more flex-cuffs out of her purse. Pointing to Kyle, she said, "You know what these are?"

"I watch movies."

"I'll take that as a yes. Snap them on Franklin and his sweetheart."

"I'm just a receptionist."

"Whatever. She means you," said Kyle.

"My name is Cassie. I need to keep the pressure on my head," she said.

"You can still have flex-cuffs on in front. Sit next to your boss or whatever he is. Move or ring anything, and I will hit you again," said Ellen. "This is not going to take long."

The receptionist quickly followed the orders.

"These are cool," said Kyle, fastening the flex-cuffs. "Where did you get them?"

248

"Amazon. They also sell body bags. Want one?"

"What's not going to take long?" asked Franklin, extending his arms.

"My questions," said Ellen. After Franklin was secure, she directed Kyle to bind his own hands. "Slip them over your wrists and then pull them tight with your teeth. He did as he was told and held out his hands at arm's length for her to inspect his compliance.

"You know what you're doing," said Kyle.

"I watch movies too. Why are you here?"

"I have anger issues. Why are you here?" Kyle asked.

"I, too, have anger issues. Amanda killed my son, and she claims he abused her. She claims that Franklin knows this. She claims this even though he recommended that my son have custody of her long ago."

"How many lives have you screwed up?" asked Kyle. Franklin immediately looked away from him.

Pointing her gun first at Franklin's forehead, and then at Amanda's forehead, Ellen said, "The question is: Did Franklin screw up or did my son abuse Amanda, as she claims? Or did you screw up and claim he did not?"

"I go with Franklin screwing up," said Kyle.

"I'm a psychologist. I make decisions based on facts that are told to me, on tests that I administer, and on declarations provided to me. My decisions are based on a more probable than not basis, based on my knowledge, training, and experience. I don't claim God-like knowledge. I do the best I can," said Franklin. Sweat beads showed on his forehead. His shirt collar was damp. "All this happened long ago, but I remember your case. Amanda's mother was concerned that Mr. Bowman was abusing Amanda. As I recall, she was concerned that he gave her too many baths. Later, much later, I learned about scarring on Amanda's private parts, possibly caused by abuse. When I was making my report, I read a declaration written by you, supporting your son. I read a declaration written by his sister, stating that he was a good parent. Long ago, Amanda reportedly made disclosures to a counselor to whom her mother took her. Then she recanted those statements the following week."

"I was a child less than three. After a weekend with him and her," Amanda burst out, nodding her head at Ellen. "I said that nothing happened because that was what grandmother and father said over and over, and I believed them. So, yes. I didn't say that I lied because I didn't think that I lied."

"Do you ever get things right?" shouted Kyle. "He convinced me that I was abused, even when I kept saying over and over that I was not."

"This is not about you, Kyle," said Franklin.

"It's about you as a hack not knowing what you are doing."

"I killed a man by accident trying to destroy my granddaughter's life, and what I am getting is advice from a kid with a mohawk. I need more than that!" Ellen shouted.

"Show him the letter, grandma. Ask him why he didn't do anything," said Amanda.

"What letter?" asked Franklin.

"You know what letter," Amanda replied. "The one you can no longer ignore."

Ellen took a letter out of her purse. Holding it with one hand, while pointing the gun with her

other hand back and forth across her captive
audience, she began to read aloud:

Dear Mr. Abel:

*Thank you for sending me the recent police reports
from Jackson County Police Department, Incident No.
11-07840. Approximately 18 months ago I conducted
psychological evaluations of both Stephen Ray Bowman and
his spouse, Kathy Ursula Washington, following allegations
that Stephen Ray Bowman, 35, had sexually abused their
minor child, Amanda Elizabeth Bowman, now 7. I did not
recommend any changes in Mr. Bowman's access to Amanda
at that time, as the findings of his evaluation were
inconclusive. Actuarial assessment revealed he was at a low
risk to perpetrate acts of sexual abuse, and he appeared devoid
of Axis I symptomatology. However, it was notable that Mr.
Bowman was found deceptive on a sexual history polygraph,
and he manifested certain problematic Axis II traits (e.g.,
marked feelings of personal inadequacy) that are associated
with an incest offender. I concluded, as did the guardian ad
litem, that the allegations of sexual abuse of Amanda by Mr.
Bowman were "completely contaminated," primarily as a
result of undue influence of the mother, Ms. Washington. My
conclusion that the child's recollection was contaminated was
based primarily upon the conclusions of the GAL and Dr. Ian
Franklin..."*

Looking at Franklin, Ellen said, "Is it true?
You received this letter and believed that Kathy
Washington lied?"

"Yes, yes. I trusted your son. Just as you did.
After I received the letter, doubts rose up in my
mind," said Franklin.

"I didn't know about any tests he took that
indicated he might commit incest," Ellen said.

"Those tests, without more information, are
really inconclusive. They are suggestive, but more

251

facts are needed. I didn't think the whole picture indicated that he committed incest," replied Franklin.

Ellen scowled and went back to the letter from Blackridge. After a few long moments, she again read aloud from Blackridge's letter: *"In sum, the new information gleaned from the July police reports and the resultant forensic interview, along with Ms. Jones' email received today, suggest ongoing problematic actions by Mr. Bowman, and they also suggest the need for further action in this matter by CPS and the court."* Stopping, she studied Franklin carefully, and finally she asked, "You read this letter?"

"Yes, I said that I did."

"Yet you took no action."

"I spoke to your son. He convinced me that it was all a mistake. He told me that the Jackson Police Department did not charge him. I thought there was no point in pursuing the matter further if the police were not."

Ellen carefully placed the letter on the receptionist's desk and smoothed it out. "I did not see this letter until Amanda showed it to me. Had I not, I would have killed her. But she convinced me, Dr. Franklin, that I needed to ask you why you read that letter and did nothing. My son did not tell me about the allegations. I believed my son from the beginning of the divorce. Why would I not? I am his mother, and I never saw him do anything like what Amanda said. I just thought Stephen was a loving father. I wanted to protect him from false accusations made by a jealous black woman, who only wanted custody of her daughter so she could get child support. That is what I thought. But – you – why did you do nothing?"

"Tell her, Ian. Tell her what you told me. Tell her that neither you nor Commissioner Goldman wanted to look bad," Amanda demanded. "Tell her that Commissioner Carpenter let me go for the weekend with her and my father, contrary to protocol. Was it because my mother was black that no one believed her? Commissioner Carpenter sent me back to live with the man who abused me. He and you, Ellen, convinced me that I was never touched."

"I didn't believe it," said Ellen. "We just wanted the truth, and I believed your mother was a liar."

"Was it because my mother was black that you didn't believe her? I've read the declarations you wrote about how my mom wanted custody to get child support, and you said that all my mother wanted was money, and she was making false accusations." She said to Ellen, "I read your declarations, grandma. You even attached an article about parental alienation. You said that was what my mother was doing, trying to alienate me from my father. All she was trying to do was save me."

"I believed your son, your declarations, and the declaration of his sister," said Franklin.

"His sister lied. They never visited her in California. I told her to help her brother," said Ellen. "That is what a family does. They support each other. Everybody lies. I just stretched the truth to help my son. I was sure Kathy Washington was lying."

"Why didn't you do anything like Blackridge asked you to do? Why didn't you investigate more?" asked Amanda.

"I did investigate more. I talked to your father. He said it was a misunderstanding," Franklin said.

253

"That is what you did? That's it?" shouted Amanda. "You discounted what a police officer saw because my father said it was a misunderstanding?"

"He said the police officer was a friend of your mother. He was never prosecuted."

"You just didn't want to tell the court that you were wrong. Because you didn't want to look bad and admit a mistake. My father did what he did for years," said Amanda.

"Others should have protected you. I am not responsible. Others should have known and spoken up," Franklin said. Desperation was creeping into his voice.

"I should have done more," said Ellen. "I just didn't want to believe it. I tried to destroy you by making it seem like you were harassing Commissioner Carpenter."

"You knew all along he was abusing me. How could you not know? You knew that I had yeast infections as a child."

"He said you placed plastic blocks inside yourself."

"How could I do that as an infant? You knew and pretended that you didn't know. You blamed my mother for lying when the truth was in front of you. You were his accomplice."

"I didn't know."

"You did not want to know."

"I was going to kill you. I killed a man, a good man, who tried to protect a woman he didn't even know. I was trying to shoot over his head, and he stood up." Ellen's voice wavered, "I am so sorry."

She put the gun in her mouth and began to pull the trigger. The bullet would have gone through the roof of her mouth except Kyle lunged forward and knocked her elbow to the side, causing the bullet to go through her cheek, taking some teeth with it.

34

Kyle Boardman opened the public entrance to the police station and walked past mannequins dressed in former police uniforms. Kyle had not thought of himself as a hero when he stopped Ellen from killing herself, but many did. Their awe and congratulations gave him the confidence he had not known before. Others followed behind him. Everyone, except Emma, went trick-or-treating with him on the night that Gary Shipman was killed. She was the youngest of the group and stayed at home with Ike.

Close behind Kyle was Randy O'Conner, son of Travis O'Conner and Jimmy McDonald. The three boys and Emma were the first ones seen by Ian Franklin when he began to suspect that children were abused by Gary and Sarah Shipman. He and the parents spent hours trying to resurrect memories that he was sure were buried in their psyches. As the parents spoke to one another and to McCoy, who was leading the investigation, more and more parents believed their children were abuse victims. They went to Franklin to uncover the truth. Mary Dugan was at the back of the group, dressed in a black ensemble with deep purple trim. The deep purple shade of her hair matched the trim perfectly, perhaps as a nod to gaiety.

The prosecutor argued that Franklin created memory resurrections. Judge Albert called it witness tampering and dismissed the case.

The duty sergeant's station, surrounded by plexiglass extending several feet above ground level, projected out from the wall. On the sergeant's right sleeve were several gold chevrons, each one representing three years of service.

"Why are you here? Get lost from a parade?"

"We're here to see Sergeant Laconia Jones," replied Kyle.

"All of you?"

"Yes, all of us. Tell him Kyle Boardman, that's me," he pointed to his chest for the policeman's clarity, "and I have brought others."

"Are you expected?"

"Long overdue," chimed in Jimmy.

"He'll want to see us," said a boy from the back.

"One at a time," the sergeant said with a scowl.

"He will want to speak to us," assured Kyle.

"What is this about? What should I say is the reason for this visit?"

"It's about the murder of Gary Shipman on Halloween night several years ago."

"You were witnesses?"

"In a manner of speaking. He will want to hear from us," insisted Kyle.

The sergeant nodded and picked up a phone, turning off the mike and audio to the lobby. It seemed to ring several times, but finally the sergeant spoke into it.

"A Kyle Boardman is here to see you and seems to be leading a children's crusade. He says you will want to speak to him."

When he hung up, the sergeant said, "Each visitor has to fill out a form." He slid some forms and pencils through a tray. He pointed to a room across the hall. "It's unlocked. Sergeant Jones said to go in there and fill out the forms. He will be right down."

The room was a small auditorium shaped room with chairs arranged at different levels. Laconia did not keep them waiting. An older woman with white hair preceded him. She was carrying a small device with legs, a stenograph machine.

"This is Ms. Bedford," Laconia said. He waited for her to set up, which she did quickly. When she nodded, he began, "Ms. Bedford was previously a court reporter, and she is now a receptionist upstairs. I occasionally use her services for witnesses who do not want us to record them. I think it best that we have an accurate record of our conversation. First of all, are you all minors, less than eighteen?"

At the back row, a boy raised his hand. "I am eighteen."

"I stand corrected. Whatever your ages, it is best that we all have a record. First things first. Hand your visitor forms to the person at the end, and I will collect them. Those of you who are not eighteen are lawfully entitled to have a parent or guardian with you here. By signing that form, you are waiving your right to have a parent with you. Do you understand?"

Many nodded; others shouted out that they understood. Laconia said, "Ms. Bedford, please note that everyone present nodded or said they understood their right, and no one asked for a parent."

Laconia collected the visitor forms that now contained each person's name, address, phone number, and email address. Before he could speak, Randy O'Connor stood up. "I can't do this. None of us should." Like his father, he had an athletic build and close-cropped hair.

"Do what?" asked Kyle. "I didn't ask you to come with us. But when you heard we were going, you joined in. What don't you want us to do?"

"Tell what happened that night. Shipman is dead. We can't bring him back, and it will just get our parents into trouble."

"Why did you come?" asked Kyle.

"I wanted to see who would show up. I wanted to see who would break our promise."

"We were children, and the promise was wrong. It was wrong to tell us to lie," said Jimmy McDonald, glancing at Kyle for assurance.

"If we tell what we know, will we get into trouble?" Jimmy asked.

"No," said Laconia. "None of you will get into trouble for telling the truth."

"Maybe not with you," shouted one of the boys. Several laughed.

"Even if what we say now is not the same as what we said long ago?" asked another.

"No, you were much younger. You won't get into trouble," said Laconia.

"What about our parents?" asked Erin. It was game day, so she was wearing a cheerleader's outfit.

"I can promise you that none of you will get into trouble. I already know what happened. I want you to write down what you remember."

"If you already know what happened, why do you need us?" asked a boy from the back row.

"To confirm what I know."

"What about our parents?" asked another. "Will they know what we said? Will they get into trouble?"

"I can't make promises about what will happen. I won't lie to you about that. I can promise you that I will do my best to have each parent treated fairly if they tell truthfully what happened."

"You have no idea what you are doing," said O'Conner, storming out of the room. Behind him, a couple of others followed, but the rest stayed in their seats.

"Will our parents get into trouble?" asked a boy with red hair.

"Screw them," said Kyle.

"Screw you," replied the boy. "Some of us love our parents."

"Again, I can't make promises because I don't know what you know. But I can tell you this – everyone will get a chance to tell what happened on the Halloween night when Gary Shipman died. The prosecutor, and ultimately a judge, will have the last word on what, if any, punishment a person receives. My job is to gather facts. Your responsibility is to tell the truth, or if you choose, to say nothing. I do not want anyone to write down anything that they know is not true. I want you to only write what you know firsthand, not what someone told you."

"I want to write about what Ian Franklin did to us," said Erin. "This ruined all our lives. I used to get taken out of class to go see him. It was like I was a dork in a special education class. I couldn't go over to my friend's home because the father was afraid I would accuse him of touching me."

"This is not about you," said Kyle.

"We all know the Shipmans did nothing to us. It was all Franklin's fault that we were treated like dorks," Erin said. Everyone nodded their heads in agreement.

Mary Dugan stood up at the back of the room. "We all know what happened. You can pretend that you are normal. But I know you are not. You are like me, only afraid to tell the world the truth. I want to write down what happened. I will tell the truth whether any of the rest of you do or not. You may not think you have anything in common with me, but you know that you do. Tell the truth and let this silence that stifles you end." Then she sat down again.

"That is the most I have heard her say since fifth grade," said Erin, and she added, "She's right. We don't look alike, but we have a common bond. I want to write what I know. We both want our truth heard."

"Erin," Mary called out, "We are far more alike than they realize. We both use clothes to hide who we are."

Erin did not respond at first, then said, "You write what you know; I will write what I know; and then we can talk."

"Write about what happened," said Laconia. "If you want to talk about Ian Franklin and his sessions, you can do that. But I am most interested in knowing what happened on Halloween night. Write what you remember about who was with you, and who, if anyone, parent or child, left. As best as you can, be accurate and tell if they came back. Don't worry if your memory is different than another person's. Just write what you know."

"You want to know what Ms. Kelly and Mr. O'Conner said?" asked Kyle.

"I want you to write what you remember, not what someone else remembers. This is not about building a case against anyone. I want to know what each of you remember. This is not about getting someone into trouble. That may happen, but it is not what good police work is about. It is about finding the truth. Sometimes the truth is that there is no one simple answer," said Laconia. He had brought with him blank witness statements and pencils. "Kyle, please help to pass these out."

"You want us to write down things?" said Jimmy with obvious amazement.

"Yes, and sign your names."

"On paper?" Jimmy held up a tablet." We use tablets. Can I email it to you?"

"But then it could not be signed by you. You don't have to write out a long narrative, and there are no points deducted for spelling or grammar."

"At least they didn't give us quills to write with," said Mary with a wink toward Erin.

"We recently upgraded," said Laconia. "Would anyone like a soda, water, or cookies?"

Several hands went up and Laconia made a call for refreshments. Now that they were there, he didn't want to leave them alone.

35

It was late afternoon when Laconia, with several uniformed officers, came to the MAACO shop to arrest O'Conner. Maggie was at the front desk. "Joe's in the back," she said. Laconia motioned for an officer to fetch him. "Don't hurt him," said Maggie.

"Not unless he hurts us," muttered one of the officers.

Joe did not resist and came out with his hands cuffed behind his back. "I am arresting you on the charge of the murder of Gary Shipman." Laconia read from a very worn card that he carried in his wallet, "You have the right to remain silent. Anything you say can and will be used against you in a court of law. You have the right to consult with an attorney and have the attorney present during questioning. If you cannot afford an attorney, an attorney will be appointed for you before any questioning. If you decide to answer questions now without an attorney present, you have the right to stop answering at any time. Do you understand these rights as I have explained them to you?"

"Yes."

Reading further from the card, Laconia said, "Having been read these rights and stating that you understand them, do you wish to make a statement?"

"Are you arresting Maggie?"

"Not at this time," replied Laconia.

"I have a lawyer lined up, Vince Jordan. He is one of the best. Travis told us about your BS interview of the kids. Jordan says it won't hold up in court. They were just kids. What do they know? What do they remember? They were kids, high on sugar."

"Some of the parents are rolling over on you as well."

"There was a lot of drinking that night."

"No one remembers you and Tiffany Kelly staying with the group the entire night. One person remembers the two of you leaving together."

"No one can put me there."

"Parents and children remember a lot. I also have a statement from Ike Kelly. After you killed Shipman, you gave your gun to Tiffany Kelly, and she gave it to him. She thought her husband would destroy it to protect her, I suppose, but he didn't."

"That's right. Kelly kept it and shot Franklin in the knee. He wanted to frame me. He wanted to frame me, not because I killed Shipman, but because I had an affair with his wife. I didn't shoot Shipman. Tiffany did. I was there, but she shot him."

"That is not what she told Ike Kelly."

"Well, she lied," insisted O'Conner.

"For moral support?" asked Laconia.

"Yeah, something just like that."

"So is Ike going to be prosecuted for shooting Franklin?"

"No, he won't be prosecuted, but you will. Whether you shot Shipman or Tiffany Kelly did, you will be prosecuted. As her accomplice, you are as guilty as she is. Either way, you are guilty of murder."

"What about Ike? Will he be prosecuted?"

"In exchange for his truthful statement, he has immunity."

"Immunity?" gasped Maggie.

"What does that mean?" asked O'Conner.

"That he, too, has a lawyer," said Laconia.

36

McBride opened the door to the police station lobby and walked to the duty sergeant's station. On the wall behind the mannequins displayed in various uniforms, in steel letters was written, "In each generation and in proud tradition, the brave have stood on the blue line to serve and protect the lawful." On the opposite wall were various photographs and plaques, detailing the local history of law enforcement from when the State was a territory to the present.

The desk sergeant knew McBride from when he was a delinquent to when he received Urban League Legacy Awards for community service and providing meals for children from low to no income families. "McBride, nice to see you not in handcuffs," said the sergeant with a smile.

"Nice to see you enjoying the life of leisure while still employed," rejoined McBride. "I'm here to see Assistant Chief Merwin."

"Are you expected?"

"I hope so. I have his lunch: ribs, greens, and mac and cheese." He held up a large bag and a smaller one in another hand.

"I can make sure he gets it."

"I'd rather do it myself. I would hate to see you tempted."

"I know you know the way, but I'll have to get you an escort."

"That is fine, but I am sure the chief wants his food hot, so have them hurry."

"A pleasure to oblige."

"A pleasure to be obliged," McBride said, and he held up the smaller bag. "I was hoping you were on duty. This is a peach cobbler I thought you might enjoy."

"You thought right," said the desk sergeant. "Put it in the tray," he said, operating a large tray similar to a bank teller's tray. Reaching for his phone, he said, "I'll speed the escort along."

Within moments, McBride was sitting in front of Merwin. "I appreciate the delivery," said Merwin. "How much do I owe you?"

"Twenty dollars and no tip."

Merwin gave him twenty-five. "I appreciate what you do for the community."

"I appreciate what you do for the community too," said McBride. "I have something extra for you. What you do with it is up to you." He slid a mid-sized envelope across the table. Inside there were photographs with date stamps.

"Does Laconia know about these?"

"He told me to burn them. I decided a more senior officer should make that decision. Like I said, what you do with them is up to you."

"Laconia is a good man," said Merwin with a smile.

"Enjoy the ribs," said McBride, making his exit.

Later in the day Knight entered Merwin's office. There was a whiff of barbecue in the air. She made a mental note to ask HR to put out a memo about the problems of excessive odors in the workplace. Excessive perfumes, colognes, smoking, and food smells were prohibited, no matter a person's rank. A direct rebuke seemed out of the question, but a not-so-gentle general reminder would get the point across, she was sure. "Did you have a nice lunch?" she asked.

"Very pleasant. The barbecue was excellent. I ate it all, or I would offer you a rib."

Uninvited, she sat down. "The performance reviews of Laconia and McCoy are long overdue. HR and I are patient, but you really need to do them. A lieutenant spot is opening up, and there is a need to reorganize."

"Your reorganization of the lobby staffing did not go so well."

"That was explained. If the night sergeant followed the proper procedure, it would have prevented the delay with getting the front door open. The tragedy occurred because he did not follow procedure."

"Not really something to put on a sympathy card, is it?"

"You have your lobby sergeants back in place. What more do you want?"

"I don't agree with your evaluations. Laconia is an excellent sergeant."

"I know you played football with him, but that was long ago."

"Because of him, a disaster was averted. He came back from his holiday and prevented an unnecessary night raid into a home where McCoy knew there were guns stored. I cannot help but think McCoy and you both wanted the disaster to occur because Amanda Bowman was the suspect."

"You can't prove that."

"You, McCoy, and Brinkmeyer induced her to wear a wire and meet with her father in the hope of getting a confession of abuse out of him. You knew she was fragile."

"She is no more fragile than a freight train. Fragile doesn't come to mind when I think of her."

"Nevertheless, she was fragile. He touched her, and she felt threatened. You know what else happened. You were listening in on the wire."

"She killed him. She claims to have had a panic attack brought on by PTSD. But this is what I know. The prosecutor's office decided not to charge her. However, only she knows what really happened."

"Whatever happened, you can't forgive her. After Abel's cross-examination of her grandmother, you still wanted her charged. You, McCoy, and Brinkmeyer wanted the prosecution to continue. If the woman hadn't confessed and tried to kill herself, the three of you would still want Amanda Bowman prosecuted."

"We had every right to our suspicions about the defense lawyer's claims made in court. It is not like they are the most neutral of people. They all do what they can for their clients."

Merwin shook his head. "Have you thought about retirement, Elizabeth? You have your twenty years in. You could retire and begin receiving benefits based upon your captain's salary. McCoy has over twenty years in. He, too, could retire and the two of you could live quite well on a combined income."

"I am married. McCoy is a man I respect, and I hope that he advances in the department as he should. He deserves to advance. If any of us needs to think about retirement, it is you."

"The two of you have taken many afternoons off together."

"So what? Having lunch with a fellow worker is common."

"Not everyone rents a hotel room to have lunch and screw a coworker, then puts the bill down on their expense account."

"How dare you? How dare you accuse me of baseless accusations?"

"Not so baseless, Elizabeth." He handed her the photographs.

"How did you get these? Were you having me spied on?"

"The photographs are real. Thank you for not claiming they are photoshopped."

"I haven't agreed they are real."

"We could have them analyzed by Internal Affairs, but that might prove very awkward for you. I was impressed at how far in the air your legs could go, but Internal Affairs might not see the humor in that. They are a rather bland lot. While Laconia was busy trying to solve a cold case, you were getting all hot with McCoy."

"Did Laconia do this?"

Merwin shook his head. "No."

"What do you want?"

"I mentioned retirement. It seems like the best option for you. If this goes further, then Internal Affairs will get involved. It is fair to say that you may receive a demotion to lieutenant. As you said, there is a slot open. Worse case scenario, you could get terminated without a pension. You charge discrimination, and a long expensive lawsuit follows with these photographs entered as exhibits. McCoy should retire as well. There are possibilities with private security firms for him to explore."

"If I were a man, you wouldn't do this. You are against me because I have tried to modernize the department. If I were a man, you would embrace my ideas."

270

"This is not about bumping your head on a glass ceiling. Equality has its price. You helped write the code of ethics and procedure manual. I can have you suspended and escorted from the building."

"You wouldn't do that."

"Elizabeth, I supported you. Now, I do not. You underestimate me, and you are now suspended. Give early retirement serious consideration while you still have the rank of captain."

Two sergeants with many gold chevrons on their sleeves appeared at his door. Each chevron represented three years of service.

"The nice sergeants will escort you out," said Merwin.

The End
January 3, 2025
Tacoma, WA

Glossary

Like any profession or trade lawyers use terms not always known to the general public. Taking the time to define them during the narrative is for many unnecessary. The following are some terms that may not be generally known.

A guardian ad litem is a person who is appointed by the court to investigate allegations and make recommendations to the court. They are sometimes referred to as the eyes and ears of the court.

Legal Financial Obligations (LFOs) are the costs imposed upon a criminal defendant after they are convicted. They include, among other things, filing fees, the cost of DNA collection, and crime victim fund fees. Restitution is separate.

"Ex parte" is a Latin phrase meaning "on one side only," or "by or for one party." An ex parte communication occurs when a party to a case, or someone involved with a party, communicates directly with the judge about the issues in the case without the other party's knowledge. An ex parte courtroom is where a party might obtain temporary orders and orders to show cause. Often the other party is not present for the hearing.

About the Author

John Cain was born and raised in Eldora, Iowa. In 1977 he received a M.F.A in creative writing from the University of Iowa Writers Workshop, He realizes now that had he spent more time trying to understand than be understood he would have benefited far more from his time at the University than he did.

After leaving the University of Iowa he had various low paying jobs with few responsibilities. He has lived in Washington State since 1979. On February 6, 1981, he was involved in a near fatal car accident. While he recovering he realized he had wasted his life. Being bruised, battered and stitched up is not fun, but it was one of the best things that ever happened to him. But for the accident he would not have decided to change his life.

In 1986, he graduated from the University of Puget Sound School of Law. . He is a general practitioner. in Tacoma, Washington In addition to his law practice He is an arbitrator for civil case of in value of less than $100,000. For a several years he was an on-call family law commissioner in the Pierce County Washington Superior Court.

He lives with his wife, four dogs, and two cats in Tacoma, Washington. He has self-published 11 John Abel mysteries.

The photograph of the author was taken by Ruth Barclay. It is a very old photograph.

"Baskerville is a serif typeface designed in the 1750s by John Baskerville (1706–1775) in Birmingham, England, and cut into metal by punchcutter John Handy. Baskerville is classified as a transitional typeface, intended as a refinement of what are now called old-style typefaces of the period, especially those of his most eminent contemporary, William Caslon." Wikipedia (citations omitted). This is the only typeface used in the book.

www.ingramcontent.com/pod-product-compliance
Lightning Source LLC
Chambersburg PA
CBHW070921260626
47162CB00007B/2753